War of the Seasons

book two

the half-blood

A NOVEL BY
JANINE K. SPENDLOVE

SILENCE IN THE LIBRARY

FOR ALPHA

CONTENTS

A MAP OF
AILIONORA

AISRAS
STONEYBROOK
STONEY MTNS
STONEY LAKE
SUNSET COVE
DOGWOOD BAY
SEA
SUNSET PLAINS
SUNSET HILLS
PINEY GREEN
AILANTHU
PINEY GREEN MTNS
BROWN DWARF TERRITORY
PEDDLER'S PORT
EMERALD COVE
SEA
CILDARA
AIBLINS
N

CHAPTER ONE

NO NEED TO ARGUE

WHAT'S WRONG?" STORY TOOK EIRNIN'S PROFFERED HAND and let him pull her up onto the wooden dock. Though he'd avoided her gaze, she still caught the yellow worry in the elf's eyes. "You've been quiet this whole trip."

"Aye, but I'm always quiet when we travel under the sea." He kept his tone light, but Eirnin's accent—Irish-sounding to Story's ears—rolled out thicker than usual, betraying his agitation. "Unlike you, I can't send my thoughts through water. Besides, you talked enough for both of us." He said the last with a wink that crinkled up the ailach—his clan's tribal tattoo—underneath his left eye.

As soon as Story cleared Ped's back, the selkie leapt out of the water and transformed from his seal form into that of an almost horse-sized, floppy-eared Great Dane. He shook himself dry, spraying Story and Eirnin with cold salt water. Blowing out a breath that fluttered his jowls, the selkie put his long, black nose on Eirnin's tattooed shoulder, begging for his fur to be scratched.

"Not a bit sorry, are you, Ped?" Eirnin obliged him with a quick scratch and gave Story a helpless smile.

Ped whined, and Story laughed, "I don't think he'll ever be okay with being number two, after me, in your hierarchy."

"He'll get over it." Eirnin patted the selkie affectionately on the neck, and Ped leaned all his weight against the elf. Like most natives of Ailionora, Eirnin was stronger than a human, which was a good thing, or else he'd have been knocked to the ground while the giant dog tried to show his affection. Sometimes it seemed the selkie didn't realize how big he was and instead thought he was some sort of lapdog.

The air whistled out of Ped's nostrils in a high-pitched keen when Eirnin stopped patting his head to reach for a saddlebag holding their gear. The elf's darkly tanned skin glistened in the hot, summer sun highlighting the swirling, black tattoos stretched over the toned muscles of his left shoulder, biceps, and forearm.

"You still didn't answer my question." Story cocked her head to one side, scattering dozens of shoulder-length, purple and black braids behind her. "I know something's got you worried, or anxious, or whatever feeling it is you're trying to hide from me."

Eirnin's shoulders tensed, but he didn't turn around. "Sometimes I don't think it's fair that only elf eyes change color." He tossed Story a soft, absorbent cloth to dry her late father's old Marine Corps Ka-Bar knife. "You can hide your emotions so much easier than we can."

"I don't hide my emotions from *you*." She pulled the knife from her thigh holster and wiped down the blade to prevent corrosion from the salt water. Later, she'd get one of the mages to make sure it was still okay. Metals were rare in this world, making her knife precious in more ways than one.

"Aye, but you don't hide your emotions from anyone, dear heart. You're nearly as bad as your sister." He pulled another cloth from the bag and used it to dry his bare arms and broad chest. He didn't bother with his legs as his cutoff leggings would continue to drip water down them until he changed. "But at least her eyes change color."

Story didn't answer and after sheathing her knife stared at him expectantly. A light ocean breeze blew against her olive skin causing goose bumps to rise along the damp surface. She felt a dribble of water run down her back from the soaked knot of cloth at her neck, holding up her brief swimming sarong.

Letting out a quiet sigh, Eirnin finally faced her. "She did it again."

"Adair? What did she do?"

"No, I mean your mother." He hung the towel around his neck. "She asked when the bonding ceremony was going to be."

"What? We're not even engaged yet!" Story crossed her arms over her chest to keep from throwing them up in the air in frustration.

"Aye, dear heart, I know." Eirnin held his hands up in a placating gesture. "But the thing is, Almera's always on my back about it. I don't know why, since dryads don't even believe in bonding."

"Yeah, well, my mom knows that humans do. Believe in getting married, that is." Story tapped her index finger on her biceps, feeling slightly annoyed, and surprisingly, it was more with Eirnin than her mother. "I might be half-dryad physically, but I'm all human in my head. Besides, she knows how seriously elves take relationships." She looked at him pointedly.

"Don't you start on me now, too. I get enough of this from

Eánna as it is." He raked his fingers through his wet, black hair, standing it up in spikes.

"What the heck does the queen have to do with us?" This time Story did throw her hands in the air and small twinges of her father's thick, Smoky Mountain accent laced her words. "And why is she talking to you about it and not me? For that matter, why doesn't she talk to me about anything, well, anything that isn't superficial, anymore? I swear she's been avoiding me."

"She'd like this business, that is to say *us*, settled." Eirnin pushed on quickly before Story could interrupt. "It's not good for the clans to see us in limbo."

"I don't see how it's any of their damn business!"

He just stared at her.

"Well, I don't!" Story took a calming breath before continuing. "This is *our* decision, elf-boy. Not theirs. Besides, don't elves usually take years of courting before they decide to bond? We've only been dating for like six months. I don't see why everyone is so concerned about us."

"They're not concerned about *us*, dear heart. It's *you*." Eirnin's features softened, and he reached for her hand. "You're the Ailesit. Their savior. *Our* savior."

"Don't call me that." Story jerked her hand away, feeling a wave of emotion roll through her. "I didn't do it for *them*. I did it for you. And Eilath and Adair." She scrubbed a hand across her face feeling suddenly exhausted. "And not everyone's happy with me for doing it."

That was an understatement. After she'd restored *The Ailes*, the tree that embodied the source of magic and immortality for the elven race, many of the elves were upset with the results. True, they had magic again after a millennium of darkness, but their immortality had returned in an unexpected manner. Whereas before the Change, elves had been immortal, male elves had been unable to father more than one child. As a result, after the Change, their race had been doomed to a slow extinction.

Until I came along.

By adding her own human blood to the dying *Ailes* tree, she'd been able to restore it, and with it, the elves' magic. They had not regained their immortality as individuals though, but could now have multiple children, thus preserving and guaranteeing their race's survival.

Eirnin's hand slid around Story's, interrupting her thoughts. He gave her hand three quick squeezes. *I love you.*

Story pressed back four times. *I love you, too.*

Lifting the corner of her mouth in what was meant to be a teasing smile, she peeked at Eirnin out of the corner of her eye. "Besides, this is ridiculous, no one's even popped the question yet."

Eirnin laughed nervously but didn't say anything, leaving Story very confused.

How could I possibly give him a bigger hint? What more does he want? What is he waiting for?

After a few awkward moments Eirnin finally spoke. His words were choppy, disjointed, as if he was searching for the correct words to say. "I'm gone all the time. You're off training with Eínlin. It feels like we've had no time together. I don't want you to feel rushed."

"I don't feel rushed." Story gave him an exasperated look. "Elf-boy, I stayed in this world to be with you. And now you sound like you're not sure you want to be with me—what gives?"

Sputtering, Eirnin jerked back as if slapped. "Not want to be with you! Where in the pits of Aisdean did that come from?" He shook his head. "Are you mad? I'm in love with you, Story Melissa of the Sorenson clan. I can't imagine not spending the rest of time with you."

"Then what's the problem?"

"There is no problem!"

"Then why haven't you asked me to marry you yet?"

"Why haven't I?" He stared at her for a few breaths, his eyes fading from yellow, to orange. Then he laughed.

"Bond with you, whatever! You know what I mean." Story fisted her hands on her hips and furrowed her brow. "I don't get what's so funny, Eirnin. Why is everything always a joke to you?"

Composing himself, Eirnin quirked an eyebrow. "You know, Story, for someone who is so very intelligent, you sometimes miss the most obvious things."

"So, now you're gonna insult me? Awesome." Pushing past him, Story tried to storm off, but Eirnin grabbed her arm and pulled her tight to him.

The world seemed to slow as she gazed into his expressive eyes. He reached up and tucked a stray braid behind her ear, his callused fingertip lingering a bit on her uniquely rounded outer ear. Story wanted to close the remaining few inches that separated their lips and forget this entire conversation. She wished she'd never brought it up; it was clear he needed more time, and she wasn't going to push him for a proposal.

He'll ask me when he's ready.

But Eirnin had other ideas. "Why do you expect *me* to ask *you* to bond with me?"

Story's eyebrows shot up to her hairline. That was the last question she'd expected from him. "You mean instead of the other way around? As in me ask you?"

"Aye." His finger traced down from the tip of her ear to her jaw, and Story found it hard to concentrate on the conversation.

"Because I... because you're..."

"Because I'm the male in our relationship?" Eirnin's finger ran along the contour of her neck before settling on her bare, sun-warmed shoulder.

"Yeah." Her eyes were half-closed as she enjoyed the feeling of his touch. It always made her feel so warm and happy, even when they were arguing.

"Do you think perhaps it is your human culture that brought you up to think like that? From what you've told me, you grew up in a somewhat male-dominated, patriarchal society."

"Yeah, but—"

"And Elves are..." Eirnin dropped his hands to his side and gazed at her, swirls of orange and purple flooding his irises.

Story stared into his eyes for a few moments, confused and not fully comprehending what he was trying to get at, until it hit her, and she gasped.

"Matriarchal!" *How could I be this clueless?* She placed her hands on either side of the elf's face. "Eirnin of the Eáchan clan, will you marry me?"

Story could see the relief wash over him as his face broke into a wide smile.

"Dear heart, I thought you'd never ask."

Closing the gap between them, Eirnin pulled Story into a deep kiss, one that she could feel all the way to the tips of her toes. At nearly the same height, it was easy for her to wrap her arms around his neck and pull him in closer. She buried her fingers in his damp hair and eagerly returned his kiss, never wanting this moment to end.

Ped, forgotten until now, whined and nudged Eirnin's shoulder. He pushed the selkie away before returning his hand to Story's hip and reclaiming her lips with his.

Thrusting his long snout between them, Ped barked loudly, and Story giggled, despite the selkie's interruption. She was too giddy over their engagement to be irritated. "I told you he didn't like—"

The sound of someone clearing his throat erupted from behind Ped.

Story fought the urge to break away from Eirnin as he fractionally tightened his hold on her.

"Whoever it is will have to learn to deal with the idea of *us*. Especially now," he murmured in her ear. Turning toward the sound of their intruder, he frowned, probably over the fact that he'd been caught off guard. The person had approached so stealthily Eirnin hadn't noticed them, despite Ped's obvious agitation.

"Easy for you to say," she whispered back, though she knew whoever it was could probably still hear her anyway— she often envied the elves and their super hearing. "You're not viewed as a catastrophe by half your race." Plus there was the cultural taboo against elves courting anyone outside their race—a taboo that should have been lifted once she'd restored the source of their life and magic. Then again, a thousand-year-old culture born of fear of extinction did not change its attitudes overnight.

"Aye, you've a point there. Still..." Eirnin raised his voice. "Oi! Whoever it is, make yourself known or go away. We don't have time for nonsense. And if you're just here to say something nasty to the Ailesit, you can go away now as well."

A thin, rangy-looking, young elf, with muddy brown hair cut short in the fashion of the hunting clan, stepped tentatively around Ped, giving the selkie a wide berth. The elf was taller than Eirnin, but then most elves were. He wore the standard hunter garb, neutral browns and greens for his trousers and jerkin to blend in with the surrounding woods, suede boots, and a quiver full of arrows alongside an elegant, composite wood bow strapped to his back. His black, Egyptian-looking, triangular ailach marked him as a member of the same clan as Eirnin.

She recognized the elf as Eisrus, Eáchan's young apprentice. The first time she'd met Eisrus had been several months ago in her quarters, when Eáchan had barged in to inform Story that as Eirnin's clan leader she was forbidding the two of them to court or bond. That had not endeared Eáchan to Story, and their frequent encounters following that episode had not been any more cordial.

Meanwhile, Eirnin had simply received permission to court Story from the queen instead, though Story knew he'd have flouted elf tradition and courted her regardless. That made her smile slightly before she focused her attention back on the young elf.

Eisrus inclined his head deeply toward Story with reverence and awe.

Well, at least he doesn't hate me...

"Ailesit." He then turned toward Eirnin and bowed his head respectfully, less than he had for Story, but more than he should have for a normal hunter of his clan.

"Eírnin." Eisrus stressed the 'i', and Eirnin's eyebrows shot up to his hairline while his face blanched. "Eachan requests your presence at the clan hall for the formal passing of the bow."

Story could only assume he meant the iron-tipped bow that was the mantle of the hunting chief's office.

Wait a sec...

Her jaw dropped open as her brain caught up with the conversation. Had Eirnin just become the new leader of the hunting clan?

CHAPTER TWO

TROUBLE

FROWNING, STORY EYED HERSELF IN THE FULL-LENGTH MIRROR
in Eírnin's spare bedroom. She was lucky that Almera
had gifted him the full-length silver and green sarong
that Story was borrowing—she'd been concerned he'd only
have skimpy ones, and by the orange gleam in his eye, she
could tell he was tempted to say as much.

*I need to remember to keep some clothes here for emergencies
like this.* Then she smiled to herself; soon enough, all her clothes
would be here for good. *And I won't be changing in the spare
room!* She adjusted her sarong one more time and frowned
again. *Well, it'll have to do.*

Showing up to a formal hunting clan dinner in dryad
clothing would only inflame the already sour feelings between
her and Eachan—as if Story was trying to flaunt the fact that
she wasn't an elf.

Closing her eyes, she focused on one of the calming
breathing patterns Eínlin, the dreamwalker clan leader, had
taught her. *In through the nose for a five count, out through the*

mouth for ten. Aside from anxiety over the upcoming ceremony, she was also feeling a surge of irritation. It felt like tonight, yet again, Eachan was trying to find a way to ruin what little time she had with Eírnin.

Story had spent the majority of their time apart training with Eínlin. After the mage had learned that she was a dreamwalker—something Story hadn't even known, but had been doing her whole life by accident—he'd been eager to work with her, developing both her abilities and his own burgeoning skill that had come with the return of the elves' magic. She smiled, thinking about all the dreams she'd had since arriving in Ailionora, dreams she'd unknowingly controlled, at least partially. Happy dreams of her father and siblings, though they had passed on the year before. Dreams with the Faerie Prince, Morrigann. Her thoughts soured.

Jerk.

He'd never outright lied to her about the dreams, though he'd led her to believe that he controlled them.

"I will always be in your dreams, so long as you welcome me."

Well, maybe he *had* hinted at her untrained ability.

Still, he tried to kill me. A lot.

And he hadn't been welcome in her dreams since their last encounter, when she'd left him imprisoned in an iron cage in the middle of his own garden, as punishment for his crimes—too many to enumerate, but attempted genocide of the elven race was reason enough.

Her thoughts were interrupted as a familiar knock sounded on the door. Aside from the fact that Eírnin lived alone, as most elves who were unbonded did, she'd recognize his knock anywhere. He popped his head inside, eyes closed, and she laughed at the familiar gesture, her mood instantly improving. "I'm decent. You can open your eyes."

He stepped the rest of the way in, crossed the wooden

floor, made smooth by centuries of feet shuffling across it, and took her into his arms. "You are never decent." He kissed her on the nose. Story leaned in to kiss his mouth, but he pulled away quickly. "Ah, ah. None of that, dear heart. We're already late as it is."

She frowned at the sight of his formal wear. It wasn't much different from everyday hunter clothing, just more layers and long sleeves that covered up his beautiful tattoos—layers that were stifling in the late summer heat as the sweat beading on his forehead attested to.

Eírnin looked at her, yellow hints of concern in his eyes. "You don't have to go if you don't want to."

Sighing, she pulled his arms from around her back before tucking his hand firmly in hers. "No, they need to get used to me. To know that I'm not going anywhere."

She tugged him out of the wood paneled room, down the narrow, plastered hall, past sparsely decorated living rooms that hadn't changed since Eírnin's parents had died decades before. Hand in hand, trailed by Ped, they followed the cobblestone streets toward the clan lodge—which looked more like an ancient stone castle, in her opinion—in the center of the island.

The sun was setting behind the vacant streets, giving the wooden buildings a skeletal cast. Story suppressed a shudder. No matter how often she walked among them, she couldn't get used to the empty homes that lined the streets and canals of every elf island. Centuries ago, they'd been teeming with life; the hunting clan alone had numbered in the thousands. Now, roughly one thousand elves were left in all of Ailionora, divided among the twelve clans.

"You're quiet." Story gave Eírnin a sidelong glance. They still hadn't talked about what had happened, about his new responsibilities. She was curious, but she didn't want to push him. It was all so sudden, but they would have plenty of time to discuss everything, including the details of their engagement, in private later that evening. If he didn't take the opening she'd given him, that would be just fine.

"Aye." Eírnin raked his fingers through his hair. "I can't get over the results from the vote." He moved his hand down and ran it across the dusting of stubble on his jawline. "We have one every ten years. I voted for Eáchan—sorry, Eachan—again. I assumed everyone else would too. She has led us well before, and with the up-coming war I thought..."

His voice trailed off, so Story took a different tack. "So, does that mean it's the Eírnin clan now?" It felt strange to say his name that way. She repeated it slowly. "Aye-ear-nin."

"Aye, that it does." He let out a deep sigh. "I didn't want this."

"I know." She didn't bother adding that she didn't want it either, and they passed the remainder of their walk in silence.

The roughly quarter-mile trek sped by far too quickly, and soon they were walking up the shallow steps and past the tall archways that lined the outer walls of the massive structure. The heavy main doors were standing open, and they stepped inside, blinking against the bright torches lit all around the great room. Story's gaze swept the space, and she forced her expression to remain neutral as eighty sets of eyes rested their gaze on her and Eírnin.

The entire clan was here, gathered around a long, plain, wooden table, which could have easily sat twenty more elves. Rows of empty tables filled the remaining space on the open floor, and Story's heart filled with sudden sadness as she thought about how close their race had come to dying out, thanks to a petty, vindictive faerie prince. Then she smiled slightly as everyone rose to their feet, and she could see the telltale, bulging abdomens of nearly every bonded female in the clan.

It would take a long time, several generations, but they would repopulate their race. Though, from the few conversations she'd had with some of the friendlier elves over the past few months, she knew adjusting to the idea of being able to have more than one child, aside from the occasional rare blessing of twins, was difficult—the very concept of cousins, uncles, and aunts, let alone siblings, was foreign to them.

"Eírnin, the clan has assembled." Eachan's voice echoed out across the hall, interrupting Story's thoughts. As one, the hunting clan bowed their heads respectfully toward Eírnin.

Story felt a flush creep up her neck. There was no official protocol where she was concerned, but most elves tended to follow the example of Queen Eánna—meaning, they treated the Ailesit with deference. Story didn't want to be treated differently, but Eachan's failure to acknowledge her presence was an obvious slight.

Not that I'm even remotely surprised.

Squeezing Story's hand three times, Eírnin walked the rest of the way into the room, never letting go of her—his way of flouting the conservative views of his clan regarding public displays of affection. Ped tromped along noisily behind them, and Story held back a smirk.

Eírnin is purposely trying to rile the older ones up.

He stopped at the head of the table, where Eachan stood waiting, holding the hunting clan's bow.

"Eírnin, the clan has voted. You are now the clan chief." She held out the bow to him, her eyes liquid silver to Story, but she knew Eírnin could see all the colors of Eachan's emotions swirling inside.

Eírnin stared at the bow for a few breaths, before reaching out and taking the ancient composite bow with precious iron tips—the only one of its kind—with all the reverence due such an item.

"I accept this responsibility." He bowed his head toward his former clan chief. "And can only pray that Ai guides my steps in leading the clan."

Story's eyes widened momentarily, and she could see that Eachan's eyes did the same. Eírnin had surprised them both by invoking the name the elves had given to the Creator. Eírnin had never been much of a believer in all the legends and stories of the past.

Though I'll bet seeing one legend come true did a lot to change that outlook. She snuck a quick glance at him, and he winked at her. Eachan saw the wink too, and a frown flashed across her features before she composed them once again, and bowing her head, she crossed to stand before the empty chair to Eírnin's right. As former clan chief, she would serve as Eírnin's first advisor, especially in the beginning during their turnover period. Story grimaced at the thought of the two elves spending even more time together.

Eírnin stared at the bow in his hands for a moment, as if feeling the weight of his new responsibility. At only sixty-four he was considered very young to be a clan leader—historically, most were well into their two hundreds. In that regard, Eachan, at a hundred and two years old, had been young herself.

The thought made Story smile—if the clan had been open to the idea of breaking tradition by electing a young leader twice in a row, based on their merit and ability, she hoped that showed they were open to accepting all sorts of new changes.

Like me...

She knew Eírnin was nervous, but he didn't need to be—he was currently the best elf for the job, as Eachan before him had been.

Eírnin let out a quiet breath before turning to face his clan. A gentle breeze blew in through the tall, narrow windows that lined the walls, cooling the stifling room and fluttering the brown and green clan banners. He hung the bow on the back of his chair, raised his arms in a supplicating gesture, and spoke in a loud, clear voice that carried across the vast hall. "My clan, please, sit. Eat. Talk. We are family."

The elves surrounding the table, left eyes rimmed in identical triangular ailachs, bowed their heads, sat, and began filling the plates before them with the different foods laid out across the table. Story let out a breath she didn't realize she'd been holding, and Ped sat on his haunches, sensing that the tension had passed. Story was pleased things seemed to go so seamlessly, and aside from a few of the younger elves, like Eisrus, no one was staring at her any longer.

The only problem she now faced was Story didn't know where to sit. She wasn't even an elf, much less a member of the hunter clan, and she didn't want to upset things more than she already had.

Before she could say anything to try to excuse herself from the meal, Eírnin motioned to the elf on his left, Eilantos, the clan leader who had preceded Eachan.

"Could we get a chair for the Ailesit, second advisor?"

Eilantos nodded his head and, without hesitation, brought a beautifully carved wooden chair from a nearby table over for Story. He seemed unsure of where to put it, so Eírnin took it from him with a smile.

"We'll just set it here next to mine." Suiting action to words, he placed the chair to the right of his at the head of the table. A hush settled on the table as everyone stopped eating and talking and turned to stare, yet again. Story sat down in her chair and kept her eyes firmly fixed on the empty space before it, while Eírnin motioned for a place setting to be brought over for her.

I'm going to kill him later.

He knew she hated this—hated breaking "rules" of any sort. But she knew he was right: some things, some traditions, needed to be rocked. And besides, they had voted for him. They had to know she was part of the deal.

Out of the corner of her eye, she saw Eilantos looking at her. He winked, then began scooping wild fowl and a breaded mixture that reminded Story a bit of Thanksgiving dressing onto his plate. Eírnin sat down and followed suit. The rest of the clan resumed their soft conversations and feasting.

Eírnin handed her a large plate overflowing with food. "Don't worry, dear heart, there's plenty more where that came from. I imagine we'll *just* manage to keep you satisfied."

The tension in Story's shoulders eased. "Look, how many times do I have to tell you? Humans need a lot of food. You guys are the ones with the freakishly slow metabolisms." Taking up her wooden chopsticks, she picked up something that reminded her of broccoli, both in smell and appearance, and crunched down on it.

Delicious!

Eilantos smiled and took a sip from his wine glass. "I've heard of your appetite, Ailesit. I had thought it was just an exaggeration the dreamwalkers had come up with to make you seem even more mysterious."

"Please, call me Story." She took another bite of not-broccoli, and after swallowing continued, "And I do eat a lot. But I swear it's normal for a human. Especially an eighteen year old."

Eilantos's eyebrows rose at that. "I didn't realize you were so young. Still an apprentice's age. Still a child like my Eisrus."

Eachan passed Eírnin a glass of wine and then sat down again, staring sullenly at her empty plate. Eírnin looked at her, almost pleadingly, and she picked up her own wine glass and took a deep swallow, pointedly ignoring the conversation. Eírnin's mouth tightened fractionally, and Story saw a quick flash of red in his eyes before he turned to Eilantos and resumed the thread of the previous conversation. "In her human culture, she would be considered an adult."

Story quickly clarified, "In all fairness, that's because we tend to live only one century, as opposed to your typical three."

"But you are half-dryad," Eilantos pressed.

"Yeah, I am. So I don't really know what that's gonna do to my lifespan, especially now that I'm tied to *The Ailes*, but I imagine I'll live a lot longer than a typical human." She shrugged, not really wanting to pursue the topic any further.

He seemed to pick up on her reluctance and changed the subject. "Have you enjoyed your time with the mages? If I've heard rightly, you're a dreamwalker, or at least studying to be one?"

Story noticed that the elves seated near their end of the table had mostly abandoned their food and were focused on her conversation with Eilantos. She set down her chopsticks and reached for her drink in order to buy some time to consider her answer. As she drank, she focused her eyes on Eilantos, and much to her surprise, she could just make out the orange sparks of curiosity and excitement in them. She was honored he'd decided to let her in so quickly. If he would trust her with his emotions, she would trust him in return.

"I guess, yes. Eínlin's been monopolizing my time. We've been trying to learn from each other. My experience and his clan's knowledge. We've come a long way. But it's nearly winter, and there's still so much left to learn..." She let out a sigh, feeling once again overwhelmed.

Taking a sip of wine, Eírnin turned toward Story. He opened his mouth as if to say something, when his fingers began to spasm around the glass, shattering it. Silver blood seeped from his hand where the glass cut into his skin, and his body began to convulse.

"Eirnin? *Eirnin?*" She grabbed his hand and tried to focus him, to get his attention. He continued to shake, his entire body seizing. Eilantos was out of his seat and at Eírnin's side before Story could blink. He pulled Eírnin out of the chair so violently it fell over with a loud crash. Eilantos lowered Eírnin to the floor gently, cradling his clan leader's head.

"Stay back!" he ordered the sudden rush of elves coming to aid or just look. From the corner of her eye, Story saw hands restrain Ped as he tried to reach his master, howling.

Story fell to her knees next to Eírnin, holding one shaking hand, trying not to get in anyone's way, but at the same time refusing to let go of him. Eilantos barked orders at the elves hovering around. She vaguely heard the healing mages being sent for, but her sole focus was Eírnin. She watched helplessly as his eyes rolled back into his head, and white foam formed at the corners of his mouth.

This can't be happening! I can't lose him. I can't!

Eírnin's body went rigid, and his back bowed up as if tugged toward the ceiling by an invisible string. She felt his hand tighten around hers.

Once. *I.*

Twice. *Love.*

And then... nothing.

CHAPTER THREE

WHO KNEW

"HE'S NOT DEAD. AT LEAST, NOT YET." EÍCETAN'S ROLLING accent, so cruelly similar to Eírnin's, struck Story as incongruous with the Polynesian vibe she always got from his clan's appearance. It also struck her as odd that she would focus on something so insignificant when Eírnin lay, unmoving, on a pile of woven mats on the floor of the Healer's home.

If she'd been asked, Story couldn't say how they arrived on the healing clan's island. It had all been surreal, like a dream. Eírnin, healthy one minute, and then seizing violently the next. And now, thankfully, breathing—if irregularly—but also comatose. Lost to the world. She had yet to relinquish his limp hand, afraid that if she did, whatever tenuous link he still had to this life would be lost.

I can't lose you too. I wouldn't survive it.

Eícetan leaned over Eírnin once again, his ailach—five thin, black stripes that ran from forehead to jaw over his left eye—almost lost in the thousands of black tattoos that covered nearly his entire body. Where Eírnin's tattoos had spiraled fluidly around his left arm and shoulder following the trail of scars a mountain troll had left there, Eícetan's tattoos followed no pattern that Story could discern. They covered his arms, neck, chest, and legs in a series of closely drawn, thin, black lines and geometric shapes.

That had to have taken years.

She was drawn from her introspection when Eícetan sat back and fingered one of the thick wooden plugs in his earlobes. "Aye, I'll need to confirm it with the other mages, Eilantos." He nodded toward the hunter standing in the doorway of the straw roofed hut. "But I stand by it. He's mostly dead. I don't know how much longer he's got. Or what's keeping him here." He looked at Story and shrugged helplessly. "There's still so much we don't know about magic. We have centuries of lore and studies, but only a few months of practical application."

Story bit the inside of her mouth and fought the desire to reach across and rip the wooden plugs from his ears. She wanted answers not excuses, dammit!

Feeling the heat from Story's gaze, Eícetan stood quickly, nearly tripping over the calf-length cotton wrap which served as his only clothing. "Ailesit, I mean no disrespect. I just don't know what caused this."

"I think I do." A female voice, with the same dialect as Eírnin's, broke in.

Story did not look up. She refused to acknowledge the speaker. Of course it would be *her.*

The speaker continued, "This acorn was found among the remains of his glass." Her arm and hand moved into Story's view, as if to separate Story from Eírnin, and Story had to force herself not to swat it away.

The hand opened, revealing a tiny, insignificant acorn resting in its palm. "This was the work of the fey."

Finally, Story looked up.

Eachan.

Something inside Story snapped as all her anger, helplessness, fear, and frustration found an available target. A primal scream tore from her throat, and Story dropped her hold on Eírnin's hand, launching herself at the former clan leader. Her hands were out, fingers curled, intending to scratch, bite, maim, punch, and most importantly hurt the stronger elf as much as she could.

"Get out!" Story grabbed a handful of the elf's short black hair and tugged, jerking Eachan against the thatch wall of the hut. "You're not wanted!" She shoved the elf hard, and Eachan just stared at her, her eyes blank silver pools, showing no emotion.

"Ailesit, you need to stop!" Eilantos's strong hands pulled her away, but she squirmed out of them and ran at Eachan again. She tackled the elf with the full force of her body behind her shoulder and hurled them both through the thin weave of the wall. They landed on the unyielding dirt outside with a thud, and Eachan's breath escaped in an audible whoosh as Story crashed down on her chest. Eachan did nothing to dislodge Story, nor block the attack she was raging.

Story raised a fist and punched the elf in the eye. "Defend yourself!"

Eachan did nothing.

Story punched her again, in the nose this time, feeling her own knuckles split, her crimson blood mixing with the elf's silver. "Fight me, you bitch!"

Several sets of heavily tattooed hands yanked her unceremoniously off the prone, bleeding elf, holding her upright between them. Eícetan stood over Story, chanting and weaving his hands through the air in a complex pattern.

"Let me go!" Story pulled against her captors, squirming and tugging, but to no avail. "I'm going to kill her!"

Eícetan extended his hand, and she could see the silver sparks of magic jumping between his fingertips as he reached for her face.

"No!" She jerked her head as far away from him as she could, her braids whipping across her face. "No! No! No!"

His hand made contact with her forehead, and she felt her body go limp. Eachan finally sat up, wiping at the blood dripping from her nose, leaving a silver smear across her cheek. Her face was still an emotionless mask, but the tears streaming down her cheeks betrayed some feeling at last.

Eícetan dragged two fingers down slowly as he closed Story's eyes. "Sleep, Ailesit. Sleep."

And so she did.

STORY OPENED HER EYES TO FIND SHE WAS NO LONGER IN EÍCETAN'S hut. A wave of panic swept over her as she took in the perfect circle of oak trees around her and the solitary, rough-hewn, stone throne in the center of the clearing. She was in a faerie ring, and worse than that, she was dreaming.

Ever since learning from Eínlin that the vivid dreams she'd had her entire life were actually born from being an untrained dreamwalker, she'd been learning to control her dreams and the places she visited in them. Showing up in the midst of a faerie ring was generally bad. Showing up by some means outside her own was flat out dangerous. She reached for her knife, and of course, it wasn't there. Her hair was unchanged though, and she was still wearing her borrowed sarong.

At least I still have control over my appearance.

Taking a deep breath, she banished the grief over Eírnin's condition which threatened to overwhelm her, tucking it away for later. She had to focus now, or risk getting bespelled, as she had the first time she'd unwittingly visited a faerie ring.

"I did not bring you here to hurt you, Ailesit." The voice, feminine and airy, like the fluttering of leaves in the wind, swirled in the air around Story, coming from all the trees around her at once.

Story whirled, not wanting to leave her back open for attack. The fey couldn't lie, but they were very adept at telling half-truths and not-lies. "Show yourself!"

All she received in response was silence. A light breeze flittered through the grove, sending out a swirl of fallen leaves, just now beginning to change colors.

"I said show yourself!"

A long moment passed, and then a soft crackling sounded from her right. Story quickly turned to face it. A tree slowly emerged from behind a tall oak and glided forward across the ground, its roots undulating over the mossy surface beneath it.

No, not a tree... a woman!

Story's eyes widened. Very tall, nearly seven feet, the tree woman's thick roots twisted up out of the ground around each other to form a trunk that narrowed and widened, following the lines and form of a traditional human female's shape. Thighs, hips, and breasts, all covered in oak bark, almost as if it were just a dress covering the woman beneath. As for the woman, as hard and unyielding as her trunk was, her arms, hands, neck, shoulders, and face were soft and smooth like human or elf skin, almost belying the madness that shone from her solidly white eyes.

She glided to a stop in front of Story and raised her delicate arms as if to say "here I am." Now that she was closer, Story could see the faint outlines of an oak leaf pattern across the surface of her skin. Her red-gold hair streamed out around her face, wild and unkempt, with what Story thought were a few branches and twigs stuck in it. When they moved of their own accord, against the light breeze, she realized they were a part of the tree lady.

"Who are you? Why did you bring me here?" Story eyed her warily, knowing better than to trust a fey. She suspected, based on the very powerful vibe coming from this one, that she was one of the sidhe—masters of the lesser faeries. She'd only met two, before now, and had no desire to encounter another. They were the most dangerous creatures of Ailionora, and that was saying something in world filled with trolls, kraken, and other unknown terrors.

Her host smiled, her features lighting up in beauty, and Story suddenly felt the desire to curl up at the lady's roots for a nap.

Story gave her head a quick shake. "None of that! Or, so help me, I'll come back here in the real world and torch this place when I wake up." She stepped away, backing into the solid trunk of an oak. It was an empty threat, and they both knew it, but Story was not about to stand there and let herself fall under another faerie spell. She'd nearly died the last time. If not for Eírnin... *Don't think about him right now!*

The tree lady's smile softened to just a quirk of her lips at the corner, and she moved to the stone throne in the center of the clearing. Her trunk bent effortlessly at what would have been the knees and hips of a human, and she sat.

"You have nothing to fear from me, Ailesit." With a

fingertip, she traced one of the unfamiliar symbols carved into the throne's armrests. "At least, not for now." Her voice was cultured and refined, much like Morrigann's had been, though hers had a wilder air to it.

Story narrowed her eyes, but didn't say anything. She would not react to threats, no matter how veiled they were, and the faerie had brought her here, so clearly she wanted to talk. Story would not humor her by acting interested.

"I am called the Autumn Princess by mortals. Though, in truth, I have not been called by any name for nearly a thousand years." Her hands tightened on her armrests slightly. "You may call me Metirreonn."

Story raised an eyebrow. "Why would I want to call you anything? I don't really see us being friends."

Metirreonn pursed her lips in annoyance, and her solid white eyes stared unblinkingly at Story.

That's creepy. Don't antagonize the crazy tree lady, Story.

As much as she wanted to lash out, Story checked herself. The sidhe had brought her here for a reason, and she'd be an idiot not to find out why.

"Fine, Metirreonn, what do you want?" She crossed her arms, trying to act nonchalant.

"I believe you know my brother, the Spring Prince."

"Morrigann?" Story dropped her arms to her side in surprise. "Don't you mean the Faerie Prince?" She felt her frown deepen at the memory of that particular faerie. So much loss and pain could be laid at his feet.

The Autumn Princess snorted and somehow managed to make that sound lovely and delicate, like a whistling wind through the trees. "This is what comes from the rest of us being locked away for so long." She drummed her fingers on the armrest. "No, Ailesit, he is the *Spring* Prince. My brother does not rule all the fey, but clearly would have you believe he did.

So typical." Then she smiled again, only this time it sent a chill up Story's spine as the tree spirit locked her milky-white eyes with Story's sea-green ones. "Though you have bound him quite effectively in that iron cage. Indeed, none of us, his kin, can release him. Well done, Ailesit. Well done."

"You didn't bring me here to congratulate me." Story felt her skin grow cold. *Morrigann's sister? Which means she's just as dangerous.* Then she remembered her encounter with the Summer Queen, their mother. *If not more dangerous!*

"You are right. I did not." Metirreonn stilled her fingers. "Spring has something of mine; he knows what it is." She smiled coldly. "I need you to bring it to me."

"And why would I do that?"

A branch from the sidhe's hair glided out in front of her, bearing a single, small acorn. "Because I poisoned Eírnin."

One of the tattoos on her shoulder coalesced into a live oak leaf, and she plucked it before standing up and holding it out toward Story. "And if you want the antidote, you will bring me what I seek."

Story lunged for the leaf, but the Autumn Princess was too quick and crushed it in her hand. "You have until Winter's first frost reaches him. Then, he dies."

Without waiting for a response, Metirreonn disappeared in a scattering of red-gold leaves and sparks.

CHAPTER FOUR

HERE COMES THE SUN

STORY JERKED AWAKE, COVERED IN SWEAT, HER LIMBS TINGLING from disuse. She was no longer dressed in Eírnin's sarong, but one of the simple, white, sleeveless shifts favored by the elf queen and her handmaidens. Looking around and seeing the familiar marble walls and columns, she noted with relief that she was in her rooms on the queen's island.

"Ailesit, you're finally awake!" Eavan, one of Queen Eánna's young handmaidens sat up from the pallet next to Story's bed. No matter how much Story had insisted she didn't need anyone to wait on her, the thirteen-year-old insisted on staying by her side whenever Story was at the queen's residence. For once, Story was glad for her stubbornness.

"How long was I out?" She swung her legs awkwardly over the side of her bed and started rubbing them, trying to regain some feeling.

"Two weeks, Ailesit." Eavan started massaging Story's other calf.

"Damn him!" Story winced at the feeling of thousands of pins and needles swarming up her legs and arms. Eícetan, like all the elves, was still trying to understand his magic now that he had access to it again. He'd clearly used more than he'd intended. "I swear, if he tries that on me again, I'll…"

"Ailesit?" Eavan stopped rubbing and looked up at her curiously. With the moonlight streaming in the open windows, Story could just make out the dots and swirls of color at the corner of the girl's eyes—the builder clan's ailach. She could also see the sparks of yellow worry forming in Eavan's eyes.

"He overdid it. Two weeks wasted!" She tried to stand and would have fallen over if not for Eavan's steadying hands. Carefully, she eased back into a sitting position. One of the techniques Eínlin had shown her was to put her body in a meditative state whenever she dreamwalked. The idea was to allow her to go weeks—or months in extreme cases—without waking, if needed. She'd never tested out more than three days before and now realized just how weak her body was after two weeks without sustenance.

As if reading her mind, Eavan dashed across the room, her straight, hip-length hair trailing behind her like a dark velvet curtain, and filled a plate from a table with breads, cheeses, and fruits. She hurried back and set the food in Story's lap.

"Thank you." Story chewed on a cracker slowly, her jaw stiff and sore from disuse. She wanted to scream. Here she was eating when she needed to be talking to the queen and planning what to do next. Eírnin's life hung in the balance!

"The Dreamwalker's been by, Ailesit. He tried to check on you, but he couldn't get into your dream." The girl passed

Story a glass of cool water, and she took it automatically, remembering the last time Eínlin had been in these rooms.

"...and that, Ailesit, is how you bring someone into the dream. At least, that is the basic concept." Eínlin stroked his flowing, white beard with a flick of his long, lacquered fingernails. "Would you like to try it?"

"Yes, I—" Story's voice caught as a familiar knock sounded at her door. Eirnin walked into her room, eyes closed, and a massive grin on his face. He was filthy, head to toe, but to Story's eyes, he had never looked more handsome. A six-week separation, due to an attempted—and she would later learn failed—alliance with the red dwarves generally had that effect on her.

She ran across the smooth, marble floor of her room and flung herself on him, wrapping her arms around his neck and her legs around his waist. Heedless of the mud staining her pristine white shift, she peppered him with kisses—kisses he eagerly returned. Despite the grime, he still smelled like apples and cinnamon. He still smelled like home.

Eínlin, realizing Story was lost to him, made so quiet an exit that even a hunter would have been proud. He could have knocked over every flower-filled vase in the room and it wouldn't have mattered; neither Story nor Eirnin had eyes for anyone but each other.

"Don't ever leave me again."

"Not if I can help it." He kissed her deeply. "Next time, you're coming with me."

But she hadn't. The queen had never allowed it, stating that it was more important for Story to train with the dreamwalkers. Story always felt as if Eánna was afraid of something. Afraid to let her leave the city of Ailes.

She choked down the remains of her meal, swallowed a gulp of water, and fought the tears that threatened to spill down her cheeks. She didn't have time for grief right now. She needed to plan. She needed to save Eírnin.

Setting aside her plate, she stood shakily.

"I need to see the queen."

Story entered the queen's garden unbidden and unannounced. She followed the meandering trails in the atrium with a haste never intended for the walkways, batting tropical plants and flowers out of her way, and stomping through water features with her bare feet, heedless of the destruction her passage caused.

Walking straight to the corner of the garden she knew the queen favored, she was rewarded by the sight of the elves' monarch and spiritual leader perched on the edge of the carved wooden bench she often shared with her consort, Eilath. Only this time, Eilath, who had been like a surrogate father to Story during her time in Ailionora, was not there. In his place sat a woman in her prime who positively radiated heat and light, as if she carried the sun itself inside of her.

Where Queen Eánna was fair and delicate, her white-blonde hair cascading in waves around her, the woman seated next to her was bold and striking in appearance. She was clothed in an orange slip dress, a short train dragging behind it embroidered with wildflowers. A crown of living sunflowers wreathed her head, and the brilliant copper hair that framed her deeply tanned face was a ragged, haphazard mess.

Story's loud and abrupt intrusion interrupted whatever they'd been discussing, and based on the rigid set of Eánna's posture, the subject had been serious. The stranger turned to look at Story, and Story gasped.

Her eyes!

The fire of a thousand suns seemed to burn inside her eyes. Story recognized them at once.

"Rhiannonn? How?" The last time she'd seen the Summer Queen the sidhe had been a thin little girl of no more than ten or eleven years old. Not a fully-grown woman in the prime of her life.

"As the year grows older, so do I." Rhiannonn stood and twirled a finely carved flute in her hand. "And good evening to you too, Ailesit. It's good to see you awake. Finally." Her voice was smooth and rich, like her children's, only steeped in far more power.

"I, um…" Story opened and closed her mouth, unsure of what to say. Even at the best of times she wasn't a fan of social niceties. Right now, the idea of doing anything that didn't involve saving Eírnin's life made her want to scream or kick something. Preferably both at the same time.

"No need to apologize. As I have been made aware of by Eánna, you are a bit upset right now, and rightly so. Especially as it appears my daughter is responsible for your distress."

Story's jaw dropped, and she looked from one queen to the other. "You know about that?"

Resting her hand on the small swell of her abdomen that carried her heir, Eánna stood up. "Eícetan's clan figured it out about two days after you went to sleep."

"You mean was *forced* to sleep."

Eánna just raised her chin and folded her arms across her chest.

Story let out a frustrated breath and motioned toward the queen with both hands. "I'm sorry, please continue."

"It seems that Autumn has been known to do this before; before the Change, that is." The queen's accent lilted and rolled like the rest of the elves', but her voice also commanded unbroken attention. "The healing mages found old records and sketches of the cause of Eírnin's condition, the acorn, and its cure, the oak leaf. Both from Autumn." Then she cocked her head to the side, regarding Story curiously. "You already know all this. How?"

Story waved a dismissive hand and began pacing. "Not important. What is important is what we're going to do about it."

The Summer Queen sat back on the bench, and Story could have sworn she smelled a faint burning from the wood beneath her. "There is no 'we', Ailesit. You will do nothing."

Story stopped pacing and whirled to face her, hands clenched at her sides. "The hell I won't!" She took two quick strides and stopped just in front of the faerie, so close she could feel the heat radiating from her in waves. Story bent over and shoved a finger in the sidhe's chest, ignoring the burning feeling against her skin. "If you think I'm just gonna sit here and—"

Without warning, Story flew backwards through the air and crashed against one of the leafy palm trees nearby. She tried to get up but found she couldn't move. She couldn't even breathe! This didn't pose an immediate danger—thanks to her dryad half she could hold her breath for long periods of time—but it did prevent her from speaking.

"Never. Do that. Again." Rhiannonn maintained her seat, but her eyes burned even hotter. "I am not your enemy, but neither am I your friend. I work for the preservation of all.

We cannot risk my husband getting his hands on a half-blood. The Uinseann is far too near, and with you in his grasp, Winter could unleash Chaos." With that, the Summer Queen rubbed a hand over her face and slumped in exhaustion.

Story felt the invisible hold on her body release. She looked at the elf queen, whose eyes were still a placid silver, but the tightness in their corners tipped Story off to her worry.

"What about my sister? She's a half-blood too."

"Rhiannonn and I both feel that Adair will not be the Winter King's target, as she is part dryad, part elf, and therefore fully a part of this world. As you are from two worlds, you would be the more tempting target—the more certain key to releasing Chaos." She pointed at a still-damp scroll that lay partially unrolled at her feet. "Almera has promised to keep Adair in Vevila until the Uinseann has passed. She should be safe from all fey there. Safer than you are here."

Story tried not to look surprised that she was getting answers, actually having a *real* conversation with Eánna. *About time!* "What the heck is the Uinseann?"

Neither queen answered, and Story pushed herself back up to her feet, dusting herself off. "Fine, then at least tell me why you let me visit my mom if it is so dangerous for me to travel now?"

Eánna scrutinized her for a moment, as if debating how much she would tell her. "You were safe during the summer, but summer will soon be over. We don't know Autumn's alliances yet—though, the fact that she poisoned Eírnin makes me wonder if she hasn't chosen her father."

The sidhe nodded in agreement. "Winter fears the Hunter."

The two queens shared a look, and then Eánna shook her

head before turning back toward Story. "Regardless, you cannot leave our protection."

The Summer Queen pointed at Story and then at the scroll on the ground with her flute. "I still think it would be safest to kill them both. Then there is no risk."

Before Story could protest, Eánna cut them both off with a slashing gesture of her hand. "We've been over this. That is *not* an option. Story will stay here. I have guaranteed her safety. She will have guards from the warrior clan at all times."

"And what is to prevent my husband from taking her?"

"The same thing that is preventing you, my friend; the iron in this city has been steadily weakening you since your arrival." Eánna looked at the faerie with true concern. "Your earlier trick has nearly drained you. You should go, while you still can."

"Wait!" Both queens turned to look at Story. "Please, can't you go to your daughter's grove and take the antidote? Make her give it to you!"

For once, Rhiannonn looked somewhat remorseful. "It does not work that way, Ailesit. We cannot forcibly take from each other, nor can we compel each other to act. We rule in our season, and that is all. We cannot go into each other's homes uninvited, and I can assure you, my daughter has not invited me into hers for a *very* long time. Nor do I expect she will any time soon."

"But she's your daughter! Can't you do anything?"

The Summer Queen blinked her eyes slowly and looked away. "I am sorry."

Her glow was fading, and in panic Story launched herself at the faerie, landing at her feet. She tried to grab on to the train of her dress, something, anything to make her stay, but all she got were some slightly singed fingers. She found herself sitting alone in the dirt at the base of the bench.

Tears streamed down her face, and all Story could feel was despair. "Are you just going to let him die? Your own cousin?"

Eánna lowered herself onto the ground next to Story and took her hand, intertwining their fingers. "Of course not." In a rare show of emotion, deep blue flooded her irises. "I've already sent two of the best hunters to the east. They will find Metirreonn's grove, and they will bring back the oak leaf."

Story's heart sank. "Two? You only sent *two* hunters? This is Eírnin, for goodness sakes!" She tried to pull her hand from the queen's grasp, but the elf was stronger.

"Story, you must understand we're massing an army here. Readying our allies, and whatever elves we have left, for the coming battle against Winter and his forces. For it will come, I have seen it." Her eyes returned to their blank silver. "I shouldn't have even sent the two after Eírnin."

Story closed her eyes and leaned the side of her head against the wooden armrest of the bench. "They won't get back in time. Summer's almost over. He'll die by Winter's first frost." She looked up at the queen trying to make her understand. "I have to be the one to go. She'll give it to me. She promised. The fey can't break a promise."

The queen sat back and eyed Story carefully. "Did Metirreonn also promise not to hurt you?"

Story ignored the question, eyes unfocused as she began to form a plan.

"You can't go, Story. She's just trying to trap you for her father. The two of them have always been close. You can't trust her. What did she say she wanted from you?"

"She didn't. She said Morrigann knew."

"You are not going." The finality in Eánna's voice brooked no argument.

Story shot to her feet, anger consuming her. Ugly tears sprang into her eyes, and her nose ran as she pitched her voice up in a yell.

"All you care about is making sure Chaos stays locked away! Making sure Winter can't get me! You'd let Eírnin die!"

The queen stood slowly. "Aye, that I would. The lives of many worlds, not just ours, depend on it." She locked her eyes with Story's, holding her with their intensity. "And they are worth more than the life of one elf. Eírnin would agree with me."

"Well I don't." Story spun on her heel and left the queen where she stood.

CHAPTER FIVE

DREAM ON

TWO MEMBERS OF EÍBHILIN'S CLAN TRAILED STORY AS SHE stomped away from the queen's garden back to her rooms.

How the heck did they know to get here so fast?

As she took in their brilliant red-dyed hair that stuck up on their heads in a fat mohawk, Story had half a mind to ask the warriors, but she knew they would maintain a stoic silence. The scarlet of their hair perfectly matched their clan ailach, a stripe that ran from temple to temple across their eyes and the bridge of their nose. The feathers adorning their hair and obsidian-tipped spears fluttered in the breeze caused by the motion of their strides. No, she was certain that these two would not be saying anything.

They stopped outside her door, and she allowed herself a tight smile. "Sorry boys, but this is as far as you get to go. I'm half-dryad you know, and I don't think your conservative elf sensibilities could handle seeing me run around naked in here."

Their normally stern faces flashed with surprise as she slammed her door on them. Locking her door, she leaned her head against the smooth wood and let out a relieved sigh. Now that she was alone, she could have a moment to think, plan, and then act.

"I assure you we won't mind if you run around naked in here, Ailesit."

Story whirled around, eyes wide in surprise. Two more warriors stood in her room, both female, clad in leather breechcloths and moccasins, like the other two, with the addition of a sleeveless leather tunic underneath the traditional beaded vest of the warrior clan. Their hair was also cut in a mohawk on the top, but unlike their male counterparts, the sides were not shaved but, instead, hung down in two long braids that reached their hips.

"You have got to be kidding me. Is this really necessary?"

"Eíbhilin thought so. He thought you might trying jumping off your balcony into the water and go on an ill-advised quest by yourself." The elf cocked her head to the side and studied Story. "I am Eazoa, and this is Easin." She motioned to herself and then to the elf next to her.

"Hi. Wish I could say I was pleased to meet you." Story stalked across her living room to the bathing room, stripped off her shift, and stepped down into the deep pool. She always thought better in the water. And underwater, she'd finally have the privacy to cry for Eírnin.

SLIDING UNDER THE SOFT SHEETS OF HER BED, STORY WAS GRATEFUL for the cool evening breeze that blew through the open archways and windows. Her first summer without air conditioning had been a hot one, and she wondered if it was due to the Summer Queen's presence. A flat, broad, wooden desk sat in the corner of her room, covered in scrolls and sheaves of blank paper. She tried not to imagine Eírnin sitting there studying ancient scrolls, drafting letters to potential allies, or painstakingly maintaining his bow. There would be plenty of time in the coming journey for her to dwell on that. For now, she needed to sleep and, in sleeping, put her plan in motion. A small voice in the back of her mind nagged at her, told her that she should listen to the queens, but she ignored it.

I'm not letting him die. Not when I can save him; I have to do this!

Story turned on her side, closed her eyes, and focused on matching her breathing with the rhythm of the water lapping against the base of the palace below. She had only to turn off her mind, relax, and let her thoughts float away. In the past, this had always been difficult for her, but this time she wasn't trying to sleep for rest; she was on a mission, and it focused her. A familiar, silver haze swept over her mind, and she knew she was in.

She was dreamwalking.

Sitting up, she looked at the archway leading to her balcony, where her guards stood watch in the real world. They were, no doubt, dutifully awake and alert. Story would do her best to change that. Though she hadn't had much success when she'd tried this aspect of dreamwalking in the past, she stood and extended a hand toward where the warriors existed in the waking world.

If I can just bring them into the dream...

Eínlin stepped out from around the archway, one hand held behind his back, while the other stroked his long, white, beard. The ends reached nearly to his waist, as did the wisps of white hair that had escaped from his topknot. He came to a stop, the long layers of his blue robes puddling around his feet. His straw sandals just barely peeped out from underneath the hem.

"I know what you are trying to do, Ailesit."

"Then you know I'm too strong for you to stop me." She wasn't haughty when she said this, just truthful. Story raised both hands, aiming them at him.

The mage cocked one bushy, white eyebrow, but made no move beyond that. "Stronger, aye, that you are." He resumed stroking his beard. "But not more knowledgeable."

Story gathered her will and pushed at him, intending to throw him far away from this dreamscape, far away from her, but she found herself... blocked. She couldn't articulate it more than that. She could still control her own appearance and her location, but she couldn't affect anything else in the dream. Things that had become simple for her over the past few months, like throwing an unwanted person from her dream, were incomprehensibly boxed away.

"What did you do to me?" Story demanded, dropping her hands and clenching them into fists.

"Are you going to fight me, Ailesit?" He shifted slightly, and his deep blue robes glinted in the moonlight—as if they were made of starlight themselves.

"If I have to." She forced her hands to open and stay loose by her side. "But I'd rather not. How are you doing this? What haven't you taught me?" She tried to keep the hurt from her voice, but everything was too raw, too painful to her right now, and even this perceived betrayal cut her deeply.

"Much." His voice held no condescension, only truth. "And there is still much left to learn. Leave off this foolish quest in which you have almost no hope of success. Stay here; continue your studies with the rest of us. We still have so much to learn from each other." He took a step toward her and extended a hand. His long, perfectly manicured fingernails, tipped in glittering blue paint, sparkled in the moonlight.

Story did not take his hand.

"'Almost no hope' means there's at least some hope." She raised her hands imploringly. "Eínlin, please, if you can't help me, at least don't try to stop me. I can't just stay here and do nothing."

"Continuing your studies as a dreamwalker is not doing nothing. Running around half-trained and as a tempting target for Winter leaves you vulnerable and dangerous to yourself and those around you." He took another step toward her, hand still extended.

"Half-trained or not, I can still control it—"

"Not always, Ailesit. You know that. Else, I would not have blocked you so easily just now." He stood before her, hand still held out, entreating her.

She just stared at him.

His voice softened. "Eírnin would not want you to risk your life for his. He would want you to stay, to train. To help keep Winter and Chaos at bay. Above all things, he would want you to be safe."

He almost had her. Almost. Until the last.

Story grasped his hand in friendship. "That's where you're wrong. Eírnin does want me to be safe, but never above all things." She smiled at her mentor. "Above all things, he wants me to be happy."

Eínlin's mouth opened to form a response, but it was too late; Story woke herself from the dream.

A large, slobbery, selkie tongue was licking her hand, and a pair of greenish-orange elf eyes, inches away from her own, greeted her in the pre-dawn light.

Story jerked back, momentarily startled. As usual. *You'd think after all the times she's done that to me, I'd be used to it by now...*

"I know, I know, 'Adair, don't do that! You'll give me heart attack!' Well, you've never had one yet. And I was worried; you weren't waking up. Come on, we've got to go. You need to pack."

Wet and naked, in typical dryad fashion, Story's half-sister jumped off the bed, flinging drops of water everywhere from her long, fiery red braids.

"I know; Eínlin's going to notice those two pretty quick." Story jerked her head toward her softly snoring guards. "How did you get them to sleep anyways?"

"Darts." Adair held out a dry bag to Story. "Hurry up! We're running out of time. Ma's got to know I'm gone by now. And who knows when they'll come busting in your door to stop us."

Story took the bag from her and tossed in her clothes, a cloak, and her old lensatic compass. "How did you know to come find me?"

"After your last visit, Ma forbade me from leaving or visiting Da for the next couple months. She's never done that before. Not even when I was just a pup." She flipped a handful of braids behind her, the bells in them tinkling softly. She was completely unembarrassed by her nudity, and Story often wished she had Adair's self-possession.

"You're only fifteen. You're still a pup." Story pulled off her shift and started winding one of her swimming sarongs around her chest and another around her waist. She might not have much to cover up, tall and bony as she was, but Story still wasn't comfortable swimming in the nude, regardless of her dryad heritage.

"Not by dryad standards. If I wanted to have my own pups now, I could. Ma had Gilroy when she was younger than me. Corcoran when she was about your age, and Mackay…" Adair trailed off under Story's disapproving glare. "Back to how I knew to come find you." She gestured toward Ped. "This fellow showed up, without Eírnin…" She shrugged; the rest was obvious.

Ever since his sister Pinni's death fighting Morrigann, Ped had been glued to Eírnin's side. Whether out of loyalty, devotion, or simply the need for companionship, Story didn't know. The poor selkie was nearly inconsolable now. Ped was still licking Story's hand and whining in a high-pitched keen. In all the madness since Eírnin's poisoning—plus her own two week slumber—she hadn't even noticed the selkie's absence.

"Actually, it's Eírnin now." Story scanned the room for her knife.

"Got himself elected clan leader, did he? Anyways," Adair continued, returning to her story, "I snuck into Ma's room, read a fresh letter from Eánna—"

She was cut off by a knock sounding at the door. Story and Adair both froze and exchanged a glance.

"Ailesit?"

It was Eavan.

Cursing the handmaiden's timing, Story grabbed her knife and strapped it to her right thigh. She motioned toward the archway with her head, and with a nod, Adair slunk back through, dragging the still-whining Ped along with her. It was quite a reach for her to get at Ped's neck, as Adair took after their mother in stature—short and curvy.

"Just a minute!" Story called back through the door, then glanced around the room to see if she'd forgotten anything.

"Ailesit? I heard voices. Is there someone with you? Where are your guards? Is the selkie back?"

"No, no one. That's just me, uh, whining in my sleep. Bad dreams." Story turned toward the archway; it was time to go.

"Ailesit, open the door!" Eínlin's voice came through, and Story knew they'd been found out. The guards on the floor stirred.

"I'm changing. Give me a minute!"

Adair waved frantically and pointed at the water below where a small rowboat was launching in their direction. A boat full of warriors. The door behind them shuddered as something or someone slammed into it.

"Guess they're going to break through. Okay, stealth time is over." Story tied the dry bag to Ped's back and twisted to boost Adair onto the selkie when she heard a body fall heavily to the ground.

"Adair!" Story's heart raced; who could have attacked them?

"What?" Adair tucked the small dart reed back into the mass of braids on her head. "Sorry, she's a bit sneaky that one."

One of Story's guards, Eazoa, was on the floor near her feet snoring softly, another dart protruding from her neck.

"Right, let's go." Adair climbed onto Ped's back and reached out an arm to help Story.

Story was glad Adair's arm was full-grown again. After a kraken had cut her old arm off several months ago, she'd had a stubby arm the size of an infant's for a few weeks while it grew back. As great as it was that her sister could regrow limbs, it was a bit off-putting to witness firsthand.

The door to her bedroom burst open and half a dozen elves swarmed in with Eínlin leading the charge, hands raised. Sparks of magic flew from his fingers, and Story found she was suddenly irresistibly sleepy, ready to slump where she stood. Adair yanked her up onto Ped, and in an instant they were airborne, leaping over the balcony railing.

Water swirled around them as they crashed through the surface, and Story again fought the overwhelming urge to sleep. Ped shifted into his seal form as elf bodies thrashed around them in the water. They'd capsized the boat when they landed. Story hoped the elves would be okay. Her eyelids were so heavy. She opened her mouth to yawn and instead received a mouthful of water.

"Story! Where do we need to go?" Adair's thoughts filled Story's mind and she tried to muddle out the answer. She knew, but she just wanted to yawn again.

"Ask me later... Need a nap." Her eyes drifted closed.

Adair grabbed her by the arms and shook hard, causing Story's head and hair to bob wildly in the water.

"We don't have time for this!"

Story opened her eyes halfway and absentmindedly noticed that some of the elves were no longer thrashing but were purposefully swimming toward them. She suppressed another yawn.

"Story, focus! I need to know where to tell Ped to go. We need to help Eírnin!"

That momentarily broke through the haze of Story's mind. *"Faerie Land... Get help..."*

Her eyes closed again, and she felt an unfamiliar set of hands grip her shoulders from behind before Adair ripped her from their grasp and shoved Story back onto Ped. Story gazed behind them as the selkie swam away, faster than anything else in this world, and took in one last view of the City of Ailes before her eyes closed once again, this time in a dreamless sleep.

CHAPTER SIX

Old Friends

STORY LAY ON HER BACK ON DRY LAND. WELL, IN THE DIRT TO be specific—she knew at least that much. She could feel the sun burn brightly behind her closed eyelids. A loud moan escaped her. She had the worst headache she'd ever experienced, her mouth felt full of cotton, and she was sweating profusely.

If this is what a hangover feels like, I'm never getting drunk.

She moaned again and cracked her eyes open.

"Finally awake are you?" Adair's thick, Welsh-sounding accent focused Story. "I know you like to sleep, but this is ridiculous. Been waiting nearly two days. You haven't slept this long since the fuath got you."

Another two days wasted! "Sorry." Story's voice cracked. "I don't think a person is meant to be forced into an enchanted sleep so quickly after waking from another." She sat up slowly, with help from Adair, and rubbed her temples with her fingertips. "They *can't* keep doing this to me."

"Well, clearly they can." Adair shoved an orange slice into Story's mouth. "You need to figure out how to put up mental wards or something." She shoved another slice in Story's mouth before she could even chew the first. "I bet your faerie friend can help you with that."

Story dodged the next slice and swallowed her current mouthful. "For starters, he's not my friend. And he's not going to want to help me at all once he finds out what I want from him." She stood up, surprised at how quickly she was recovering.

Looking at the half-eaten orange in Adair's hand, Story felt her stomach grow cold. "Where did you get that?"

Adair pointed at one of the trees in the wild orchard behind them. The orchard was penned by a living, rambling, wooden fence, and there were thousands of trees spread out as far as the eye could see. There were trees of every fruit imaginable: cherry, peach, pear, pomegranate, and of course, orange, to name a few, all in various stages of growth and bloom.

"Wait, you can see the orchard?" Story was surprised. It had been invisible to Eírnin when they'd come to restore *The Ailes* last spring.

Maybe when I caged Morrigann his wards fell?

"Aye, of course. Should I not be able to? Because I can. Why? Can't you? Oh, that's a shame. It's lovely, all sprawling and wild, yet there seems to be some order to it. I don't quite understand, but I love—"

Story grabbed Adair's upper arms. "How much did you eat?" When Adair didn't answer her immediately, Story gave her a shake. "Tell me! Now!"

Adair's normally green eyes gained swirls of yellow. "Not much. Only an orange or two. I don't eat as much as you. I'm not human, remember?"

Story dropped her sister's arms and heaved a sigh. "Never eat fey food; didn't mom teach you that?" She scrubbed a hand across her face. She had no idea what eating from Morrigann's garden would do to them, but she was certain it couldn't be good. The last time he'd had any sway over her, she'd almost died.

Heck, I practically helped him kill me!

"I don't guess there's anything we can do about it now." Story pulled out her compass from the dry bag and let out another sigh. "Come on, time to visit my friend."

"Hello, friend." Story smiled, feeling at peace for the first time since Eírnin had been poisoned. Her compass pointed unerringly at *The Ailes*, the great tree that was the source of the elves' magic. She rested a hand on the smooth trunk of the tree and stood on her toes to smell one of the exquisite silver blossoms. *Heavenly!* Red apples peppered the branches of the tree, and Story could have sworn she heard the echo of her own heartbeat in the roots of the tree. It was the first time she'd been back to visit *The Ailes* since her blood had saved it.

In a way, she was tied to the tree, and it to her. It was happy and healthy, she could feel that. But she could also feel an echo of her own sadness over Eírnin's plight.

"It's not your fault. There's nothing you could have done." Story leaned her forehead against the bark, feeling the magic prickle against her skin. "My friend, I'll need your help in one thing, though. If you can." She pictured what she needed in her mind and felt warmth wash over her. The tree would help her.

Smiling again, Story patted the trunk one last time, loathe to leave, but she knew she had to. She really couldn't afford to delay any longer. Every minute brought Winter's first frost ever closer.

Adair stared at *The Ailes*. She'd been standing speechless since they'd arrived, and for the girl, that was saying something.

"It's real." Her voice was quiet, hushed.

Story quirked an eyebrow. "You knew it was real. You watched me plant the apple I brought back in the queen's courtyard. You've visited the sapling growing there."

"Yeah, but this is amazing. It's *real*." Adair shook her head. "I can't explain it. I… I can feel it. The magic in my veins is dancing. Does that make any sense?"

Story smiled and took her sister's hand. "It does. Now come on, time to visit the inmate."

Adair continued to stare at the tree until it was out of sight and they were stepping into the clearing at the heart of Morrigann's home. Even then, Story had to snap her fingers in front of Adair's nose to get her attention. Though the sidhe was caged, he was still dangerous, and they needed all their senses alert and ready.

"I know you're out there. You may as well come forward," a silky, cultured voice rolled out from the center of the clearing. "It's not like I can do anything to you from in here."

Ped growled and Story stiffened at the sound of the Spring Prince's voice—so lovely and refined, seductive and musical. She took a deep breath and motioned for Adair and Ped to stay behind her as she stepped into the clearing. It was a perfect circle, a faerie ring with a wooden throne in the middle that looked like it had grown there. An iron cage surrounded it, its thick bars bent and twisted together at the top. Ped's growl deepened, and Adair gasped... then giggled, as only a fifteen-year-old girl could.

Oh great. I really don't need more complications right now.

The reason for Adair's reaction was obvious. Seated on the throne at the center of it all was Morrigann, playing a spry tune on his gold violin. His skin, lightly dusted with gold that glimmered faintly in the sunlight, radiated magic. His blonde hair was streaked with gold as well, and his finely chiseled body, plainly visible since he wore only a leafy green kilt, looked like it had been sculpted from stone. He locked his glittering violet eyes with Story's and smiled as beautifully as his sister had.

And yet, Story was completely unmoved. Adair giggled again, and Ped began to whine, but Story felt nothing for the sidhe, except perhaps a bit of sadness. He might be putting on a fine show, but he looked... diminished. When she'd last seen him at the height of spring, he had been nearly as bright and full as his summer mother, but now he had faded. Had Story never seen him in his full glory, she might have been taken in by this attempt to portray strength, but she knew what he was truly capable of, and this was nowhere near it.

"Oh, don't look at me with those pity-filled eyes." Morrigann slowed his bow, his song becoming mournful. "You don't get to feel sorry for me. You put me here. What did you expect? That you could leave me in a cage surrounded by this much iron and nothing would happen to me?"

Story bit back an instinctual apology—he was responsible for so much death and sadness. What she'd done had been for the greater good. In her opinion, he'd gotten off easy. "How do I know you don't look like that just because it's nearly autumn and your season's been over for a while?"

He curled up the corners of his mouth in a smirk and released his violin. "You don't." With a wave of his hand the instrument began playing a familiar tune on its own.

My lullaby! She narrowed her eyes in irritation but did not say anything. He had lured her with the tune before, and she would not give him the satisfaction again. After all, the last time he'd played this for her, she'd wound up on top of a sacrificial altar as he tried to plunge an obsidian blade into her heart.

He adjusted his position on his chair, hanging a leg over one wooden arm, and propped his head against his hand. "So, my dear, sweet, *simple*, girl, to what do I owe the honor of your presence? Not that I'm complaining—I always do love our time together." He glanced past Story's shoulder and widened his eyes with curiosity and excitement. "And who is this? I must say, Story, your choice in traveling companion has greatly improved. I'm glad you've left the elfling. You were no fun when he was around."

A deep-seated rage boiled up inside Story, but she pushed it down, calming herself.

You need his help. Don't do anything to jinx this!

She opened her mouth to answer him, but Adair beat her to it, pushing past Story and getting perilously close to the bars.

"I'm Adair. I'm Story's sister. Well, half-sister." Adair flipped her braids over her shoulder and giggled. "I'm also a dryad. Well, half-dryad—"

Story yanked Adair back and glared at her. "Now is *not* the time."

Morrigann grinned. "Well, Story, I can see where you get taste in clothing from. Quite a change from when you first arrived in our world." He gestured toward Adair with his free hand, and Story suddenly felt very exposed. She was still in her swimming sarong, and Adair wasn't wearing much more. The worst part was she knew Morrigan was just acting this way to throw her off balance. He knew she wanted something, and he knew the fact that Eírnin wasn't with her was significant. Yet, he was still going to try to make a game of this. Like always.

He ran a finger along the surface of his gold violin and smiled to himself, as if he had some deep dark secret, which, Story was certain, he probably had several, when she realized something important:

Metirreonn hadn't had an instrument!

She'd never seen Morrigann or his mother without their instruments. Even if they were just sitting quietly in the background, unused... they were *always* there.

I bet that's what he has!

Adair had wandered up near the cage again despite Ped's best attempts to block her. Hauling her sister back once more, Story whirled Adair around to face her. "So help me, Adair, if you don't do exactly what I say from here on out I *will* send you back to Vevila."

Maybe I should, she's a half-blood too...

The girl's eyes widened and became a mixture of yellow and blue. Story sighed and let go of her arms, indicating with a nod of her head that Adair should go back to the clearing's edge. It was bad enough that she was risking her own life. She couldn't risk Adair's too. At the first chance, she would send her back home with Ped, where she'd be safe.

Even if I have to tie her down to the selkie!

Decided, Story turned back to the cage. "I need your help."

"I'd gathered that much. Why else would you come visit me?" He leaned around her and winked at Adair. "Unless you're matchmaking—"

A dull thud sounded, and Morrigann looked down to find Story's knife embedded in the wood of his chair, a mere inch from his thigh. He hopped out of the seat as if he'd been burned, and Story dropped her throwing arm, willing him to feel the fire in her eyes.

"Stop enchanting my sister." She flicked her eyes to the still quivering knife. "Next time I won't miss."

Morrigann held up his hands in a placating gesture. "Calm down, no need to be throwing iron around. I'm not enchanting your sister."

Story narrowed her eyes.

"Honest! You know I can't lie. She simply ate too many of my oranges. It'll wear off in a few days." He stretched his arms over his head, showing off the chiseled lines of his muscles. "And if it doesn't, well then, I can't help it if the girl likes me. Just look at me."

Story gave a disgusted groan, and he curved his mouth up in a half-smile. "Besides, she's not the one I'm interested in." He gave Story a knowing wink.

"Seriously? When have I given you any reason to think I might be remotely interested in you?"

"I seem to recall—"

"Any reason when I had control of my own mind." Story crossed her arms. "Look, you know I'm not here for a social call. I need something from you."

Morrigann made to sit in his throne again, saw Story's

knife, and opted to lean against the armrest instead. "I know." He waved a hand in her direction. "Proceed."

"I need you to take me to Metirreonn's grove. Eírnin's been poisoned, and only one of her leaves can save him. I don't know the way there. I need a guide. I need you." She didn't feel a bit bad about not telling him the full truth—that she was trading him, or whatever it was Metirreonn wanted, for Eírnin's life. *Nope, not one bit. And now to sweeten the deal.* "I'll have to let you out of your cage to guide me." *I can always put him back...*

Morrigann paced the length of his cage, which wasn't much—no more than five steps in either direction. She bit her lower lip and tried not tried not to fidget. The seconds seemed to drag on, as though they were hours.

Finally, he stopped and faced her, a rare, serious expression on his face.

"Let me get this straight, you want me to help you get to Cildara and steal one of my sister's leaves for an elfling I care less than nothing for."

"Yes." Story inwardly flinched at his casual disregard for Eírnin's life.

"My sister, who hates me and blames me for imprisoning her these last thousand years—and rightly so, I might add."

Story's eyes widened. *Well, that explains why Autumn is pissed at him... but now I only have more questions.* "Yes." She took a step closer to the bars.

"And nearing the autumn equinox, no less, when she will be at both the height and the heart of her power, and I'll be at my lowest?"

"Yes." Story's palms began to sweat. Perhaps he didn't value his freedom as much as she'd banked on.

Morrigann leaned in toward the bars, but did not touch them, maintaining a few inches of separation. Still, she knew the proximity had to be draining him, so she leaned in closer, leaving about a foot of space between the two of them.

He smiled, and Story felt a flash of hope.

"No."

CHAPTER SEVEN

A Thousand Miles

WITH A FLASH OF SPEED BORN OF HER TIE WITH *THE AILES*, Story shot her left arm through the bars, wrapped it around Morrigann's neck, and yanked him within a hairsbreadth of the iron. Smoke rose from his cheek at the mere proximity of the bars. Touch would leave him with a lasting scar. His blackened and burned hand, from when Eírnin had stabbed him with her knife last spring, attested to that fact.

Lowering her head to his ear, Story dropped her voice to a whisper. "Don't think for a moment that just because I let you live last time I won't hesitate to destroy you now." He pulled against her hand, but this close to the iron he was too weak to resist as she held him fast.

"But how would that help you save the elfling?" His words were slow and came out in labored gasps.

"It won't. But it would definitely make me feel better." She needed him to be absolutely certain of the seriousness of her threat. With a flex of her fingers, Story jerked Morrigann's cheek against the iron bar. A scream tore from his throat as his flesh burned. Story held on tighter to his jerking head; she knew she wasn't acting rationally, but she didn't care. She'd already lost everyone she cared about once before. She would *not* go through that again.

Cool hands wrapped around her arm, pushing it into the cage, allowing Morrigan's face to move free of the bars.

"Story, no! Not like this." Adair reached her other arm through the bars and pried Story's fingers from the faerie's neck. "Eírnin wouldn't want this. You need to stop!"

Story blinked and shook her head to clear it. Adair stood before her, a look of shock on her face, and Story felt a rush of anger and shame shoot from her head to her toes. Beyond her sister lay Morrigann, clutching his cheek and staring at her with wide glittering eyes. He would forever bear a scar on his cheek.

From me.

She suddenly felt nauseated.

Breathing slowly to calm her racing pulse, Story ignored Adair's accusing gaze and gazed down at the sidhe.

"Well?"

He stood up slowly and dropped his hand. An angry black burn streaked across the length of his cheekbone, a finger's width across. "I will take you to Cildara on one condition." He raised the index finger on his burned hand to punctuate his words.

"And that is?"

"Once I get you to my sister's grove, you will release me from my servitude. I will be free. No more cages." He touched his cheek with a wince.

Story didn't even hesitate. "Agreed."

The Spring Prince shook his head and kept his distance. "Not good enough. I know something of you humans; you can make and break promises like the shifting of the wind. You must swear an oath. On the *The Ailes*."

Story stepped back, completely unprepared for this. She did not give her word lightly, but she also knew she'd come here willing to promise Morrigann anything, knowing that she could go back on her word if needed, even though the thought made her sick to her stomach.

What am I becoming?

This was different. If she swore this oath, that meant he would be free to once again wreak havoc on Ailionora. Could she do that? Could she put Eírnin's life above everyone else's?

Haven't you already done that just by leaving the safety of the queen's protection?

"Decide soon, little human. Before I change my mind." Morrigann smirked, the new burn on his cheek somehow enhancing his good looks rather than detracting from them. It gave him a roguish air.

Taking a deep breath, she let it out slowly. *In for a penny, in for a pound, right?* "I swear, on *The Ailes*, that once you have seen me and my companions safely to Metirreonn's grove, I will release you from your obligation to me."

"And..."

Story pressed her eyes closed, feeling sick over her next words. "And I will not imprison you again."

There has to be some sort of loophole!

But even as she said the words and felt them bind her to the sidhe, she knew there wasn't. If she did not release the Spring Prince upon completion of his part of the bargain, it would destroy her.

Morrigann smiled and raised his arms in a less than humble shrug. "Well, aren't you going to let me out?"

THEY STOOD ON THE BEACH ALONG THE MASSIVE LAKE THAT BORDERED Morrigann's garden. Story's knife was back in her thigh sheath, but Morrigann looked even more diminished than he had before. At her request, *The Ailes* had loaned Story the power to bend one of the bars far enough for Morrigann to climb out of his cage. Still, the passage had drained him significantly. His skin still glowed, but it was much fainter now, and his hair seemed to have lost some of its brilliance.

Morrigann noticed both Story and Adair staring at him, and he frowned. "What did you expect? You know iron drains my kind, and now I don't know how far I'll be able to take us."

Story exchanged a confused look with Adair. "What do you mean how far you'll be able to take us?" Story waved toward the water. "Aren't we going to swim?"

"Oh, you'd like that, wouldn't you? Shove my face into iron, make me climb past it, and then lure me into a sea full of salt." He crossed his arms across his chest, which in turn flexed his biceps, presumably to show them off to his traveling companions. "Honestly, what have I ever done to make you so vindictive?"

Story placed her hands on her hips and glared. "Oh, I don't know? Should we start with all the times you tried to kill me? And then *did* kill me?"

He rolled his eyes and threw his arms up in exasperation. "Well, yes, but you came back to life, so that hardly counts."

Story leaned in and jabbed a finger in his chest. She opened her mouth to retort when Adair interposed herself between them and pushed them apart.

"Oi! Look you two, knock this bickering off. It isn't helping anything. Let's just go." Suiting action to words, she stripped off her sarong and stepped in the water.

Morrigann didn't wink, didn't smile, didn't even stare. He simply picked up Adair's sarong and held it out to her.

"We're not swimming, little dryad, or have you forgotten what salt does to my kind?"

"Then how are we getting to your sister's place?" Adair took her sarong from his hands and reluctantly began winding it back around her body.

"Yeah, I'd like to know that too." Story still had not relaxed her posture.

"I'll take us there," Morrigann said simply, as if that explained everything. "Get on the selkie. I don't know how far I can get us as my power's almost completely drained. In my season this would be no problem at all. But now…" He shrugged.

Story boosted Adair onto Ped's back, but before she climbed on herself she turned back to Morrigann. "So help me if you—"

"Ailesit!" His violet eyes glittered menacingly. "I have given you my word. I can do *nothing* to harm you, or your companions until I see you safely to Cildara." He leaned in and raised his index finger to her face. "Believe me, if I could harm you, you would *not* be standing here right now."

Story was taken aback by the vehemence in his voice. He'd been, at times, flirtatious, teasing, kind, seductive, playful, even while being murderous—but he'd *never* shown his temper so baldly before. It scared Story, and she was very quickly reminded that just because she'd beaten him once, it had taken the loaned strength of the world to do so. Even now, weakened and drained, Morrigann was still a sidhe, Lord of the Spring, and very *very* dangerous. Without another word, she climbed onto Ped's back.

Morrigann stepped toward Ped, and the selkie growled. When the fey reached out his hand, Ped snapped at his fingers.

"Will you get that beast under control? I can't do this if he's trying to eat me."

Adair leaned forward and whispered into Ped's ear. His loud snarls turned into low growls and eventually dwindled to silence. His ears drooped, and he whined softly. Adair continued to whisper into his ear and motioned Morrigann forward. The Spring Prince extended his hand once again, and while the selkie's neck flinched at the fey's touch, he did not shy away or attempt to bite him again.

"Hold tight. We'll go as far east as my power will take us." He raised his other arm and flicked his wrist in a circle. Gold sparks shot out around them, and they were suddenly surrounded by a cloud of tiny pixies. Story's heart leapt, and she couldn't help the smile that blossomed on her face. She'd always loved the pixies; loved to dance with them, to play with them, to simply be with them.

But the pixies had no time for play now. They swirled around the group faster and faster in concentric circles while Story felt squeezed tighter and tighter. The lake and surrounding mountains disappeared, and all she could see was a swirl of glittering gold. The pixies flew faster still, and the pressure surrounding them was so intense Story thought she was going to implode.

Abruptly, the gold sparks drifted away, and Story felt as

if she'd just burst from the end of a tube. She took a deep, relieved breath and heard Adair and Ped do the same.

Morrigann dropped his hand limply from the selkie's neck and stumbled a few steps before collapsing face first into the forest's thick undergrowth. The pixies that had swirled around them lost their glow and dropped. Upon hitting the earth they dissolved in a shower of gold sparks. Story felt a momentary pang of guilt as she realized those pixies were gone for good.

Adair slid off the back of the selkie and ran over to Morrigann's side. "He's still alive!" Story didn't know if she should be relieved or not. "Come on, Story. Help me move him—he's heavier than he looks."

Story patted Ped's neck. "I don't suppose you could help us—"

She found herself flat on the ground as Ped puffed out his jowls before turning and showing her his hind end.

"Okay. Guess that's a 'no'." Standing up, she dusted herself off before rubbing her backside. She hadn't broken anything, but that had hurt.

She frowned as she bent over and picked up Morrigann's arms while Adair hefted his legs. "Can't we just drag him?" Story puffed as they wrestled his limp body over the underlying scrub brush to a dying meadow. "And shouldn't he weigh like practically nothing? He's a faerie for goodness sakes! I thought they were just glitter and malice in a pretty package."

Adair grunted as she lifted his legs over a log. "I don't know. I never realized the Sidhe were this dense. Of course, I've only met one other, and the Summer Queen didn't let me lift her. Not that I asked. Not that I wanted to. She's scary. Don't you think she's scary?" Adair paused for a breath, and

Story took the opportunity to dump her end of the limp Spring Prince onto the browning grass.

"That's good enough." She brushed her hands together to get rid of any residual dirt and looked down at Morrigann. His appearance surprised her—he looked completely normal. He was still attractive, only in a very cursory sort of way. His features, the shape of his jaw, his form were all still pleasing to the eye, but his skin had the pale, unhealthy pallor of someone who never went outside. His hair hung limp against his head, dull and straw-colored. His face had a haggard look to it, as if he hadn't slept in days. Overall, he appeared as if he was suffering from a slow, wasting disease.

A pang of guilt flared in Story's gut again, but she clamped it down and turned away from the faerie, taking in their surroundings. It was a forest, like so many others in Ailionora, filled with evergreens and deciduous trees, some of which already had leaves changing color.

It'll be winter soon…

"I wonder where we are?" Story reached for her compass, but then realized how useless it would be. The compass always pointed toward *The Ailes*, not north.

Adair finished adjusting Morrigann, trying to make him as comfortable as she could. Then she joined Story at the edge of the clearing, licked her finger, and stuck it up in the air. After a few seconds, she put her finger back in her mouth as if tasting it.

"We're near Emerald Cove. Which means the biggest nearby village is Peddler's Port." Adair smiled, as if over a memory. "It's been *forever* since I've been to Peddler's Port. The last time we were there Da and I—"

"Wait a sec, did you just *taste* the air to figure out where we were?"

"Aye, that I did. Why? Can't you do that too? All dryads can. We can sense all the water around us at all times."

"Guess I missed out on the 'water tasting' gene. I suppose it was a package deal with the 'breathing underwater' gene." Story shrugged. "So that's how you knew where we were? You could taste Emerald Cove from here?"

"Yes and no. I could taste Emerald Cove, but I could also taste Peddler's Port, and I could taste our surroundings. Without licking them of course. That would be odd."

Story felt her eyes grow wider. "You tasted everything? Not the water?" *Because yeah, that's not weird at all.*

Adair started to laugh, and Story felt better. *She was just teasing me!*

"Don't be silly, Story! Of course I was tasting the water. Just about everything has water. You have water, so I can always tell when you're near by the taste of the moisture in the air. I can tell when anyone I know is near. You know what's odd?" She pointed at Morrigann. "He doesn't taste like anything. I don't know if that's because he's not like us mortals, or if he's got some sort of ward up."

Story glanced over her shoulder at Morrigann. "Have you ever been able to 'taste' fey?"

Adair shook her head. "No."

"Maybe they aren't made up of water then."

"But that wouldn't make sense; they're the essence of nature!"

Story shrugged. "Look, I don't even pretend to begin to understand them. So, are there any other dryad skills or abilities I should know about? Things you guys, um, I mean, we, can do with water?"

"Aye." Adair cocked her head to the side and gave Story an appraising look. "And quit trying to avoid the topic."

"What?" Story raised an eyebrow. "What topic am I trying to avoid exactly?"

Adair crossed her arms across her chest. "You know what I mean: Eírnin."

"I don't want to talk about it." Story turned away.

Reaching out a hand, Adair rested it on Story's arm. "You need to. You're not acting like yourself. What happened in Faerie Land? That wasn't you."

Story shrugged her hand off. "How am I supposed to act? Like everything's okay? Like I'm not about to lose everything all over again?"

"You still have me and Ma."

Story didn't know how to answer Adair without hurting her feelings. Nothing she said would be okay. *It's not the same. I love you but not like I love Eírnin. It's just not the same...*

The awkward silence extended until Adair finally realized Story was not going to speak.

"Eírnin wouldn't want you to act like this. Raging around, hurting others." She paused and then bit her lower lip. "Hurting yourself."

Whirling around, Story stuck her index finger in Adair's face. "I am *sick and tired* of people telling me what Eírnin would or would not have wanted for me. What about what *I* want for me?" She dropped her hand and ignored the bright yellow and blue swirls in Adair's eyes. "Besides, none of us are really in a position to know what Eírnin would want, are we?"

Adair had no answer, and as the first silver tear slid down the girl's cheek, Story spun around once again and jogged in the direction Adair had indicated Emerald Cove was. She needed to swim. Well, mostly, she needed to not see her little sister cry. She knew she should apologize, that she should stay and comfort Adair, but her heart could only take so much breaking.

CHAPTER EIGHT

EMPTY

*E*IRNIN PULLED OFF HIS TUNIC AND DOVE FROM THE PIER INTO *the water. He surfaced and shook his head, scattering a halo of water droplets around him. He looked up at Story with* mischievous orange eyes as he treaded water. "Aren't you coming in? I thought you wanted to swim."

Cocking her head to the side, Story quirked the corner of her mouth up in a half-smile, admiring the view before her. "Maybe I just wanted an excuse to get your shirt off."

He laughed. "You don't need to contrive reasons for that!"

"I know." Her half-smile blossomed into a full grin, and she dove in after him. Not surfacing, she yanked his leg and pulled him down under with her. He didn't fight her, but instead reached out. Finding her, he pulled Story tightly to him. The orange in his eyes rapidly shifted to purple. Eirnin's lips met hers and—

Story forcefully banished the memory and kicked against the bottom of the cove, pushing herself to the surface. She needed to breathe again, and memories like that caused nothing but pain right now. She'd been trying to review the things Eínlin had taught her those first few days—after that swim she'd decided to take him up on his offer of training to become a dreamwalker.

"Do you think I should do it?" Story and Eirnin were back on the dock now, kicking their feet back and forth in the water while Ped swam nearby, occasionally surfacing for a scratch on the head from Eirnin.

"Do what?" Eirnin turned to look at her, sparks of orange curiosity in his eyes.

"Work with Eínlin on the dreamwalking stuff. To learn from each other." She turned back to look at the setting sun. "He said that there's so much we could unlock together. That it'll take a lot of time and hard work, but that with his knowledge and my experience we could make up for centuries of lost time."

Eirnin interlaced his fingers with hers. "Aye, it sounds like a good thing then. You'd learn to control your ability, and he'd learn how to use his. All the mages of his clan would."

"And you could definitely use some dreamwalkers in the coming war, eh?" Story bumped his shoulder with hers.

"I won't deny it. Aye, dreamwalkers will be a great asset when the time comes. We need any advantage we can get. Winter will be a formidable foe."

"Why?" Story raked her fingers through her braids, trying to reign in her sudden impatience. "Why are we going to fight him? I mean, all anyone has said the past couple weeks is 'prepare for the coming war' and 'Winter is going to unleash Chaos and destroy everything.' But no one's bothered to say why or how he's going to do this." She gave him a sidelong glance. "It's like you all know something I don't."

Eirnin shook his head. "You know I'd never keep something like this from you. I don't exactly know the details myself. The

Summer Queen said he was coming and we needed to prepare. So we are preparing."

"So we're just going to go off to war on the word of a faerie?"

"They can't lie."

"I know that! But doesn't anyone know more? Isn't anyone the least bit curious?" Story blew out her breath in frustration.

"Eánna knows all the details there are to know. As do the clan leaders. But they aren't sharing the information, and it's not my place to ask."

"Well, maybe it's mine!"

But it hadn't been.

As Story dove back to the bottom of the cove, remembering how the queen had flatly refused to answer her questions, then taken to avoiding her when Story kept at her over the following months. In fact, the most information she'd received from her was during her last meeting, when Eánna and Rhiannonn had forbidden her to leave the queen's island.

Why does Winter need a half-blood? And why does he want to unleash Chaos? And who or what is Chaos?

There was still so much she didn't know!

And why won't they tell me?

She kicked harder, propelling herself to the bottom before finally settling cross-legged on the rocks and sand.

I bet Morrigann knows…

She thought about the unconscious sidhe in the meadow, how he looked one step away from fading away into nothing. How she'd purposefully burned him on the iron of his cage and then nearly destroyed him by trying to force him to help her. She thought of the fallen pixies whose lights had gone out, never to return.

I don't care. Eírnin's worth a million of them.

But was he worth the world? All the worlds and everyone in them?

Yes!... and no. No one is worth that. Except to me, he is.

Story grabbed a handful of sand in frustration. She didn't even know her own mind. *Because I haven't had a chance to sit and think or process what's happened.*

Ever since Eisrus had brought the news of Eírnin's election as clan leader, she felt like she'd been caught up in a storm, unable to do anything other than react to the next blow that was sure to come. In the interim, she'd allowed her emotions to lead her completely.

She thought about her unprovoked attack on Eachan, and her willingness, or rather—if she was honest with herself—her satisfaction at hurting Morrigann. She felt her face burn with shame once again.

What am I becoming? I don't know who I am anymore.

She could almost hear her father chastising her again, as he had when she'd ridden his motorcycle without permission and laid it down on a turn, mangling the bike and nearly herself in the process. She'd blamed the bad breakup with her first boyfriend for her actions, but her dad had never been one to let her off easy.

"Don't you go haring off on an emotional bender. I know you're young, but that don't mean you can just say or do whatever you want with no consequences. Just because somethin' is what you want, it don't mean it's the right thing to do. Once you do or say somethin' it's done. You can't take it back."

He'd promptly grounded her for a month... and also taken the time to teach her how to ride a motorcycle safely.

She felt tears well up in her eyes and drift away in the

gentle current. It was the first time in months she'd felt sadness over the loss of her family, but it was also the first time in months she'd felt she truly needed her father. Not just for his wisdom but for his comfort and strength.

So what am I going to do?

She released a handful of sand and watched it disperse in a light cloud.

I've made such a mess of things.

She'd already decided she was going to continue on to Cildara. She was sure that if she didn't, Eírnin would die. Metirreonn had almost certainly set it up that way. And, if the queens were correct, it was a trap for Story. But by knowing it was a trap she could plan to defuse it. For that she needed information, and if the enmity between the siblings was what she thought it was, she was fairly certain she could get Morrigann to give her the information she needed.

As for Adair, well, her sister wouldn't like it, but she had to go back to Vevila. It was bad enough that Story was out and about, providing a tempting target for Winter; they didn't need two half-bloods running around.

It felt good to have a chance to sit and process things instead of just reacting blindly. Decisions made, she kicked off the bottom of the cove and swam back to shore.

"ADAIR, YOU HAVE TO LEAVE. YOU HAVE TO GO BACK TO VEVILA."

Her sister's mouth hung open, half filled with the raw fish she'd been snacking on. Story's fish was cooking over the night's campfire—she only ate sushi when she had no other choice. Adair's mouth snapped shut, and she swallowed her food whole.

"Why?" Her eyes clouded in yellow worry, and she stayed uncharacteristically quiet.

Story smoothed her knee-length, pleated wrap-skirt around her, considering her words. "I don't really know all the details, but I do know half-bloods are Winter's targets right now." She fingered the laces of the lavender archery vest that Mister Tilpasse, the gnome tailor, had made for her last spring. "That means you need to go back to Mom until the Uinseann—whatever that is—passes." She met her sister's eyes in an attempt to convey the truth of her next words. "I don't want you to leave, but you're both in danger and a danger to everyone by being here."

"No!" Adair shot to her feet and threw the remains of her dinner on the ground. "You can't make me. I'm going with you whether you like it or not. You need my help!" She put her hands on her hips. "Besides, you're a half-blood too."

Story stayed seated and rotated her fish over the fire; it was nearly done. "Yeah, but I have a guarantee from the Autumn Princess for my safety. You don't." It was a blatant lie, but she planned to get such a guarantee, and she needed Adair back under the water and safe. "As for needing your help," she glanced over at the meadow where she knew Morrigann still slumbered, "I'll be okay. I needed to calm down, center myself, and not be led so much by my emotions. You helped me see that." She lifted the fish off the flames and blew on its sizzling surface. "And by doing that, I've realized I can't risk the life of everyone in the worlds by having you here with me."

Adair crossed her arms and stuck her chin out defiantly. "You are not the boss of me."

"Real mature, Adair." Story bit into her fish. *Gross.* She

only ate seafood under duress. Her thoughts drifted off to a memory of food.

Eirnin placed a slice of tangy cheese on top of a cracker, then topped it off with a berry before passing it over to Story.

She raised an eyebrow and just looked at the food. "Oh come on, you really don't need to feed me constantly."

He continued to hold out the cracker as the flickering flames from the hearth fire revealed the orange amusement in his eyes.

Story crossed her arms stubbornly. "I'm not hungry." Her stomach rumbled loudly. The elf laughed, and Story cracked a slight smile before opening her mouth obligingly and allowing him to place the cracker inside. It was a taste explosion—sweet, tangy, and salty all rolled together. Delicious.

They both reclined back onto their elbows, the soft crocheted rug beneath them protecting them from the cold tile floor of his home. Stacking another cracker, he passed it to Story and she laughed. "You know, you're really encouraging this whole 'high maintenance' thing."

He shrugged and piled another cracker for himself. "What can I say? I like maintaining you."

They finished eating in companionable silence, and then Story finally spoke what was really on her mind. "I wish you didn't have to go."

"I know, dear heart. Me too. But you know I have to."

"I do. But I wish there was someone else who could go."

"I'm the only elf the centaurs trust. The only one who's bothered to build up a relationship with them over the last few decades." He slid closer to Story and put his arm around her shoulders. She leaned her head against his, snuggling against him.

"I wish I could go."

"Aye, me too. But right now your training is more important. You've learned so much. Besides, you can always visit me in my dreams, right?" He winked at her, and she laughed.

"True, but it's not the same. It's never the same." While she was fully aware in the dreamscape, Eirnin was always asleep. So she could visit him, see him, but never talk to him. Not the way she could with other dreamwalkers.

She leaned against his chest and hugged him tightly, unwilling to let go. But she knew, all too soon, the sun would rise and she would have to, and he would be gone again for weeks.

His hand slipped into hers, and she felt him give three gentle squeezes.

"I love you too."

"Hey!" Adair stood before her, snapping her fingers in Story's face. "Don't you blank out on me like that when I'm talking to you. You don't get to order me around! I'm grown up now, and I'm not going anywhere."

Story jerked back, fighting the urge to slap Adair's hand out of the way. "I could tie you to Ped."

Rolling her eyes, Adair stepped back. "Don't be silly. I'm coming with you. Unless you escort me back to Vevila yourself, you're not getting rid of me." She didn't need to add that if Story did that, she'd most likely be stuck there too. Never mind the fact that every day she spent doing that was another day closer to death for Eirnin.

Story opened her mouth to answer when a branch snapped directly behind Adair. Then several more cracked in quick succession, sounding like a line of firecrackers going off. Story shot to her feet and shoved her sister behind her while unsheathing her knife in one smooth motion.

What she saw caused her to lower her hand. Adair pushed past her, impatient as always. "What is it—oh!"

Four thin tree stumps stepped out from the woods and trained their burning yellow eyes on the two girls.

"It's all right. It's just wood sprites." Story sheathed her knife, struck by the oddness of her words. The first time she'd met this sort of fey they'd been torturing Eírnin and had attacked her when she'd tried to stop them. "They're probably just here to check on Morrigann."

Adair took a hesitant step back. "Wood sprites are never all right."

"They're his." Story waved in the general direction of the slumbering sidhe. "He's bound to help us, so therefore, they are too."

"Uh, Story..."

"What—" Story's words died on her lips as she turned back around and saw that the tree sprites were no longer silently standing at the edge of the clearing but were suddenly closer, long branchlike arms gripping rocks, poised to throw. Identical smiles split the bark across their faces, and Story's stomach plunged in a sickening feeling of déjà-vu.

"I don't think they're here to help."

CHAPTER NINE

KISS WITH A FIST

IN A FLASH, STORY'S KNIFE WAS OUT AGAIN, BUT THE WOOD sprites didn't charge her or Adair. Giving the girls a wide berth, they ran toward the meadow. Toward Morrigann. Something didn't sit right with Story about this, and a shared glance with Adair confirmed she felt the same way. In unison, they whirled and chased the fey.

"They'd better not hurt him!" Adair yelled.

"They'd better not take him!" Story yelled back. She didn't know what was going on—if they were here to rescue their prince, or something else less pleasant. Either way, if they took him, she'd be without her guide to Cildara.

Morrigann wasn't far, so the chase was short. Breaking through the trees ready to attack, the girls found Ped standing between the Spring Prince and the wood sprites, growling menacingly.

Story didn't hesitate and used the momentum of her running to jam her knife deep into the bark of the nearest sprite.

It exploded in a scattering of orange sparks and earth, coating her. Adair reached into her hip bag and threw a handful of salt at another. It collapsed on the ground writhing as the salt burned through its bark. Story finished it off with her knife, putting the sprite out of its misery.

The two remaining sprites, one bearing fresh scars on its trunk from Ped's teeth, shrieked with their loud, hollow cackles, dropped their stones and melted into the treeline without a trace.

"I didn't know you cared." Morrigann's voice drifted up weakly from the meadow floor. Ped directed his growls toward the faerie, snapped his teeth at him, and then stalked off toward their camp.

"I don't care." Story sheathed her knife once again, fairly certain the wood sprites were gone—for now. "Your only value to me is in saving Eírnin's life."

Morrigann, still lying on his stomach, tried to roll to his side. He was too weak and only ended up crushing one of the flowers that had begun sprouting around him. *Well, that's a good sign, I guess. He can still make things grow.*

Adair dropped to her knees and helped him sit up, and he thanked her with what seemed like sincerity. She blushed, a bluish tint coloring her cheeks, and would have responded except Story cut her off.

"Adair, could you please go back and check on the camp? Looks like we'll need wards set up after all."

Adair looked like she was going to argue, but Story crossed her arms and shook her head firmly. The dryad rose to her feet gracefully and with one last warning look at both of them slipped through the trees to their camp.

Alone with the sidhe, Story suddenly felt nervous and

uncomfortably vulnerable. She gripped the hilt of her knife and reminded herself that he was weakened and probably couldn't enchant her right now if he wanted to. *But still...*

"Let's make a rule right now that you won't enchant me or bespell me or whatever it is you did the first time we met."

Morrigann frowned and leaned heavily on one arm for support. "There's no need for that. I can barely make a flower grow much less—"

"Humor me."

"Fine." He rolled his eyes. "I promise I won't bespell you while I'm guiding you to Cildara."

"Or Adair."

He flashed her a wicked grin, his new scar stretching across his cheek in a thin, dark line. "I already told you she's not the sister I'm interested in."

Story sighed and sat down on the ground next to him, tucking her bare feet under her. "Why is it never easy with you?"

"Who says I'm not easy?" He winked and blew her a kiss.

He's just trying to get under my skin. Focus.

"Why did the wood sprites attack you? Aren't they your little spies? Don't they work for you?"

"Not any more. Once you released my family from Aisdean, I no longer commanded all the seasons, and therefore, I no longer command all the fey." He shifted position and leaned against his other arm. "The wood sprites serve my sister. She will very shortly know we are on our way. I hope you have a plan to sneak in once I get you there."

Story looked away toward the night sky, refusing to meet his eyes. She was a terrible liar, and he didn't need to know that she didn't need a plan. "I'll figure something out between now and then." She turned back to him and cocked her head to the side. "Now tell me, who is Chaos, why is Winter hell-bent on releasing him, and why would that be a bad thing—aside from the fact that, generally, chaos by its very nature is not a good thing?"

"Exactly so. Chaos, as you say, is not a good thing. He was imprisoned by the Creator back at the forming of the worlds and ever since then has striven to escape his chains and unmake everything the Creator has made."

"You mean destroy all the worlds."

"Yes."

Story pondered this for a moment and then asked, "So where do I fit in all this, and why does Winter want to destroy everything?"

"Not everything. Just everything that isn't faerie."

"But then why release Chaos? He's not going to give the fey a pass, is he?"

"It's a very long story, Story." His eyes glittered and the corners of his mouth twitched.

"I bet you've been waiting to say that ever since you met me, haven't you?"

He smiled, almost brightening. "I have." Then he let out a slow breath and eased onto his back. He appeared pale and weak again, as if the very effort of talking was draining him.

"Well, I'm all ears." Story arranged her skirt around her and shivered as a cool breeze blew through the meadow, a chilly reminder that Winter's first frost was fast approaching.

Morrigann pointed a finger up at the night sky. "Do you see those three bright stars?"

Story angled her head to the side and tried to see what he was talking about. There were thousands of stars. Unable to get the proper angle, she hesitated a moment before finally laying down on the tall grass next to him, careful not to touch the faerie, even accidentally.

"Which three?"

"The three brightest, nearly in a line." He picked up her hand, sending a jolt of heat through her. Using her index finger he pointed them out. "Uistean, Uasail, and Uaine." They were obvious now. "Every thousand years they align in what is known as the Uinseann."

Story's eyebrows rose at the familiar term, and she extracted her hand from his, trying not flinch while doing so. She'd forgotten how good his touch felt. *Stupid sun faerie!*

"What does that have to do with Chaos?"

"Everything." Morrigann threaded his fingers together and rested them on his bare chest. "About two thousand years ago, the centaur Cadwaladr made a prophecy. He said that during the Uinseann, which always coincides with the winter solstice, Chaos would be released and all the worlds would be unmade." He paused as if waiting for another question, but Story didn't speak; she was finally getting information and wasn't about to derail his train of thoughts. Or rather, his memories.

"As you can imagine, my family and I were not too keen on this because if we are destroyed we cease to exist. Unlike mortals, we don't have a happily-ever-after life to look forward to. So we decided to discover the means to release Chaos so we could prevent it.

"We searched for centuries and found nothing. Finally, when there was only a scant hundred years left, my mother suggested turning to her friends the elves for assistance." He glanced at Story, a wry smile on his face. "It would be a gross understatement to say my father was horrified by the very notion, and I think perhaps a bit envious of the close friendship my mother maintained with the elf queens. Even Winter craves a bit of Summer all to himself." He shrugged. "We all do."

Story nodded her head in agreement. She certainly desired summer's warmth above winter's chill.

"They argued, and in a fit of pique, my father handed off his horn to my sister and left to search on his own." He paused to rest, taking a few slow breaths.

Story rolled onto her side and propped her head on her arm. "I guess he found what he was looking for?"

Morrigann heaved a sigh and spared her a glance before returning his gaze to the sky. "Indeed." He laced his fingers behind his head and considered his next words before continuing. "Far in the south where Winter almost always reigns, buried deep in the snow and ice, was one of the gates to Chaos's prison."

"One of the gates?"

"Every world has one."

"What do they look like? And why didn't you look there for information to begin with?" Story raised an eyebrow, curious what the gate in her home world might be.

"Because we didn't know what we were looking for. We just knew the gates existed. It was pure luck that my father even found the gate in Ailionora." He stretched his arms out for a moment, and Story froze, afraid he was trying to place one around her.

The last thing I'm going to do is snuggle with this creep.

But he simply replaced them behind his head and kept talking as if nothing had happened.

"As to what our gate looks like, it is two concentric rings of stone monoliths with lintels. They're covered with ancient symbols and writing I didn't recognize, which means they're older than me." Which was saying something, since the Sidhe were among the most ancient beings in the world.

Story pondered his words, tapping her fingers in a rhythmic pattern against the cool ground. "It sounds kinda like Stonehenge in my world. No one really knows who built it, and now it's fallen almost completely apart." *Could Stonehenge really be our gate? I wonder if they look the same in every world?*

"As I recall, our gate was in disrepair, too. Of course, when I saw it I didn't have much time to pay attention to my surroundings as we were busy imprisoning my father."

"*We* as in you, your mother, and your sister?"

"Yes, it was a family affair."

"You've never gone back since then?"

Morrigann shook his head slowly.

"Why not?"

"Fear."

Story sat up. "What?" *Morrigann is afraid of something?*

"I was afraid. I didn't want what happened to my father to happen to me." He shrugged as if this explained it all.

"I don't understand."

"I don't know why I keep forgetting how simple you are."

Story's face flushed and anger boiled in the pit of her stomach, but she bit her tongue. The faerie continued as if nothing had passed.

"Chaos is locked away, but the gates are where that barrier is the weakest. It's where his influence can be felt the strongest."

"But then why even have a gate?"

"Because Chaos had to get put *into* prison somehow, didn't he? But gates, portals, doors, whatever you want to call them all work basically the same way. And, like a closed door to the outside, you can still see sunlight seeping in around the edges. The taint of Chaos is like that; it seeps out of the cracks in the gate. It seeped into my father as he spent years trying to learn the meaning of the symbols on the pillars." Morrigann sighed and glanced over at Story, and she thought she could detect true sadness in his expression.

"In the end, Winter became Chaos's creature, completely bent to his will. My father was mad. He hardly recognized any of us, much less what he was doing, or how he was working to destroy *everything*. Chaos had tricked him into believing that only the mortals, those beings of flesh and blood—most importantly the elves—would be destroyed. The fey would be safe, and the sidhe would rule second only to Chaos."

"So it was a self-fulfilling prophecy." Story tucked a loose braid behind her ear. "In trying to prevent Chaos's release, Winter became the means by which it would happen."

Morrigann nodded his head in agreement, so Story asked the question that had been bothering her ever since the meeting with the queens. "Why does Winter need me?"

"To sacrifice you."

Story snorted. "I've heard that from you before."

Morrigann smiled slyly and reached out a hand to brush her cheek. "Yes, only this time it's more than just one drop." Story raised her chin before he could touch her, so instead he dropped his hand and rested it on her knee. "This time, Winter must drain a half-blood in the center of the mound until their blood flows freely to all the pillars circled around them."

Story brushed his hand off her knee, ignoring the warm tingling sensation that lingered after his fingers were gone.

"I hardly think you, or any mortal for that matter, could survive something like that." He shifted his head to the side to meet her eyes. "And being a half-blood from two worlds? Oh yes, you do make a prime target for my father." Then he smiled and leaned toward her, and she felt herself drawn in to him. "But never fear, sweet Story. Once my service to you is complete and I'm free, I'll kill both you and your sister to prevent Winter from ever getting his hands on you."

A LOUD CRACK FILLED THE AIR AS STORY'S HAND FLEW OUT and slapped Morrigann's face. The impact was so hard the sidhe was knocked back down onto the ground, where he stayed, clutching his stinging cheek.

"Don't you *dare* threaten my sister!"

"It wasn't a threat." Morrigann raised a corner of his mouth in a half-smile. "It was a promise."

Story had her knife out and poised over Morrigann's chest before he even finished his sentence. The faerie froze and stared at the tip of the knife just over his heart.

"I wouldn't do that if I were you, simple Story, and not just because you'll lose your guide to Cildara."

Story's hand shook as she held the knife. "What do you mean?" She sat back on her heels.

He shrugged as if he hadn't just been a hairsbreadth away from his destruction. "It's a little known fact about my family that has been lost to common knowledge over the ages, but quite simply put, you can't destroy a Season. It's nature. It will happen. It has to happen." As Story opened her mouth, he hurried on. "Unless you're Chaos, of course. But then you're not. As I was saying, you can't destroy a Season. Were you to plunge that knife into what you surely believe is my shriveled, blackened heart, you would destroy me, but not Spring."

His eyes glittered in the starlight. "And the Season would need a place to go, having lost its host. *You* would become Spring." He gave her a menacing smile. "And I don't think either of us wants that."

Story scuttled away from him. "You mean, I would have turned into a faerie, one of the Sidhe? I would have become *you*?"

"Yes, but not nearly as good looking, I'm afraid."

She re-sheathed her knife. *Guess I'll have to figure out some other way to protect Adair.* Because he was right, she did *not* want to turn into him. And after some of her questionable choices lately, who was to say she wasn't well on her way already?

"Going back to the previous subject that did not involve us threatening or trying to kill each other, how exactly did you imprison your dad?" Story crossed her legs underneath her and ignored the slight chill of the ground. "I mean, if it was almost the winter solstice, wouldn't he have been the strongest of the four of you? Even if you ganged up on him, you and your sister would only equal him in strength, and your mother would have been completely useless."

Morrigann slowly rolled to his side and propped his head up on his arm, looking up at Story with real interest. "Perhaps you're not quite as simple as you've always led me to believe."

"You're avoiding my question."

"I am." He narrowed his eyes toward the distance, as if choosing his next words carefully. "Winter gave Autumn his horn before he left. This allowed us, in a way, to use a small part of his own powers against him and cast him down into Aisdean."

Story scrubbed her hand across her face. "Then I don't understand what the problem is? He's not out."

Morrigann shook his head. "I spoke too soon. Simple still." He sighed and flopped onto his back. "When you restored *The Ailes* you broke open the gates to Aisdean, releasing all of my family, each in their season. First my mother, then, with the first falling leaf, my sister. The first chill of Winter will herald my father."

"So put him back in!"

"It's not that easy. It would take all three of us. And after what happened last time, I doubt my mother and sister would trust me again." He said this matter-of-factly, as if it was of no consequence, but Story was beginning to learn that Morrigann understated things that were important to him.

She bit her lower lip, knowing she'd already pushed him far, but she couldn't help asking one more question. "Why did you imprison your mother and your sister? They didn't want to release Chaos, did they?"

Morrigann's face clouded, then became an impassive mask. "That's none of your business." He turned his back to Story, a clear signal that he was done talking for the night.

STORY WALKED ACROSS THE CIRCLE THAT ADAIR HAD DRAWN IN the ground—a simple ward to keep the lesser fey away. The fire had died down, so Story added a few logs then crossed to check on her sister. She was sleeping, curled up next to Ped, who was also snoring loudly. Selkie were the only creatures on Ailionora that slept more than Story did, but she didn't begrudge them that—they stayed awake for sometimes days at a time when swimming in the oceans. She picked up her wool cloak from a fallen log and lay down next to Adair, spreading her cloak over both of them.

The weather was changing; the nights were cooler now. She shivered and not because of the chill in the air.

I'm running out of time!

There was also the very real threat of Morrigann once his service to her was completed.

And I can't destroy him either.

She shuddered when she realized how close she'd come to doing just that not only earlier this evening, but months ago, after he'd killed her, and she'd returned and imprisoned him. Story had thought at the time she was being benevolent and kind—perhaps teaching him a lesson. She'd had no idea what the consequences would have been if she'd followed her initial instinct that Ailionora would be better without him in it.

I need to find a way to imprison him again without me being the one to do it.

And then it hit her—she almost laughed out loud. Why hadn't she thought of this before? The answer was so obvious!

She closed her eyes and deepened her breath, slowing it down in time with Ped's snores. She needed to sleep. She needed to dream.

Story opened her eyes to see the crowning tops of a perfect circle of oak trees. She sat up and twisted around. Sure enough, there was the solitary stone throne at the center of the faerie ring. She was back in Cildara.

She got to her feet and dusted herself off. "Metirreonn?" She looked around and saw nothing, not even a fluttering of leaves. "Metirreonn!"

A scattering of red-gold leaves and sparks coalesced over the throne, and suddenly she appeared, the Autumn Princess, as if she'd always been there. Her roots were dug deep into the earth, and her hair was redder now than before, as were many of the leaves there.

"You're running out of time, Ailesit."

"Hello to you too, Metirreonn." Story put her hands on her hips. The sidhe had gone right to the point, so she followed suit. "I need a promise from you. Two actually."

The princess raised a perfectly shaped eyebrow over her milky-white eyes. "I rarely give promises."

"You'll give me these, or our deal is off."

Metirreonn laughed, and the sound echoed through the leaves of her trees. "You *are* amusing, Ailesit. I can see why my brother likes you." Her face sobered. "We do not have a deal. I have leverage. Or does your elf's life mean so little to you?"

Maintaining her poise, Story refused to give in to the bait. "I think I'm the one with leverage." She cocked her head to the side. "Autumn, where is your instrument?"

The sidhe froze, her fingers gripping the armrests of her throne. After a few moments of silence, she relaxed slightly. "What do you want?"

"Two things: first, that you will let me and my traveling companions leave Cildara safely, once I've delivered what you want." Story paused, giving the Autumn Princess a moment to consider.

Metirreonn finally nodded. "It will be as you say. You have my personal guarantee of your *safety* until you leave my home."

"And that means no more wood sprite attacks either."

Metirreonn frowned. "Fine." She drummed her fingers on the stone. "Though I can only control *my* faeries. Anything else…" She gave an almost imperceptible shrug, and Story decided not to press the issue. Her second request was the most important as far as she was concerned.

"The second promise is that after I've delivered Morrigann to you, and you get your instrument back from him—because I'm assuming that's what he's got—you'll imprison him until after the Uinseann has passed." Story's stomach twisted nervously. She had no idea how Metirreonn would react to the request, or if she could even do it. She was banking on her holding enough of a grudge against her brother that she'd agree, but with the fey, Story had learned to never make assumptions.

The faerie threw back her head and laughed. "Is that all? Oh, Ailesit, I will do you one better. I promise that my brother will be imprisoned until the end of time."

Story knit her eyebrows together. She only needed Morrigann restrained until Adair was no longer a target for Winter. "No, that's not entirely necessary—"

"It is done." The Autumn Princess stood up, or rather, unbent her trunk, and undulated over to Story, towering over her. "Now, little human, it is time for you to go."

Before Story could say a word, she was thrust from the dream into darkness.

"DO YOU LOVE ME?" A SOFT, ALMOST GIRLISH VOICE SOUNDED FROM nearby as Story slowly opened her eyes. She was laying on a soft carpet of fallen red blossoms, under a spidery, sprawling tree. As she looked around, she could see the trees that dominated this garden, but she could not see the source of the voice.

"Always the same question, Ealis."

Story's eyes widened; that was Morrigann's voice! She also knew this was still a dream, but not her dream. *Morrigann's dream?* What did the Prince dream about tonight?

Rolling onto her stomach, she crawled over to a large mossy stone, hedged by a massive fern. She peered through the fronds and saw Morrigann and a girl, presumably the owner of the other voice. Their backs were to her, and they sat at the base of one of the moss-covered trees with red flowers. A small stream trickled by their feet, and Story could see large, brightly-colored fish swimming. A small, white arch bridged the stream, though it seemed superfluous to Story as it would have been easy to step over the water without it.

"And always the same answer, my love." Her accent lilted and rolled in a manner similar to the elves, and the girl—no, young woman, now that Story could see her better—turned her head and reached out a pale hand toward Morrigann's dusty golden cheek.

Yeah, definitely a dream. He hadn't looked that healthy since, well, springtime.

Ealis left her hand on his cheek for a moment while he leaned into it, his eyes closed. Then she dropped her hand, and the motion shifted her loosely-wrapped, pale pink robe off her shoulder. She looked down at her porcelain-like hands, now folded daintily in her lap, a cascade of thick, dark, perfectly straight hair tumbled over her shoulders, masking her features from Story.

Morrigann shifted closer to her, and it was then that Story realized he was not wearing *anything*. She stifled a gasp and focused on keeping her eyes on the young woman, who appeared to only have recently put on the silk robe. Story's eyes widened; she found herself very glad she hadn't arrived any earlier.

Morrigann reached out with one hand and lifted her chin. He placed a tender kiss on her red painted lips, and then smiled against them. "You know how I feel about you." He took her hand, so small and delicate in his glittering gold one, and placed it over his heart. "You're everything to me."

She pulled back and clasped her hands again, this time looking straight at him. "Then why won't you say it? Why won't you say you love me?"

She looked at him for a few moments, and when he said nothing, she swept her hair up into a thick bun at the top of her head and pinned it there with two finely carved wooden sticks. As the tiny train of flowers that trailed down from the sticks fluttered in the breeze, Story noticed the woman's point-ed ears.

She's an elf!

The elf was also a dreamwalker, judging by her black, pinwheel ailach. However, she was not one who Story recog-nized, and she thought she knew them all.

What is she doing here?

The elf moved to stand, and Morrigann's hand shot out

and closed over her wrist. "Please wait." She stood there, awkwardly, looking down at him as he gazed up at her pleadingly. "I can't say it. I *can't*."

"Why? Because it would be a lie?"

"No! Because… I just can't."

Ealis reached over with her free hand and gently disengaged Morrigann's fingers one by one. "I have wasted centuries of my life with you. Waiting for you. Loving you. I'm done. We're done." When her hand was free, she winked out of the dream, as if she'd never even been there.

Morrigann stared at the place where she'd stood, a contorted look of pain washing over his face.

"I love you still."

His whispered words were almost lost in the breeze, and Story leaned closer, trying to hear better. She leaned out too far and fell through the fronds of the fern.

Morrigann jerked up at the sound, and for a moment their eyes locked, filled with the shared pain and understanding of great loss.

Then his face clouded over with anger, and he surged to his feet.

"Get out!"

He thrust his hands at her, and once again, everything turned black.

S TORY SLOWLY BLINKED HER EYES OPEN AND RAISED HER HAND to block the sun streaming in through the trees overhead. She felt bruised and battered, and not just from sleeping on the cold, hard ground. It occurred to her rather painfully that since Eírnin had been poisoned she had yet to pass a full night without purposely dreamwalking or being thrust into sleep through some sort of enchantment.

This can't be healthy for me.

She felt a draft at her back and realized that Adair and Ped were gone, probably awake for hours now, swimming and fishing in the cove for their breakfast.

Her body ached but her mind whirled as she remembered in a rush everything that happened last night. Metirreonn's guarantee of safety for herself, Adair, and Ped had lifted a huge weight from her shoulders. Strangely though, the fact that Morrigann would be imprisoned forever did not further ease her burden. If anything, she found herself feeling guilty.

Stop that! He wants to kill Adair!

But after her visit to his dream last night, seeing the depths of his anguish when the elf had left him... Well, to be honest, she hadn't thought him capable of that level of feeling. She'd accused him of condemning the elves to die because of his jealousy over their ability to feel, live, and love. He'd laughed at her and accused her of knowing nothing, of jumping to conclusions. And apparently she had. It seemed the sidhe *could* feel, and strongly. Why couldn't he tell the dreamwalker he loved her? Had he cursed the elves out of spite over being rejected by one of their own?

Her eyes felt gummy and puffy, but she forced herself to keep them open and look at the fire pit, now nothing more than a few charred logs. As her eyes focused she could make out a pair of feet—and not dryad feet. She followed them up, and before she got to his face, she knew who was sitting on the other side.

"Good morning, Story." Morrigann's eyes were cold and hard, and he gave her a tight, humorless smile. "Sleep well?"

"COME ON, PED. YOU'VE GOT TO LET HIM RIDE." STORY SCRATCHED the selkie behind his ears. "He's still not strong enough to walk very far, and every minute we wait is a minute closer to Winter."

The selkie just stared at her, seemingly unswayed. Story leaned her head against his long nose and stared into his dark brown eyes. "Don't you want to help Efrnin?"

The selkie blew through his nose and jowls—his

equivalent of a sigh—and Story knew he'd allow it, but only because of his love for the elf.

"Well, you haven't bothered to ask me what I think." Morrigann looked up at her from his seat on the log, a single eyebrow cocked in expectation.

Story knew he was referring to more than just their current transportation situation. Adair and Ped had shown up with breakfast shortly after she'd awoken, effectively cutting off Story and Morrigann's conversation. So the confrontation Story both feared and wanted had been delayed until later.

Rolling her eyes, Story crossed her arms over her chest. "Fine, what do you think?"

"I don't want to ride the beast." He a made a show of examining his fingernails, as if they were the most fascinating things in the world.

She faced the faerie and put her hands on her hips. "I don't care."

He stood slowly and mirrored her position. "I don't care that you don't care."

She took a step forward and stuck a finger in his face. "Well, I don't care that you don't care that I don't care—"

"Stop!" Adair wedged between them and shoved them apart. "I care." She looked up at Story. "Quit being a bully! I lost Eírnin too. That's no excuse to behave like this!"

Behind Adair, Story could see Morrigann cross his arms and smirk, but before the smile had finished forming, Adair whirled around. "And you! Stop pushing her buttons. Quit trying to make everything difficult just because you think it's amusing."

She stepped out from between them and turned to face them both. "You're acting like pups. Spoiled, selfish, bratty pups. I expected more from both of you."

Story felt her face flush in embarrassment. Adair was right, she had been acting like a bully and a petulant child, determined to have her way regardless of the consequences. It was time to act like the adult she supposedly was.

Morrigann merely shrugged. "That's your fault then. I never claimed to be anything other than spoiled, selfish, and bratty." He winked at Adair, and then tried to pull himself onto the shying Ped. "A little help please, Story?" He bared his perfect teeth at her in a parody of a smile.

Story swallowed her pride, determined to be the grown-up here. She squatted down and threaded her fingers together to form a stirrup for him to step on.

Leaning over, he whispered in her ear, "If you *ever* enter my dreams uninvited again, when I kill your sister I will do it slowly, and I will make you watch." Then he blew Adair a kiss before placing his foot in Story's hands.

Despite his weakened state, his foot was still warm, like a ray of sunshine. As he stood in her hands and lifted his other leg to swing over Ped's back, Story straightened and used the momentum from her legs to boost him up. But instead of stopping, she pulled up with her arms as hard as she could, launching the Spring Prince up and over the selkie where he landed on the ground in an ungraceful heap.

Story allowed herself a small smile as she crossed her arms and looked down at the furious faerie.

NOW I'll start acting like an adult.

Much to Adair's disappointment, they skirted the gnome village of Peddler's Port and continued their journey east toward brown dwarf territory. Story had considered stopping in Peddler's Port for some more supplies, but she didn't want to risk a delay by what would certainly be the overly hospitable innkeeper's insistence that they stay for a night (or three) and that Adair sing for the villagers. Besides, as long as they stayed near water, they would be able to find enough food to survive.

As they traveled, Adair chattered ceaselessly about anything and everything—except their journey—with the other two occasionally responding to her. Morrigann, however, hadn't spoken a word to Story, and she was only too happy to respond in kind. Late in the third day of their journey, Story finally broke the silent standoff.

"Where are we going, anyway?" Story cast a sidelong glance at Morrigann as he rode atop Ped, both the selkie and the faerie clearly uncomfortable with the arrangement.

"To Cildara."

"Thanks, Sherlock, I already had that much figured out."

He raised a questioning eyebrow. "My name is Morrigann."

"Yeah, I know, it's just a—you know what? Never mind." She suddenly felt depressed, remembering all the times she and Eírnin had had similar conversations. He'd always found human turns of phrase amusing. "I meant, how are we getting there?"

"I know what you meant."

Story frowned, not rising to the bait. He always had to make things difficult. Why did men think that was cute? Being obnoxious was not cute. "Well?"

"Well, what?" He looked at her innocently.

"Are you going to tell me or not?"

"Or not."

"What? Why? Is it a big secret or something?"

"No. *You* wish to know, so *I* don't wish to tell you."

Adair shook her head at Morrigann, who in turn shrugged. She looked at Story. "Cildara is somewhere in the eastern portion of the Piney Green Mountains. Like his home," she stuck a thumb at Morrigann, "it changes location." Then she frowned at him. "There, was that so hard?"

"No," he smiled. "And you did it so very well, little one." Adair wrinkled her nose in irritation and spun back around to continue walking at the forefront of their small group. Story was glad that the effect of Morrigann's fruit had finally worn off her sister.

"And yes," Morrigann continued, directing his words at Story, "since I'm sure you're wondering, I do know where Autumn's grove currently resides."

"Wonderful." Story reached up to scratch Ped's ear. "So tell me, what instrument does Metirreonn have?" It was a dangerous question; it might tip him off that she knew he had it, and that it was what his sister was really after. Though, if he hadn't figured that much out on his own, he wasn't nearly as smart as he thought he was.

Morrigann's violet eyes flashed as he narrowed them. "Why do you ask?"

Yup, he's suspicious. "Well, you have a violin, your mom has a flute, you said your dad had a horn, so I assume your sister has an instrument too." She pasted what she hoped was an appropriately curious yet innocent expression on her face and waited for an answer.

The faerie regarded her for a moment, eyes narrowed, before answering. "Autumn's instrument is a harp."

Story buried a small smile. She noticed he was very careful not to say that his sister actually *had* a harp; he only named what her instrument was.

He definitely had her harp.

ANOTHER WEEK PASSED, AND THE DAYS GREW COOLER. NOT QUITE cold yet, but summer had gone, and autumn was in full swing. Their little party settled into a routine as they traveled along the shoreline. After that last conversation, Story and Morrigann ignored each other, and Adair took to going on long swims just to escape them. Story couldn't blame her; the tension was palpable.

Each night Story built a fire, Adair drew a ward—though Story knew it probably wasn't necessary—and they cooked the day's catch over the flames. Morrigann never ate with them. Story didn't know if that was because he didn't need to eat, or because he didn't like fish. Regardless, his brilliancy was coming back. He still looked like a normal human, but he no longer carried the pallor of death over him. There was a healthy glow to his skin, his cheeks were filled out, and his eyes were no longer sunken. If Story hadn't known what he was supposed to look like, she would have supposed him to be at the peak of health.

Their routine changed one night when Morrigann produced his violin and began playing a sprightly tune. Story tried to ignore it, to focus on her dinner, but found her foot was tapping along of its own accord. Then Adair was singing along, making up the words as she went, telling a story about an unfortunate gnome in a battle with spriggans over his corn crop. While the story itself was not funny, the way Adair told it—or rather sang it—coupled with Morrigann's cheery playing had Story laughing and up on her feet clapping along.

Morrigann played another song, and Adair kept right on singing. Her voice soothed away Story's worries, and before she knew it, Story was dancing around the flames of the campfire with happy abandon, laughing along with Adair, caught up in both the magic of the faerie's playing and the dryad's singing. It reminded her of the wild faerie dances she'd had with the pixies when she'd first come to this world, and while she had learned not to trust the fey, at times she still found herself missing her dances with the pixies.

As she whirled around, she found that if she squinted, the sparks from the flames looked like pixies. Adair, still singing wordlessly, grasped her hands and they spun each other round and round before letting go and pinwheeling apart, laughing. Dizzy, Story stumbled and would have fallen had Morrigann not caught her. His violin disappeared as he let it go, taking the music with it.

"Careful there, simple Story. Don't you know better than to dance in a faerie ring by now?" He smiled down at her, genuine enough, but Story still jerked away from him.

"That wasn't a faerie ring, that was..." The truth was Story didn't know what it was, but the combination of faerie and dryad magic had been a soothing balm to her aching heart and frazzled nerves.

Morrigann raised up his arms. "Calm down, I was only joking." Then he extended one hand to her. "Can we call a truce?"

Story looked at it warily, keeping her own hands by her sides. "You mean until you're free to kill us?"

"Obviously."

"Why?"

He looked at his hand meaningfully, and when she still did not take it he threw both his hands up in the air, frustrated. "Because I'm *bored*." He exhaled noisily. "You used to be so fun. And now you're just mopey, and angry, and overly sensitive—"

"Because I don't take well to death threats made to my family, I'm overly sensitive?"

"Exactly!" He beamed, clearly oblivious to her sarcasm.

Story sat down on the log, irritation spreading through her, and crossed her arms over her chest. Adair shook her head at both of them and left to go swimming in the shallows with Ped.

Morrigann regarded Story curiously. "I take it you don't want a truce?"

"Who was the dreamwalker?"

His features shifted instantly to a blank mask. "I don't know who you mean."

"Do you want a truce or not?"

He stood quietly for a moment and finally seemed to come to a decision. He sat down next to her, so close that Story's hair stood on end from the faint magic charge that emanated from him.

"Yes, I want a truce. For now."

"So who was she? The elf in your dreams? And why do you hate the elves so much? I mean, if you loved her..." Story cocked her head to the side and caught a glimmer of grief as it washed across his face. Without thinking, she placed a hand over his and gave it a quick squeeze, and was immediately surprised by her own actions. "Look, I didn't plan to spy on you or anything. I was just suddenly there, and I didn't mean—"

Morrigann interlaced his fingers with hers, and her eyes widened. *What's going on? He promised he wouldn't enchant me, so what's this?*

"Thank you." He sounded sincere. "Her name was Ealis."

Was Ealis? That explained why Story didn't know her. She was just a memory—truly just a dream.

"What happened to her?"

"My sister..." Morrigann paused, considering his next words. "She gets jealous very easily."

Story's breath caught, but she didn't pull her hand away. He seemed to need it, and by the glow emanating from where their hands joined, she guessed the physical contact was somehow helping him heal.

"When you say jealous..." She didn't quite know how to phrase it, so she just went for it. It would be awkward in any case. "Do you mean she was jealous of you? Or that she was jealous of Ealis?"

Morrigann didn't even bat an eye. "She didn't like when I was with others... romantically and reacted... poorly... whenever she found out."

At this revelation, Story tried to jerk her hand away, but he clung to it tightly. "Don't you judge us by your mortal code of morals. Autumn and I are not siblings in the way your kind are; any more than two trees would be considered siblings. It is the only term in living language that comes close to describing our relationship. Or I suppose you could call us consorts, if that would make you feel better."

Story stopped tugging and just stared at him, completely confused. "I don't understand."

"I don't expect you to." He slid closer to her, so that their hips and legs touched down to their ankles. Story tried to move away, but found she couldn't. The same faint glow formed where their legs touched, and she stifled a yawn. She knew she should try to pull away again, but she wasn't bothered by his touch anymore. It actually felt nice. Warm and comforting.

"Try me," she said, fighting another yawn.

Glancing at her for a moment, Morrigann nodded. "Very well. My family is a family only in the loosest sense of the word. Long ago, when the worlds were created, this world only had two seasons: Summer and Winter. They were a matched pair and complemented each other perfectly. And my understanding is they were very much in love.

"Eventually—and I still don't know what possessed them to do this—they decided to create two more seasons, milder versions of themselves, but also a pleasing combination of both their attributes. People often forget that Autumn holds as much of Summer's warmth as I do."

Story felt a burst of warmth flow from him, then a quick shock of cold. "And that I am as much a part of Winter as is my sister."

"So you were a matched pair." Story yawned so wide she thought she'd crack her jaw. She couldn't understand why she was becoming so sleepy so suddenly.

"Indeed. They created us in their image, so we could be just like them—perfectly complementary in our traits. We were literally made for each other."

"Except you didn't love her." It wasn't a question. Story could tell by the set in his jaw that "love" was not how he'd describe his feelings for Autumn. She clenched her jaw to stifle the next yawn.

Morrigann gave her a sidelong glance. "You can't help who you love, Story. You certainly can't force two beings to be in love, no matter how 'perfectly complementary' they are."

"But she loved you?"

He shrugged. "I don't know if Autumn even understands what love is."

"And you do?"

He didn't answer.

"Was she, Ealis, the elf maiden from the legends?" Her eyelids felt so heavy.

"Yes."

"Why did you do it? Why did you betray her? Condemn the elves to extinction? Do you hate them that much?"

Releasing her hand, Morrigann stood up and scooped her into his arms. "Goodnight, Story. Thank you for the physical contact. I needed that. I'll be able to walk on my own now for the rest of the journey." He laid her down on her cloak and then tucked it around her snugly.

Story was dimly aware that he'd avoided her question, and that he'd taken her strength without asking, but she also knew she was too tired to care.

CHAPTER TWELVE

COMPASS

THE DINNER ON THE TABLE SET FOR TWO HAD LONG SINCE GROWN *cold, though it remained untouched. Story paced the smooth, tile floor of Eirnin's dark living room, the late summer sun having set hours ago. Her bare feet rustled across the cool surface. It should have had a calming effect, but as the minutes passed by, she only found herself feeling more anxious and angry.*

Where is he? she wondered for what had to be the hundredth time in the last hour. She knew he was at council, but this was ridiculous! How could they keep him so late when he was leaving so soon? It just isn't fair!

"Life isn't fair," her dad used to always say. Well, it was trite then and it was trite now.

At last, the front door creaked open. Eirnin slid quietly inside, clicking the door shut, his back to her.

She stopped pacing. "Where the heck have you been?"

Even as the words left her mouth she knew she sounded nagging and overbearing. What she really meant to say was "I'm glad you're back" and run into his arms. But it was too late now.

Stiffening, Eirnin turned around, his elf eyes easily able to see her despite the darkened room. "I'm sorry, dear heart, I thought you'd be asleep by now. I was trying to be quiet."

Story tilted her head to the side and raised an eyebrow. He'd just avoided her question, and quite obviously at that. Now she really was upset. "Well, I'm clearly not." She fisted her hands on her hips. "And you didn't answer my question."

"You mean your demand?" He took off his cloak and hung it on a hook near the door.

Story just looked at him. Actually, she gave him the *look. The "stop playing around with me if you know what's good for you" look that females of all races seem to know from birth.*

Facing her, Eirnin crossed his arms over his chest and tried to give her "the look" back. It didn't work. He blew out a loud breath and flopped his arms to his side in frustration. She couldn't see his eye color in this light, but his body language told her. He was nervous and annoyed.

"You know where I was: war council." He strode toward her and opened up his arms to hug her. "I'm sorry I'm late—but you know how these things go. Someone starts talking, and before you know it, it's the middle of the night."

Story didn't move and didn't give him any outward invitation to come closer to her, so he stopped short.

"Who with?"

"What?"

"Who were you in council with?"

"The usual: all the clan leaders, their advisors, and the queen."

Story narrowed her eyes and noted the little fidgets in his hands. "What aren't you telling me?"

Eirnin frowned. "Just leave it alone, Story."

"Tell me!"

"Leave it!" He walked over to a wooden chair, sat down, and began unlacing his boots.

She blinked back tears, feeling slapped. He'd yelled at her! He never yelled at her. Realization dawned. "You've been with Eáchan! I bet she invited you over for another 'private' council session."

Eirnin sighed. "It's not like that—"

"Wait, so you really were with her?" Story felt the bottom drop out of her stomach. "And you tried to hide it from me? What's going on with you two?"

He stood up, one boot in his hand. "Nothing! It was just council! I'm the only one who's interacted so closely with one of the Sidhe in living memory, and she wanted to talk about that." He started pacing with an odd gait, still wearing one boot. "Honestly Story, I don't understand what the problem is; I have private council with Eánna all the time and you don't care."

"Eánna isn't one of your ex-girlfriends!" Story was so angry she could feel herself shaking, and the tears that threatened to spill before were streaming down her face now. Traitorous, angry tears. "And Eánna hasn't been trying to break us up from the moment she met me." Eirnin opened his mouth to speak, but she cut him off. "And most importantly, you've never tried to hide those meetings from me!"

"Of course I didn't want to tell you about this meeting, because I knew you'd react just like this. Nothing is going on!" His voice was as loud as hers now, echoing off the stone walls of his great room.

"Don't you yell at me!"

"Why not? Are you the only one who gets to be angry here?" he shouted back.

Tears streamed down her face, and Story made a futile wipe at her nose; this was not how it was supposed to go. It was like she was in a bad play and was watching herself from the wings, unable to stop herself from saying these terrible words. *"You know what, Eirnin? Nevermind. If you want to be with her so bad, just go, be with her!"*

Eirnin's step stuttered, a confused expression frozen on his face. *"What? Are you mad? Where did that come from?"* He moved to her side and made as if to put his hand on her shoulder. *"Dear heart, what's wrong with you?"*

She flinched away from his touch, backing up to the door. *"Yup, that's right, I'm crazy. It's all me. Why would you want to be with crazy, screwed up, overly emotional, human me?"*

Flinging the door open, Story stomped out into the cool evening air. *"Go be with perfect Eáchan for all I care!"* She slammed the door shut behind her, but not before she caught the look on Eirnin's face: a mixture of pure confusion and devastation.

Whirling around to run before she could give in to her instinct to take Eirnin in her arms and apologize for everything, she slammed right into Eáchan. The elf steadied Story while she gazed at her with her implacable silver eyes.

"I'd be more careful, Ailesit." The ghost of a smile flitted at the corners of Eáchan's lips. She released Story's arms and resumed her trek to her own home a few streets away, leaving Story standing alone at the end of the gravel path leading to Eirnin's door.

Story had no idea how much Eáchan had heard, but she knew it had been enough. Bursting into tears, she walked heavily over to the bridge that led to the queen's island and back to her rooms. She listened for the sound of Eirnin's footsteps behind her so she could apologize, but there was only silence.

Story sat in her empty tub, still dressed, and still crying. The chilly tile of the pool cooled her hot, flushed skin, but instead of comforting her, it only made her feel more alone.

Why had she said those things? She didn't mean them—not even a little bit! She'd just been angry, and she'd lashed out at the closest target. Unfortunately, that target had been the person she cared for the most in all the worlds.

It was like Josh all over again! She driven not just him, her best friend, but all her other friends away after her family had died, afraid to be close to anyone. Why was she doing it again?

A soft knock sounded at her bathroom door.

"Come in," she sniffled, unreasonably irritated by the interruption of her pity party. She should have known Eavon would come check on her before too long.

But it wasn't Eavon.

Eirnin stepped down into the deep tub and pulled her into his arms.

"I'm so, so sorry," she sobbed into his shoulder, her tears starting back up again with a vengeance.

"Shhh." He smoothed down her braids with one hand and squeezed her tighter with the other. "I'm the one who's sorry. I shouldn't have yelled at you."

"No," she wiped her nose on his shirt, "I'm the one who started the yelling. I'm sorry." He pulled away just far enough to hold out a handkerchief to her—he'd come prepared. She gratefully accepted it and blew her nose before continuing. "I know there's nothing going on between you and Eáchan. I know you love me. I'm just... I'm just

crazy right now. I don't know what's wrong with me." She looked at him, pleading with her eyes for him to understand.

He stroked her cheek with one hand and kissed her forehead. "Dear heart, you're not mad. You're worried and upset about yet another separation after it seems like I just got back from the last trip." He quirked up one corner of his mouth in a sad smile. "And truth be told, I am too. We're not behaving entirely rationally right now. We're neither of us perfect."

She chuckled, "Well, maybe you aren't, but I am." She snuggled deeper against him. "I love you. I'm really, really sorry for my behavior."

"I know, and I am too." He pulled her tighter to him. "I love you so very much." Then he raised an eyebrow and nodded at the empty tub before them. "You know these things work better when they're filled with water, right?"

Story poked his ribs with her index finger. "Quiet, you."

"What? I was just saying—"

She silenced him with a kiss.

Story pulled out her compass from its pouch but didn't open it.

Have I lost my way?

She was dreaming, of that she was certain.

That was our first big fight as a couple.

She wasn't controlling the dream—at least not consciously.

I need to find my center.

The world filled in around her, like an artist's sketch

coming to life with color, and she found herself back in Eícetan's hut.

What would Eírnin think of me now?

She didn't turn around right away, afraid of what she'd see in the Healer's home. But eventually longing got the better of her, and she looked.

Will he even recognize me?

And there he was, just as she'd left him, slumbering peacefully on Eícetan's pallet.

Eírnin.

She was by his side in two steps and dropped to the floor next to him, taking his hand in hers. She was shocked by how warm it felt, even in the dream—she'd assumed it would be icy cold with the poison coursing through his veins.

"I don't know if you can hear me, elf-boy." She traced a circle on his skin with her thumb. "But I'm going to talk anyway. I know you probably wouldn't have gone about things the way I have, and I'm starting to see how badly I've been behaving." She paused and bit her lower lip, fighting the swell of emotion building inside of her.

"I can't excuse what I've done. I feel like I've made a deal with the devil. Two devils actually." She laughed weakly, knowing he'd appreciate her poor attempt at humor, then sighed. "I don't think there's any going back now, though. The promises made on all sides are binding."

She ran her fingers through her braids, keeping her free hand wrapped tightly around his. "But I'm going to try to make things right." Her voice cracked on the last word, and she looked at his face, taking in his gently closed eyes, strong nose and brow, square jaw, and the cleft in his chin— something Will and Katie had always called a chin-butt. The memory of her willful and spunky younger siblings, dead over a year now, cracked her resolve. The tears she'd been struggling to keep at bay broke through her flimsy dam.

Story clutched Eírnin's hand, squeezing it in a repeating pattern of threes, and cried.

CHAPTER THIRTEEN

ALL THINGS MUST PASS

WHEN STORY WOKE UP THE NEXT MORNING, SHE FELT strangely refreshed. After what had happened with Morrigann and her dreams and memories of Eírnin, she'd expected to feel even more drained. But somehow her contact with the faerie had rejuvenated her as well, and she'd had the best night of sleep she'd had in weeks.

A good crying jag always made her feel better, even when it was within a dream. *Can't keep stuff bottled up for too long or the pressure will kill you*, her father always said.

Her hip was starting to ache from lying on one side for too long. She rolled over to relieve the pressure and found herself nose to nose with Morrigann.

"Good morning, Story." Morrigann's eyes were bright and vibrant, and he waggled his eyebrows. "Sleep well?

"Yes, actually." She fought the urge to jerk away from him. He was only doing it to make her feel uncomfortable, and she wouldn't give him the satisfaction. "Your doing?"

"I'll never tell."

"Afraid to admit to doing something nice?" She raised an eyebrow. "Or was that payment for the cuddling last night? You going to explain what the heck that was?"

"Actually, I was waiting for you to finally wake up. You humans do sleep a *lot*, did you know that?" He waved a hand in the air as if it was inconsequential. "Now that you are no longer snoring, I can tell you that my pixies have informed me we will shortly have guests."

"What?" Story jumped to her feet. "Who? And where's Adair?"

"She and the selkie are capturing some more of that vile fish you all seem to favor." Morrigann leaned on an elbow. "As for the 'who', my pixies tell me it is the hunting party Eánna sent to find the elfling's antidote."

Elves! Hunters!

Story's eyes widened in panic, and she immediately began scouting for a place to hide or run to before his words caught up with her.

"Wait, so they're not after me?"

"Not to my knowledge, no."

"Change of plans then." She began straightening her attire, smoothing her skirt and peasant blouse, and tightening the laces on her vest. Times like this, she was supremely grateful for her low maintenance hair—her natural curl would have been a nightmare on this journey. Then she paused, "Wait a sec, how do you know about Eánna sending a hunting party?" *And what else does he know?*

"My mother and I have always been close." He sat up and cocked his head to the side. "Spring, like Summer, is the bringer of life. We have ever been allies."

"Is that why you locked her up in Aisdean for a thousand years? Because you were so close?"

Morrigann's mouth turned down at the corners, tugging at his scar, giving him a decidedly menacing appearance. "Did you want me to have my pixies delay them so we can slip away?"

Story shook her head. "No, at the very least I need to talk to the hunters. Maybe we can even help each other." A surge of hope filled her at the thought of potential allies; things would go a lot smoother with a couple of hunters along. Assuming they weren't the sort of elves who viewed her as the harbinger of destruction.

Morrigann's frown blossomed into a smile, and Story was instantly alert. "How wonderful! I *do* love a good brawl."

"What—" Story stopped speaking at the sound of someone entering the clearing behind her. They were already here.

"Ailesit!" a familiar voice called out to her. "What are you doing here?"

Story closed her eyes and let out a long breath as she slowly turned.

No, not her. Anyone but her!

"Eachan." The elf's name tumbled out of her mouth before she could stop it, and the two of them stood staring at each other across a scant ten feet of meadow.

Story felt shock, anger, and trepidation course through her. Eachan's eyes remained impassively silver to Story, and she had to settle for the twitch at the corner of Eachan's mouth and the slight narrowing of her eyes to let her know that the elf was as out of sorts as she was.

Eisrus stepped into the camp next, taking up position a step behind and to the right of Eachan. His face showed all the emotion Eachan's had hidden, and his obvious delight and reverence at seeing Story, in the wake of his initial surprise and confusion, was almost enough to overwhelm her.

"Are you two just going to stare at each other all day?" Morrigann called up from his reclined position. "Because this is really getting quite boring. I'd hoped for so much more."

Story gave him a warning look. "You're not helping."

An ostentatiously false look of hurt crossed the faerie's features. "I don't know why you're getting angry with me." He stretched out before slowly rising to his feet, brushing non-existent dirt off his chest and arms—presumably to call attention to them. "I'm not the one who poisoned the elfling." His eyes shifted subtly toward Eachan.

What? No... she loves him!

And yet, as Story met Eachan's eyes, the elf said nothing to counter the faerie's insinuation.

And the fey can't lie...

Story was across the clearing and grasping Eachan's shoulders in the blink of an eye. "Tell me you didn't do it. Tell me you didn't try to kill him." Story stared up into her silver eyes, pleading, and finally saw Eachan's colors for the first time. Pink and blue swirled through the silver, and Story released the elf's shoulders in disbelief.

Ashamed? No! No! No! She can't have done it! She can't...

Eisrus backed away from his master, eyes swirling too many colors to name as shock coursed through him. His voice emerged as a whisper, "Eachan, what have you done?"

Eachan dropped to her knees and looked up at Story, silver tears leaking from the corners of her eyes. "I cannot deny what your companion has said, Ailesit."

Story felt the handle of her knife pressed into her hand and watched as Eachan guided it to her own throat. Their eyes locked and Story saw, for the first time, the full depth of Eachan's emotions. Her hurt, her pain, her guilt, her sadness, her torment... her unrequited love. Story's hand shook as her own emotions battled with each other.

She poisoned Eírnin! She deserves to die!

The knife quivered in her hand, its point digging into Eachan's skin.

No! Look at her, she hates herself for it—she can't have been in control of herself when she did it.

A small bead of silver blood formed at the blade's tip.

I don't care! She poisoned Eírnin! She deserves to die!

Story stared at Eachan's blood, transfixed.

Think about what you're doing! Are you really going to KILL someone?

Eachan closed her eyes, accepting her fate.

Who am I?

The knife fell to the ground with a muffled thump. Story staggered back, one hand flying up to cover her mouth while her other arm snaked around her own waist, as if to physically hold herself together.

What did I almost just do?

Morrigann made a disgusted sound. "What? I do *nothing* to you, and you burn my face and threaten to destroy me, whereas *she* tries to kill your precious little elfling and gets a pass?" He crossed his arms over his chest and scowled. "It hardly seems fair."

Story ignored him and kept her eyes on Eachan, who was coming shakily back to her feet, surprised to still be alive.

"Why?" Eachan dabbed her finger at her neck, fingering the slight wound.

Story dropped the hand covering her mouth. "Killing you won't bring him back." She bit her lower lip, hesitating. "But leaving you alive might. I could really use your help." Then she stepped forward and extended her hand toward the elf.

"Oh honestly!" Morrigann threw his hands in the air. "You'll offer *her* a truce, and not me?" He flung himself down onto a tree stump. "Unbelievable."

Eachan eyed Story's hand for a moment and then, hesitantly, took it. Her grip was gentle at first, but then suddenly tightened as if Story was her lifeline. She went down on one knee and looked up at Story, hints of green tinting the corners of her blue irises.

"Ailesit, I pledge myself to you. I will follow you. I am yours to command." She touched her forehead to their joined hands, and Story felt a surge of magic course through her and wrap itself around their hands before settling deep into her body.

Astonished, Story helped Eachan to her feet. "What did you just do?"

"I don't rightly know." Eachan unclasped Story's hand then stared at her own. "There is still so much we are learning about magic." She let her hand drop down to her side and returned her gaze to Story. "But I think it's safe to say my promise is unbreakable."

Eisrus dropped to his knees and reached for Story's hand. She jerked it back before he could touch it. "Oh, heck no, kid. Are you crazy? Get up."

He stood and glanced between the two of them, confused. "But as Eachan's apprentice, I should strive to emulate all the things she does."

"Aye, but swearing fealty to someone is not one of those

things, Apprentice." Eachan placed a hand on his shoulder. "You show great trust in me by your willingness to do so after what you just found out."

"Yeah, about that..." Story crossed her arms across her chest, her mind still reeling from the events of the last few minutes. "Why did you, you know... poison..."

"Yes!" Morrigann called over loudly from his place on the tree stump. "Why did you try to *kill* the elfling?"

"Thanks, Morrigann, I got this one."

Story felt, more than heard, the two elves behind her move and glanced back in time to see them both whip their bows off their backs, arrows trained on the Spring Prince.

"Whoa, whoa, whoa! None of that!" Story yanked down on both their arms and the arrows fired harmlessly into the dirt. "We're all on the same side here. He's... a good faerie." She looked back at the sidhe. "For now." She cursed herself silently; given his diminished state, until she'd said his name, the elves hadn't realized who or what he was.

Eisrus spat in the dirt before him. "The only good faerie is a destroyed faerie. Especially *that* one."

Eachan merely regarded Story curiously, lowering her bow. "I don't rightly understand, but of course, as you say, Ailesit."

Story let go of Eachan's arm and gave what she hoped was a commanding look to Eisrus.

Chastened, he lowered his own bow. "I'll leave him be. For now."

"I think we need to catch each other up on everything that's happened so we're all on the same sheet of music here." Story looked at each member of the group in turn. Eachan inclined her head in agreement, Eisrus eyed Morrigann warily but still nodded his head, and Morrigann simply waved a hand in her general direction as if to say "whatever."

The elves sat down cross-legged opposite the faerie, and Story leaned against a tree between Eisrus and Morrigann, making a loose sort of circle. Story noticed that Eisrus kept glancing around, as if he was worried about being attacked.

Story put a reassuring hand on his arm. "It's okay. We're safe here." She pointed at the wards around them, and Eisrus looked pointedly at Morrigann.

The sidhe looked toward the sky in disgust. "Those only work on lesser fey. Obviously."

Still, Eisrus kept scanning the treeline, and more often than not, his eyes lingered in the direction of the shoreline. *Ah,* Story felt the hint of a smile. He'd always seemed to perk up whenever Adair was around, during the few encounters she'd witnessed between them. Story buried the smile she felt and turned toward Eachan.

"Why don't you tell us what happened?"

The elf sighed and then spoke, her rolling accent thicker and more difficult for Story to understand than usual. "Aye, that's the problem—I don't rightly remember. Eírnin had just been elected clan leader, as I knew he would be, so I went out to hunt." She closed her eyes and then opened them slowly, pink tingeing the edges. "In truth, I went out looking for a mountain troll to kill. I was upset, and I wanted to vent my frustration." Nobody said anything at this admission, so she continued. "I'd left the iron-tipped bow behind, as it was no longer mine to use."

She ran a hand through her short cropped, inky black hair, making it stand on end. "But I was careless... and I'm not quite sure what happened next. I had the acorn and put it in Eírnin's wine, and I don't know why I did. I was in a haze. It was as if I could see myself doing it, but I was powerless to stop. It wasn't until he started convulsing—" She broke off and scrubbed her face in her hands. "Well, you get the point."

"I do, better than you know." Story gave her a half-smile and glanced over at Morrigann. "I was once bespelled by the sidhe too. I tried to assist in my own execution, as a matter of fact. If Eírnin hadn't showed up when he did... Well, you get the point."

"How many times are you going to bring *that* up?" Morrigann gazed skyward and let out a dramatic sigh. "Honestly, Story, you've got to learn to let go. You can't go on staying mad about inconsequential things forever."

Eisrus shot to his feet. "Inconsequential? This is the Ailesit you are talking about; the savior of the entire elf race. How dare you!"

Reaching out, Story placed a calming hand on the elf's arm, ready to restrain him if needed. Even at his weakest, the Spring Prince was still a dangerous foe. Eisrus subsided, but continued to glare at Morrigann. The faerie just smiled demurely in return.

Adair chose that moment to enter the campsite, a soaking wet Ped at her side, breaking the awkward silence that had descended.

Eisrus's eyes lit up, and a large smile crossed his face before he quickly sobered his expression. But he couldn't hide the green and purple swirling in his eyes, and noting Eachan's slight frown, Story suspected she could see his colors too.

Taking in their odd grouping, Adair dropped her string of freshly caught fish by the fire.

"Well then, what did I miss?"

"I'M NOT GOING! WE'VE ALREADY HAD THIS DISCUSSION. YOU CAN'T make me!" Adair crossed her arms over her chest and glared at Story with red and blue eyes.

"Actually, yes, I can." Story mirrored her pose and glared right back.

"Oh yeah, how? You going to make good on your promise and tie me to Ped?" Adair jerked a thumb over in the selkie's direction.

"Eisrus," Story called over her shoulder.

He was at her side in an instant. "Yes, Ailesit?"

"Would you mind escorting my sister back to Vevila?" Story nodded toward Adair. "I've cleared it with Eachan already. You'll both ride on Ped, so the trip should be relatively short. A couple days at the most." She turned to look at the young hunter. "It's very important that Adair makes it back to our mother safely. Once there, you can either come back on Ped—if he'll bring you—or you can stay there and wait for our return, and perhaps learn a little bit about another culture while you're at it."

His eyes brightened, almost solidly orange, except for a few purple flashes. Story smiled, her suspicions confirmed. Adair, on the other hand, was either completely clueless or not interested in him at all. Story honestly didn't know which one it was, because usually Adair was very perceptive in these matters. Then again, she was "boy crazy" at the moment, only not so much around the elves, as most had not exactly welcomed her as one of their own.

Eisrus broke into her thoughts, nodding his head eagerly and saying, "Yes, Ailesit. Whatever you need!"

He moved to Adair's side, doing his best to look serious and authoritative. Adair's mouth opened and closed as she stood there, for once at a loss for words.

A chilly wind blew through the camp, and Story shivered. "I'm done arguing with you, Adair. I need you to do this. We're still a couple weeks from Cildara, and Morrigann can't move us again. We're running out of time."

"But it's not fair! I want to help save Eírnin!" Adair blinked rapidly, fighting back tears. "He's like a brother to me. He's family."

"Life isn't fair. You're going."

Adair's face crumpled, and she buried her face into Eisrus's chest and cried. He wrapped an awkward arm around her and looked to Story for guidance. She swallowed past the lump forming in her own throat and motioned toward the water. He nodded, turning them both toward the shore. Adair didn't fight him, and for that Story was grateful.

She'll understand once she's calmed down. But the words sounded hollow in her mind.

After a few steps, Morrigann called out to them. "Wait. I have something for you."

Eisrus paused and glared at the sidhe, yellow and red flooding his eyes. "I don't need anything from *you*. You've done quite enough for my kind."

Giving a sour smile, Morrigann shook his head. "Elfling, if I'd wanted to harm you, I'd have done so by now."

Eisrus's eyes flared red, and he opened his mouth to retort, but Eachan silenced him with a look. "Do as he says, Apprentice."

Morrigann held out a closed hand but made no move, forcing the elf to walk back to him before he opened it slowly. A glowing gold orb, the size of a small marble, sat in the palm of the faerie's hand.

"What is it?" Adair peered around Eisrus's shoulder, her gaze riveted on the gold ball. Her face was still streaked with tears, but her eyes were dry.

The faerie smiled at her. "It's a small bit of the Sun's warmth." He looked at Eisrus. "Take it."

"Why, so you can track us?" The elf's eyes were solidly yellow, and Story didn't blame him. She'd learned the hard way to never trust the fey.

"No, you simple minded fool."

Story shot him a warning glance, and he sighed loudly before continuing in his haughty demeanor. "It's so when you arrive in Vevila and release it, it will find its way back to me." Morrigann returned his gaze to Adair and smiled again. "That will let both me and your sister know that you are safe from the clutches of the *evil* faeries who want to kill you." He glanced at Story, his smile fading as a rare, more serious expression crossed his face, though he still directed his words to Adair. "Then, perhaps, if you remain there until the Uinseann is past, there will be no need for any faerie to harm you. Ever."

Story's eyebrows shot up to her hairline. He hadn't promised anything, per se, but his meaning was clear: so long as Adair was safely kept in Vevila until after the winter solstice, he—Morrigann—wouldn't try to kill her. She snorted as she realized that he *couldn't* hurt Adair while she was in the middle of a salt-filled ocean anyways. Useless promise indeed. Still, the thought behind it was nice.

Whoa there, Story, don't trust him. Don't EVER trust him. Nothing he does is "nice."

Eisrus looked at his master, and when she nodded her head, he held out a slightly trembling hand. For all his bluster, the young elf was afraid of the Spring Prince.

And rightly so.

Morrigann placed the orb in the elf's hand tenderly, as if it was a precious child. It flared brightly for a moment in Eisrus's palm and then sank down into the flesh, leaving a small, flat circle of gold.

Raising it up to his face, Eisrus's eyes faded to a placid green. A gentle smile crossed his features, and he stared at the gold warmth emanating from his hand with something akin to longing. Adair leaned in closer, her nose almost touching his hand, wearing the same enraptured smile on her face.

"It will stay there until you release it."

Eisrus didn't answer the faerie, still staring at his hand. Morrigann snapped his fingers before the elf's eyes finally gaining his attention.

"How do I—"

"You just release it. It can't leave you until you command it to go."

Eisrus didn't look as if he ever wanted the orb to leave.

"You will *have* to command it to go in order for it to work."

After the elf finally nodded his head in acceptance, Morrigann stepped back, and Eisrus and Adair absentmindedly walked toward the water, still staring at his hand in awe.

"Don't worry. They'll get used to the feeling eventually

and be themselves again. Meanwhile, until they do, they'll be safely underwater, away from fey danger."

Story gave Morrigann a sidelong glance and saw that Eachan was doing the same thing. "Thank you."

The sidhe sniffed. "For what? It serves my purposes to know your sister is safe."

Story just shook her head as she walked over to Ped. She reached up to scratch him behind his ears. "I know you want to stay too, but this is the best way you can help me help Eírnin. So, thank you." She kissed him on his whiskery nose, and he returned it with a fat, slobbery lick up the side of her face. Then he turned around and followed the two youths down to the water's edge.

Story faced her new traveling companions and had to stifle a laugh. Morrigann and Eachan; both of them thought Ailionora would be better off without her in it.

She grinned, feeling a surge of hope. These were the last two people in all the worlds she thought she'd ever find herself allying with. If that could happen, anything could!

CHAPTER FOURTEEN

OUT TO GET YOU

"WHY DID YOU DECIDE TO, WHAT DID YOU CALL IT? PLEDGE fealty to me?" Story asked Eachan, finally interrupting the oppressive silence that had been shrouding their journey the past few days. "I thought you didn't like me."

"I don't. That hasn't changed." The hunter flitted her eyes over to Story momentarily, then returned to scouting a trail only she could see, weaving around the massive trunks and thick underbrush. "But you spared my life, when, by rights, it should have been forfeit. I owe you."

She paused for so long that Story thought she was done talking, but then Eachan resumed the thread of the conversation. "And not only did you forgive me for what I've done, but you were willing to join with me—someone who has only ever wished you ill—in saving Eírnin... well, I suppose I must finally acknowledge that you do truly care for him. That you're not the completely selfish girl I once took you for."

Story didn't know quite how to respond to that. Was it a compliment or a rebuke? Walking behind her on the narrow trail, Story couldn't see her eyes to gain any sort of insight on her emotions. "So, you finally approve of me then?"

Eachan snorted. "Absolutely not. I think you're rash, arrogant, and overly emotional. Far from a suitable companion for an elf of Eírnin's stature." She nodded on the last bit to punctuate her words.

"But you would be suitable for him." It wasn't a question.

"Aye, of course. As hunters, we share the same cultural background and knowledge base. As elves, we are equals."

"So, being the Ailesit doesn't win me any points?"

Eachan glared down at Story from her perch atop a giant log. "The fact that your blood is red does not make you a suitable companion for Eírnin. If anything, it makes you less of one."

Not intimidated, Story held out her hand to the elf for assistance in climbing up. "Would you feel the same way if it was another elf, not Eírnin, who we were talking about?"

Eachan's mouth twitched, and she said nothing. Grasping Story's hand, she pulled her up onto the log and leapt down the other side.

Pulling himself up and standing shoulder to shoulder with Story, Morrigann said in a loud stage whisper, "I'm *so* glad that awkward conversation is over." Then he nimbly hopped off the log. "I have a wonderful idea: let's all talk about how Eachan cares so much for the elfling that she poisoned him."

He held out a hand to help Story but she ignored it, jumping down on her own, careful of where she landed on her bare feet. It would soon be cold enough to warrant shoes again, but she was determined to avoid them for as long as possible— she'd grown to enjoy the feel of earth under her toes.

Morrigann was not to be dissuaded. Taking up his

position behind Story again, he called out to Eachan. "Was it because you'd rather see him dead than let him choose to bond with another?"

Eachan whirled around and fixed Morrigann with a scathing look. "How about instead we talk about how you nearly eradicated my entire race for nothing more than your own amusement?"

Story let out a loud sigh. She was beginning to understand how Adair must have felt traveling with her and Morrigann. "Just stop it, both of you. We're all on the same side here."

"For now," Eachan and Morrigann said in unison. This led to another glare between them, which, thankfully, resulted in another long silence.

STORY HAD A HARD TIME FALLING ASLEEP THAT NIGHT. PERHAPS IT was the ground, so much colder than it had been before. She tried to convince herself it was only from being at a higher altitude now that they had reached the slopes of the mountains, rather than the fast approaching winter.

Or perhaps it was the guilt over sending Adair away. Thankfully, she knew her sister was safe now—the bit of sun had returned to Morrigann earlier that day, letting them know Eisrus and Adair had made it safely to Vevila.

Perhaps it was the guilt of proceeding on the journey herself, and therefore risking unleashing Chaos. Or maybe it was the guilt of her planned betrayal of Morrigann, even though she knew he was plotting the same for her.

Regardless of the reason, she couldn't fall asleep. She

flopped onto her back and gave a loud sigh. Eachan fidgeted at the sound then settled back into the rhythmic breathing pattern of a solid sleep state.

Lucky.

"I can help you with that."

Story nearly jumped out of her skin. Morrigann was stretched out beside her. *He's worse than Adair when it comes to personal space!*

"How long have you been there?" she demanded, a flush of embarrassment creeping up her neck.

"Long enough to know you're having trouble sleeping." He propped his head up on his hand and gazed at her, his violet eyes glittering in the firelight. "I can help you fall asleep if you'd like."

Story eyed him warily. "Why?"

"Do I really need a reason?"

"Yes. You don't do anything without an ulterior motive."

He smiled slowly before answering. "Fine. My reason is you humans are so very fragile." He reached out a finger toward her cheek, but she stretched away to avoid his touch. His hand dropped to the ground as if that was what he'd intended to do. "If you don't get enough sleep, you'll be practically worthless tomorrow. You'll slow us down. The sooner I get you to Cildara, the sooner I'm free."

"And the sooner you can kill me."

A demure smile was his only response.

"I'm not going to have to cuddle with you again, am I? Because that's not happening."

He gave a light chuckle that sounded like the soft patter of rain. "I *will* need to touch you for this to work." She flinched, and he rushed on, "But the 'cuddling' as you call it is not strictly necessary. It just makes it that much more pleasant." He held out his hand toward her, but she eyed it warily.

"What exactly is 'it'?"

"I'm surprised you haven't figured it out yet, but then—"

"Yeah, I know, I'm simple. Got it. Moving on." Story narrowed her eyes.

"I am Spring. I bring life. And when I am weakened, I seek after life. And you, my dear, are full to the brim with life!" He cocked his head to the side and eyed her. "A more recent change, I think, perhaps due to your bond with the Ailes. In any case, you strengthen me, and in return, I give you a good night of sleep."

"Ah, so you aren't being altruistic. It's just a side effect of you getting what you want."

He shrugged.

What could it hurt? I do need to sleep...

Story reached out and took his hand, interlacing their fingers. A golden glow blossomed where their skin made contact, and she felt herself yawn. "Don't think this means I like you. Or that we've got a truce. Or that I trust you."

Morrigann leaned in, his honey sweet breath wafting over her. "I wouldn't *dream* of it."

Her lids drooped closed, and Story fell into a deep, blissful sleep.

WALKING DOWN MAIN STREET, THE SNOW FALLING SOFTLY AROUND them, Josh threaded his gloved fingers through Story's.

Josh? Story looked around, confused. She hadn't really given much thought to Josh, her oldest friend, in months—not since her mother said she'd get her letter delivered to him, letting him know she was still alive and well and not to worry about her. *He's better off without me around anyways.*

"Any idea of where you want to eat before the party?" Josh raised his eyebrows; they were as fiery as the rest of his closely cropped hair.

I remember this night... It was their first date, back when things in her life had been much simpler. They'd been close friends since childhood, and then suddenly when they were sixteen, it had blossomed into something more.

Looking around, Story pointed at a little restaurant. "There's Nick and Nate's. They serve the best pizza this side of the Mississippi."

Story knew she was dreaming now, but didn't mind; it was a nice escape.

"That sounds perfect." Josh gave her hand a squeeze, and she froze. The action was too familiar. Too much like Eírnin.

Josh must have seen the look of pain wash across her face, because he let go and placed a tentative hand on her shoulder. "Is everything okay?"

"No." She felt tears slid down her cheeks, and she looked away from Josh, unwilling to meet his eyes. *Why can't I stop crying all the time?*

The memory of her friend evaporated into nothingness, and Story continued down Main Street, past the Mercantile and the pottery shop where she'd bought her favorite mug.

She missed that mug. Its blue glaze had been streaked to look like tall, willowy trees.

She turned a corner and nearly ran into Eínlin. The dreamwalker merely raised the bushy, white eyebrow over his pinwheel ailach and then pivoted to walk with her, his blue robes flaring out around him. They walked through the snow together, down the streets of her grandad's hometown. She'd spent every holiday and most every summer there. Her granddad had taken her and Josh deer hunting every autumn, though she'd been horrible at it. Josh, on the other hand, had been an excellent bow hunter and always bagged a large white-tailed buck. But given that he shared the deer jerky they made later, she didn't begrudge his luck. Too much.

"So, this is where you are from." Eínlin gave an appraising look at the different homes of various sizes built into the mountainside.

"Yup, good old Waynesville."

"It's very different here." The elf's straw sandals left strange tracks in the snow.

Story gave a short laugh. "That's putting it mildly."

"No wonder you ask the oddest questions." He ran his hand along the hood of a yellow Volkswagen Beetle, his fingers leaving furrows in the snow. "So much metal. It almost seems wasteful."

"Why are you here, Eínlin?" Story glanced at him out of the corner of her eyes. "Not that it isn't nice to see you, but after the way I left..."

He stroked his long beard with one hand as they turned back onto Main Street. "Queen Eánna wanted to make sure you were all right. I've been trying to find you ever since you left." He glanced at her. "You were hiding quite effectively."

"I wasn't trying to. At least not purposefully. Though I guess I've always been able to keep people I didn't want out of my dreams." She gave him a wry smile. "I'm sorry for worrying you."

"And I'm glad you decided to let me visit. There is still so much to learn about your abilities. About all our abilities." He stopped walking, and Story followed suit, facing him. "I don't suppose you'd be willing to come back and let the hunters get the cure for Eírnin?"

One corner of Story's mouth raised in a nervous smile. "Not for all the worlds."

His eyes closed, and he let out a deep sigh.

Story gripped his shoulder. "But don't worry, I'm with Eachan now, and we're working together."

Eínlin's eyes shot open. "What?"

"It's true. So I'm not completely without protection, right?" Story decided not to mention Morrigann. No need to worry them more than necessary. "As for my sister, Eisrus has taken her back to Vevila, where she'll stay until after the Uinseann."

Eínlin's hand continued to stroke his beard, his long fingernails flashing under the streetlight. "I would like to show you something. May I?"

"Sure." It was not as if he could do anything to her in the dream. Could he? Morrigann had said that nothing permanent could be done to a person physically in a dream, but hadn't she woken up with a burned tongue once?

Before she could change her mind, the mage took her hand and the scene around them shifted. They were no longer in North Carolina. Sprawled out before them was a snow-swept gnome village. The icy wind sliced through her hair, and Story's gaze was immediately drawn to the fires that con-sumed the thatched roof of every building and then to the flee-ing gnomes themselves. Instead of fighting to put out the fires, the stocky earth people were carrying their smaller children and pulling on the arms of those too big to be carried.

They weren't running from the fires.

Massive, white furred, ape-like creatures were raging through the streets. When they encountered a gnome, they didn't even hesitate before pulling them apart, occasionally stopping to eat one, but generally tossing the bloody gnome pieces aside and reaching for the next one. Story felt bile rise in her throat as she watched one of the snow-apes lift a scream-ing child toward its mouth. Closing her eyes against the horror before her, she screamed, "Stop! Make it stop!"

The whistling wind ceased, and Story felt nothing. Cracking her eyes open, she couldn't see anything but white and emptiness. She only knew Eínlin was with her because he still held her hand. Opening her eyes fully, she turned toward the Dreamwalker and swallowed the lump in her throat.

"What was that? And why did you make me watch it?" Story blinked back tears. "I'll never be able to forget what I saw."

"I know, Ailesit, and I am sorry." Eínlin released her hand and began walking down the empty white space. Story kept pace at his side, still stunned and horrified by the vision.

"What I showed you was a memory of ages past." The elf's sandaled feet swished across the non-existent floor of the dream. "You have seen but a taste of the brutality that Winter once unleashed on this world after he was tainted by Chaos." He raised a bushy, white eyebrow as he regarded Story. "He will do worse this time."

"What were those things?" Story fought to keep the trembling from her voice.

"JoBran. Roughly translated, snow elves or elf-eaters."

"Those were *elves*?"

"No, not elves. That's why I said roughly translated. In your world, you'd probably call them snow humans or some derivative."

"Wait, you mean like snowmen? As in abominable snowmen?" Story's surprise momentarily overtook her fear of the creatures.

Eínlin stroked his beard and regarded Story curiously. "I've never heard that name before, but yes, they are abominable." He stopped walking and faced her. "Knowing the risk now, will you reconsider? Will you come back?"

Story knew this question was coming, knew it was the only reason he'd shared this information with her—to try to scare her into doing what he wanted. What the queen wanted.

"No. I won't."

Sighing, he closed his eyes. "Aye, I knew you wouldn't." He turned and walked away from her, fading from the dream. "Be careful, Ailesit. The lives of all depend on you."

Chapter Fifteen

HARD HEADED WOMAN

AREN'T YOU BOTHERED BY THE FACT THAT I'M RISKING ALL THE worlds by being out here?" Story directed her question at Eachan since she already knew how Morrigann felt on the matter.

The elf's shoulders stiffened but she kept pressing up the mountainside. "Aren't *you* bothered by that, Ailesit?"

"Kinda." Story grabbed onto a low hanging tree branch to help pull herself up the steep slope. The images from the memory Eínlin shared with her flashed through her mind, but she banished them away before they could make her ill. "But only if I think about it too much, so I'm trying not to think about it."

"I expected as much from someone like you."

Story felt her eyebrows shoot up to her hairline. "Excuse me? The other day my actions were 'noble and selfless' but now you're looking down on me for it? Can we say hypocritical much?" She paused to take a breath. "And you have done nothing to try to get me back to safety. Shouldn't making sure Winter can't get me take higher priority over getting an antidote for Eírnin?"

"Do you want to know what I think?" Morrigann called from behind them.

"No!" Story and Eachan said in unison.

Before he could respond, a loud shriek, like rocks being torn in two, rent the air. They all froze, and the hair on Story's arms stood on end. It was very close—twenty feet at the most, through the trees.

I know that sound...

"Mountain troll," Eachan whispered, confirming Story's suspicions. "Fully grown by the sound of it." Yellow flooded her eyes, and Story looked back at Morrigann to see even he looked worried.

"Let's go around," Morrigann hissed, pointing to the side. Story nodded emphatically. She'd encountered a troll once before; it had interrupted her first kiss with Eírnin, and the troll had scared her witless. That one had just been a child.

Eachan crept quietly to the right, and Story was moving to follow her when they heard an even worse sound: someone was screaming.

Without thinking, Story immediately spun toward the sound and powered up the slope. Someone was in trouble!

Eachan lunged for her. "Ailesit! No! You can't risk it. It's too dangerous!"

Slipping out of her grasp, Story kept running until she reached the edge of the trees. She peered through them at the scene beyond. A thirty-foot-tall pile of moving boulders, arranged in a rough humanoid shape, was holding a shrieking person in its massive hand.

The parallels to what she'd seen in her dream were sickening, and Story gripped the trunk of the tree and tried to calm her racing heart. The troll was moving its hand steadily toward the black maw of its mouth. The person screamed again and struggled to get out, but to no avail.

Eachan slipped in beside her. "Ailesit—"

"Can you hit its knee from here?" Story whispered.

The elf gave her a scathing look and had an arrow nocked and ready to fire before Story's next breath. She let the arrow fly, and it hit true—dead center of the knee. But instead of falling to pieces as Story expected, the troll whirled toward their hiding place with lightening speed and bellowed.

At least it's not still trying to eat that guy anymore.

Eachan had another arrow nocked and shot before the troll finished turning.

"Move!" Morrigann shoved Story out of the way, causing Eachan's third arrow to fly askew and hit a tree. The faerie yanked them both out of the way just before a massive boulder foot came crashing down where they had been.

Story dodged another flying tree, pulling Morrigann behind her. "What I wouldn't give for some da'nan right about now!" The horse-like animals were smart as well as deadly to trolls.

"Not going to happen while I'm about!" Morrigann called back. Da'nan didn't like faeries.

Eachan shot two arrows at once this time. Both flew true, and the troll bellowed again, this time dropping its prey as it reached down to tug the arrows from its knee. Its size was making the troll almost unstoppable.

The body fell through the air, and Story darted out to try to catch it.

"Story, NO!" Morrigann lunged after her, but she slipped his grip and arrived just in time for the person to drop neatly into her arms. Actually, he didn't so much drop into her arms as nearly flatten her, which shocked Story, since with her added strength from *The Ailes* she should have been able to catch him easily.

What's this guy made of, bricks?

The troll noticed her movement and reached a massive hand for both Story and the hairy man pinning her down.

"Come on, guy, get up!" She pushed him, but he just groaned. "Eachan! Do something!"

The hand came closer.

"I am!"

What's that supposed to mean? Is she letting the troll kill me? Story made another desperate attempt to dislodge the body atop her, to no avail. She closed her eyes tightly, waiting for the crushing hand.

Not how I expected to go...

Before she could think of anything else, she heard the twang of Eachan's bow once more and the loud yell of the troll. This time the cry was different; it lengthened until it sounded like rocks being torn in two again.

I know that sound too!

Story peeked through her lashes in time to see three new arrows sticking out of the troll's knee, and then it crumbled. Story bent over the head of person moaning on her legs, sheltering her own head as best she could with her arms. The troll literally fell apart in a shower of stones and boulders, leaving only a heap of small rocks around them.

Coughing, Story waved the dust away from her face.

"Hey, a little help here you two? This guy weighs a ton!" She coughed again from the grit in the air.

Eachan was the first to reach her. The elf made a disgusted face when she saw the person on Story's legs, but still leaned over and grabbed his hairy arms. "I'm sorry for trying to stop you before, Ailesit... I thought you were going to—"

"Plunge headlong into a fight with a mountain troll?" Story grunted as she pushed against the weighty fellow. "Do I look stupid to you?"

"Yes." Morrigann grasped the hairy man's legs, and with their combined efforts, they were able to move him off of Story. "You're lucky you weren't crushed by one of the falling boulders."

Story stood up slowly, brushed herself off, and straightened her clothes before turning to the faerie. "And why did *you* try to save me? I thought you wanted me dead. You never agreed to keep me alive, you only promised not to kill me yourself."

"Only until I get you safely to my sister's grove—don't forget that important bit."

Eachan stepped in front of Story and leveled an iron-tipped arrow at Morrigann. "You will *not* harm the Ailesit on my watch."

Morrigann's eyes flitted down to the arrow, mere inches from his chest, and then back up to Eachan's face. "Impressive. Where did you come across that much iron?"

"This arrow was given to me by the queen in case your sister needed some additional *persuading* to help us out." She pulled back further on the string. "I don't mind testing it out on you first, little faerie."

Story reached out a staying hand and gently lowered Eachan's bow. "You don't want to do that. Trust me."

Eachan glared at Story, and her eyes flared red momentarily, fading to silver as she returned the iron-tipped arrow to her quiver. "Fine. You're in charge." She stepped away from the two of them and moved to examine the prostrate person on the ground.

"You didn't answer my question." Story crossed her arms and looked at Morrigann with narrowed eyes. "Why didn't you let the troll kill me?"

The faerie merely smiled, stepped forward, and leaned in toward Story's ear until he was only a hairsbreadth away. His warm breath tickled the skin at the base of her neck and sent a shiver of magic down her spine.

"I'll never tell," he breathed, before pulling away and giving her a mischievous wink.

Before Story could respond, the person on the ground groaned loudly and sat up, blinking his heavy-lidded eyes.

"Ach!" He spit out a mouthful of dirt and grit and lumbered to his feet. The top of his head stopped just short of Story's chin, making him about as tall as a gnome.

Except, he didn't look like a gnome; he was far stouter. While the gnomes were a hardy people, this individual was abnormally wide—a solid mass of muscles. "Built like an ox" was the phrase that came to Story's mind, but even that seemed inadequate.

He had wiry brown hair, brown skin, brown trousers, and brown boots and gloves. It was all so monochromatic at first Story thought he wasn't wearing anything at all, and it took even longer to notice he wasn't wearing a really furry shirt—that was actually his natural chest and arm hair. As he stretched, she saw that his back was nearly as hairy as his chest. And he smelled badly, as if he'd never had a bath in his life, and judging by the layers upon layers of dirt caked on him, he probably hadn't.

"Who saved me?" His voice was deep and throaty, his accent thick and strong, reminding Story of someone from Eastern Europe. He looked at Story, focused on her ears, and smiled broadly, showing several rows of broad, flat teeth—perfect for grinding, though grinding what, Story didn't know.

"Ach!" He spat on the ground. "It must be you, Miss! Thank you. I thought I was troll lunch for sure, Miss."

"Why would a troll want to eat a gnome?" Story cocked her head to the side, confused. "Trolls eat rocks... right?"

He let out a loud laugh and bent over, slapping his knee. "Ach!" he spat again. "You are funny, Miss. What are you?"

"None of your concern, Master Dwarf." Eachan stepped forward and grabbed Story by the arm. "Let's go."

Story dug in her heels and yanked her arm back. "Just one second... Dwarf?"

The dwarf didn't answer; instead, he stared at Eachan, anger and loathing clear on his face.

"Ailesit, please, can we just go?" Eachan tried to pull Story away again, but she flashed the elf a warning look, and Eachan dropped her arm. "Fine, have it your way."

The dwarf perked up. "Ailesit?" He eyed Story with as much curiosity as she'd given him. "Ach! So it's true? The elves got their magic back?"

Morrigann snorted, and the dwarf whipped his head around as if seeing him for the first time. "And who are you?"

Story placed a hand on the dwarf's shoulder. "Maybe introductions all around are in order? We need to make camp for the night anyway. Would you join us, Master Dwarf?"

"Ach," he spat, "I'd love to, Miss."

CHAPTER SIXTEEN

UNINVITED

THEY SAT AROUND THE CAMPFIRE, STARLIGHT SPARKLING overhead, Morrigann playing a soft tune on his violin, and Eachan waxing her bow string. Story ate a salad of wild greens and berries, while the dwarf—whose name was Dagen—munched happily on some rocks. She hoped he wasn't eating the troll; it struck her as a bit weird for him to be eating something that had been trying to eat him first.

"So back to your question, Miss," Dagen said between bites. "Trolls love to eat dwarves, Miss. They do eat rocks, but then so do we. So, Miss, it would be like you deciding to set aside your salad and eat a rabbit for dinner."

Story nodded her head. It made sense when he put it that way; except the rabbit didn't try to eat her in return. "Okay, then tell me, are you fairly tall for a dwarf? I just expected you to be much shorter..."

He cocked a wiry brown eyebrow. "Why? Have you met many short dwarves, Miss?"

"Well, no, you're the first dwarf I've ever met—"

"You'll have to forgive her, Master Dwarf," Morrigann interrupted. "She comes from a land that has gotten what few stories that remain of Ailionora so far wrong, it's really quite comical."

Story shrugged; he was right. Some of the faerie tales and legends held true, but others were way off. "Okay, so dwarves aren't short—"

Eachan snorted, and Dagen shot her a nasty look. Story continued, "But you are long-lived, right?"

Eachan snorted again, and Dagen burst to his feet. "Ach! Have something to say to me, hunter?"

Eachan waved a hand at him. "Sit down, Master Dwarf, before you hurt yourself." She returned to working on her bow without sparing him a second glance. Dagen glared at her a moment longer before settling down among his rocks. He crunched down on one and pulverized it in his mouth.

So, elves and dwarves not getting along—at least we got that one right.

"In answer to your question whether we are long-lived, Miss, the answer is yes and no, Miss." He narrowed his eyes at Eachan. "Ach! I wouldn't expect *some* to understand, Miss." He pursed his lips in a frown and retuned his gaze to Story. "Some, Miss, well, they never bother to learn nothing about any others what aren't their own kind, Miss." He ground a rock between his teeth, scattering shards down his beard. "Ach! Except for what they could use them for, Miss."

This time it was Eachan who shot to her feet. "Just what are you implying, *dwarf*?"

"Just what I said, *elf*." He was back on his feet, hands

fisted on his hips, glaring up at Eachan. "Ach! You elves never care for no one but yourselves."

"That is a lie! Even now, we are working to gather an army to keep Winter from destroying all the worlds. An army you dwarves have failed to join." She jabbed a finger in the dwarf's chest. "Who's the selfish one now?"

Dagen grabbed her hand tightly in his gloved one. "Don't touch me with your filthy elf hands, hunter!" He flung her hand out of his grasp and stepped back. "Ach! And how do we know you elves aren't trying to trick us? We are not so stupid, hunter, we know you want to kill us all permanently and have all the metal to yourselves!"

Eachan's eyebrows shot up to her hairline. "Idiot! It isn't a ploy. Winter approaches, and he brings Chaos with him, the unmaker of all."

"Ach!" The dwarf spat at her feet. "You lie like the filthy elf you are!"

Story was about to step in before they came to blows, but surprisingly, Morrigann beat her to it. "She does not lie, Master Dwarf." He placed his hand on Dagen's shoulder where it glowed momentarily. The dwarf let out a deep breath and slowly sat back down, his calm restored. Morrigann reached out to do the same to Eachan, but after one warning look from her, he retreated back to his side of the fire.

The dwarf scratched his chest absentmindedly and glanced at the faerie. "Ach! How do you know? And how do I know you're not lying to me too?"

Story answered this time. "Because he can't lie." She motioned for Eachan to sit back down, and the elf obliged, her vivid red eyes slowly fading to smoldering embers of anger. "This is Morrigann, the Spring Prince."

"Ach!" Dagen's smile split his thick, short beard. "Truly?"

Well that's new. She'd ever seen anyone happy to meet one of the Sidhe before.

The dwarf stood up again and extended a hand. "Sir, it's a great honor, truly a great honor."

Morrigann smiled at the dwarf, shaking his eager hand, while Eachan mumbled "Idiots, all of them," under her breath.

"You see, Story, some people appreciate me the way they ought." He winked at her over his shoulder, and Story rolled her eyes.

"Master Dwarf, do you believe us now?" Story said.

He nodded his head emphatically and seemed a bit sad when Morrigann released his hand. He did strike Story as a tad simple-minded, but perhaps that was just because he was coming across as a child in his behavior—not the young man he appeared to be.

"Okay, now that that's settled… how old are you, if you don't mind me asking?" Story picked her salad up and took a bite.

"I just had my first birthday, Miss." He crunched down on a rock, and Story spat out her mouthful of food.

"What?"

"Ach! Last week, Miss, I turned one. I thought my short beard would have made that obvious," he said around a mouthful of pebbles.

Morrigann sat down smoothly next to Story, and she slid away from him to ensure he wasn't touching her. The corners of his mouth turned down in a pout, but he didn't move closer. "Dwarves and gnomes are cousins of a sort."

Story nodded. "Yeah, I figured that much out on my own. They're both earth people."

Morrigann shook his head. "No, you don't understand. While the gnomes are tied to the earth for their magic, making them excellent farmers—"

"—Who your spriggans love to torment."

Morrigann continued on as if Story hadn't spoken. "Gnomes still procreate in the typical mortal fashion."

"And dwarves don't?" Story looked at Dagen, who took that moment to belch before grinning at her. Then he proceeded to shove more rocks in his mouth and chew.

Eachan made a disgusted sound in her throat and jumped to her feet, mumbling something about hunting. Story nodded, acknowledging her departure, and looked back at Morrigann expectantly. "Well?"

"No, dwarves don't." Morrigann slid an inch closer to Story. "Dwarves spring from the earth fully formed. They're mature with a full beard by their third year and are fully grey by their seventh year. It's rare to see one older than eight, and a ten-year-old is positively ancient."

Story's eyes widened. "What? They are literally born from the earth?"

Morrigann slid closer again, and Story, in turn, moved further down the log, away from him. She knew what he wanted, and she wasn't interested in falling asleep yet.

"Yes, you can ask Dagen all about the specifics of how it works when it wakes up." He indicated the dwarf with a nod of his head, who, to Story's surprise, was sprawled atop his rocks, snoring softly. "But essentially, when a dwarf is ready to procreate, it gives up some of its blood in the birthing caves of their mines, and there you go, new dwarf."

He slid closer, but Story was too busy thinking to slide away from him again. "*It*? Don't you mean *he*?"

The Spring Prince chuckled and moved close enough that they were touching again, only this time, there was no soft glow from him drawing on her life essence. "Oh, simple Story, dwarves are all 'its'. They don't procreate after the 'normal' fashion, ergo, they don't need genders."

"Well, by that logic, neither do the Sidhe, but you still have them."

Morrigann moved his head side to side in a non-committal way. "Yes and no. *I* am male, but Spring is not."

"But I thought you were Spring?"

"I am."

"I don't understand."

Morrigann chuckled and gave her a beautiful smile. "Oh, simple Story, if you were to destroy me and become Spring, would you also change your gender?"

"I certainly hope not! I don't want to be a guy." Then she blushed when she realized the potential perceived insult. "Not that there's anything wrong with that..."

Morrigann's loud musical laughter filled the space, and Story relaxed.

"So, the red dwarves to the west, are they 'its' too?" She glanced at him and was surprised by how near his face was to her own. The last time they'd been this close... She banished the dangerous thought.

"Yes, even the red dwarves, though they're decidedly more delicate in their features." She felt his hand brush across her hip as he settled it on the log on the other side of her. "I think it's the lack of beards and body hair."

He leaned in closer and swept a few braids out of her face, tucking them behind her ear. His hand lingered there, tracing the outline of her ear with his fingertips.

"What are you doing?" A warning flag went up in Story's mind. This was too much like their first encounters, months ago. She knew what came next. She also knew she should move away, but her legs wouldn't listen to her.

"I've always been fascinated by your rounded ears. So different. Exotic even." His hand continued to trace down her neck, and his thumb followed the line of her jaw.

Echoes of Eírnin, his touch and memory, filled her mind. Story was riveted in place, transfixed by the faerie's smoldering gaze and the warmth emanating from him. He felt like the sun on this chilly autumn evening, and she craved the warmth and life that was coming off him in waves. His lips grazed hers, and she felt a jolt of heat down to her toes, warming her to the core.

She closed her eyes and inhaled his honey sweet breath, relaxing against him, as she felt his arms encircle her. It felt so nice, like she was surrounded by a blanket of sunshine.

His mouth pressed harder against hers, and he gently teased her lips open, filling her with life and warmth.

Her hands crept up his back feeling the heat of his bare skin, pulling him closer, wanting more more more—

"Ailesit!"

Story jerked away feeling instantly diminished and chilled from the break in contact. Eachan stood on the other side of the fire carrying a dead rabbit by its ears. A shocked expression was on the elf's face as she took in the scene before her.

Morrigann tried to pull Story back toward him, and her hand shot out almost of its own accord, slapping him hard across the face. He released her arms then, and she shot to her feet, backing away from him. "You promised you wouldn't enchant me again!"

He held his cheek where she'd hit him, and a smirk crossed his face. "I didn't."

CHAPTER SEVENTEEN

CROSSROADS

ILESIT, WAIT!"

Story ignored Eachan and crashed blindly through the woods, feeling foolish, guilty, angry, and used. And that was just scratching the surface. Hot tears leaked out of the corners of her eyes; she felt lower than a worm.

How could I do that? How could I let him kiss me? What am I going to tell Eírnin?

Strong fingers wrapped around her upper arm, pulling Story up short. She whipped around hand raised to lash out, but Eachan caught her wrist.

"Ailesit, it's just me!" She released Story's hand, and it dropped to her side. "The cursed faerie is still back at the camp." She took in Story's tears, the stricken look on her face, and her expression softened. "Don't blame yourself over what happened back there."

"What?" Story scrubbed the back of her hand across her

eyes, trying to compose herself. "No, I let him… I didn't want to, but I still let him. I don't understand—"

"Ailesit!" Eachan gripped her shoulders and gave her a quick shake. "Stop! That was *not* your fault. It was his. And I should never have left you two alone." She released Story's shoulders and lowered her head in seeming embarrassment. "I knew he would try eventually, but I thought with Dagen there…" She kicked a rock deep into the forest. "Curse that blasted dwarf and its inability to stay awake for even a few minutes!"

Story stopped crying, but her heart was still racing, and her head was spinning. *Why is Eachan being nice to me?*

"Look, Eachan, I really appreciate what you're trying to do here, but I really screwed up. I'm still responsible for my own actions." Story began walking up the slope, trying to calm her breathing.

Keeping pace with her, Eachan raised her hand and waggled it in a "so-so" gesture. "Aye, in most cases yes, that would be true. But when the fey are involved, oft times different rules come into play."

"I'm not sure I understand what you mean. He said he wasn't bespelling me."

Eachan kept pace with her up the mountainside. "You've been traveling with the Spring Prince for how long now? Several weeks? A month? Most wouldn't last a day around him and his charms."

Story started to contradict her, but Eachan held up a hand. "He's a faerie, for Ai's sake. And not just any faerie, but a sidhe—Lord of the Spring, bringer of life. Every living thing is drawn to him whether he enchants them or not."

Sniffing, Story wiped her nose with her sleeve. *I really*

need to remember to carry a handkerchief or something if I'm gonna cry like this all the time.

"But that's crazy! I'm still in control of me. I could have stopped it."

"Could you? Did you try?" Eachan stopped walking and leaned against a tree.

"Yes! At least, I think I did…" Story trailed off under the elf's frank gaze.

"But you couldn't?"

"Well, no." Story bit her lower lip, thinking. "It was like my mind was screaming at me, but my body wouldn't listen? It was really weird, but I didn't feel enchanted. I know what that feels like—your mind doesn't resist then." She canted her head to the side, eyeing Eachan. "Why aren't you affected by him?"

Eachan didn't answer at first, but Story could see bare hints of pink embarrassment tinting her eyes.

"Who says I'm not?" Eachan pressed on before Story could respond. "But the difference is, he doesn't pay me any mind. He hasn't tried to kiss me—"

"Only because he knows you'd probably stab him if he did."

Eachan stared at Story for a moment, locking eyes, and then the elf did something Story never thought she'd see: Eachan grinned and then laughed, full and hearty. "Aye, that I probably would. But not until I'd kissed him good and thoroughly. Might as well make it worthwhile, eh?"

Story laughed with her, and it felt good, like a burden had been lifted. Just as quickly, she sobered. "Why are you telling me this? You could have let me agonize over this, thinking

I'd gone and cheated on Eírnin." A part of her still kind of felt like she had.

Shrugging, the elf wouldn't meet Story's eyes. "If you two decide not to be together, I'd rather it be for a real reason, and not because of fey magic and trickery."

"So what you're saying is you want to break us up honorably? And then steal Eírnin for yourself?"

Eachan nodded. "Something like that." She leaned in toward Story, lowering her voice again. "I know you say we need the Spring Prince to find Cildara, but I know how to get us there without him."

Story raised a questioning eyebrow.

"The dwarves know the way. They have ever been friendly with the sidhe. Though Ai knows why." Eachan curled her lip in disgust as she nodded toward the camp and slumbering Dagen. "You saved its life; it owes you a favor. Call it in. Have it take you to Cildara, and we can be free of the cursed faerie."

She sounded sincere, and it was a good idea on the surface, but the problem was Story couldn't get rid of Morrigann yet. She had to trade him to Metirreonn for Eírnin's antidote.

Should I trust her with that information? Sure, she was being friendly now, but that could change.

A twig snapped, and they both glanced around quickly but saw nothing. In that moment, Story decided she couldn't trust anyone right now, least of all herself.

"I can't get rid of him," she whispered, leaning back in toward Eachan. "He swore an oath to get me to Cildara. He can't kill me until he does."

"I don't like it!"

"I don't like it either, but that's the way it is."

Eachan considered her words then nodded once, curtly. "It will be as you say." She checked over her shoulder again. "But I don't trust him. Especially not with you."

Story reached out and gripped the elf's shoulder and Eachan returned the elvish friendship gesture. "Me neither." Story frowned. "Give me a few minutes out here to think, and then please ask Morrigann to come see me."

"Ailesit?" Eachan's eyes flooded with yellow in the moonlight.

"Don't worry, I'll be fine. We just need to set some new ground rules is all." Story smiled. "And if that doesn't work, I've always got my knife."

The corners of Eachan's mouth twitched up in the semblance of a smile, and she gave Story's shoulder one last squeeze before returning to the camp.

Story continued walking and wished for a lake or deep river to swim in so she could organize her scattered thoughts.

STORY COULD JUST MAKE OUT THE CAMPFIRE BURNING FURTHER DOWN the hill. Morrigann's frame as he sauntered over to her was unmistakable. She inhaled a deep breath, mentally rehearsing her speech again.

"Already want more, Story?" The faerie stepped around a massive tree and leaned against it, presumably to show himself off better. "Can't say I'm surprised—"

"Stop." Story held up a hand. "This," she pointed between them, "is never gonna happen. If nothing else, please get that through your little golden faerie head."

He cocked his head to the side. "I don't see why not. When we're not trying to kill each other, we get along famously." He shrugged. "Why fight it?"

Story's jaw dropped. "Look, I don't know how much clearer I can make this for you: *I. Don't. Want. You.*"

He pushed away from the tree and took a slow, languid step toward her. "Some part of you *must* want me, or else you wouldn't have kissed me."

"*You* kissed *me!*"

He stepped closer. "You kissed me back."

Story refused to back down. "I did not."

"Believe what you'd like." He shrugged again. "I didn't bespell you. Your responses to my advances? That was all you."

Clenching her jaw, she tightened her hands into fists, resisting the urge to smack him again. *He is always so frustrating!* "Yes, physically, a part of me *is* attracted to you, but who wouldn't be? You said so yourself: everyone, even Winter, craves Summer's warmth."

Morrigann pursed his lips, considering. He nodded. "You make a valid point."

Story released a breath she didn't know she was holding.

"But—"

Story cringed. *But what? There is no but!*

Taking one last step toward her, Morrigann reached for her face. She flinched away, and he let his hand fall harmlessly to his side. "We're just two lonely people, looking for some comfort in each other. There's nothing wrong with that."

Story barked a short laugh. "Nothing wrong with that?

There's *everything* wrong with that!" She shook her head. "I'm going to marry Eírnin. I love *him*. Not you. *Never* you."

It struck Story that he was the first person she'd told about her engagement. Not even Adair knew yet.

Morrigann's eyes widened briefly, and then his expression hardened as he laughed derisively. "So you think the elfling is your one true love? That everything will be perfect with him; that is, if you can save him?"

"I never said he was my one true love. I think it's a bit silly to think there's only one possible person out there for you." Story raised a hand forestalling Morrigan's next comment. "But I chose him, and he chose me, and we love each other, and that's that. I know it won't be perfect, shoot, it hasn't been so far, but that's normal. More importantly, we're happy." She leaned toward the faerie. "And I don't even understand why we're having this conversation. Unless, like a kid, you just want something you can't have."

"You really ask why?" Morrigann smiled down at her. "Oh, Story. Simple, simple, Story." His violet eyes sparkled, and he leaned in closer. "I like you."

She opened her mouth to protest, but he stopped her words with a finger over her lips. "I may want to kill you, for the good of all, but I *like* you. I always have. It wasn't all a ruse." He drew his finger lightly across her lips. "You're so full of life..."

He dropped his finger, and Story's lip flinched from his touch. "Well, I don't like you, much less want to be with you."

"Don't lie to yourself, Story; we'd be good together." Morrigann leaned back and crossed his arms. "We're more alike than you're willing to admit."

"We're nothing alike!"

He raised an eyebrow and tapped the scar on his cheek, and Story felt her face flush. To cover it, she quickly added, "Besides, I've seen what happens to girls you like. You betray and kill them."

He recoiled as if she'd slapped him. It was a low blow, but she needed him to understand how serious she was. She opened her arms in supplication. "I just want to get to Cildara and get the antidote for Eírnin. I'm tired of fighting you and waiting for you to betray me in one way or another.

"I can't trust you, Morrigann. Even if there was no Eírnin in my life, for that reason alone, I could never be with you." She dropped her arms and gazed up at him, pleading. "Please, promise you won't try to kiss me, draw energy from me, or basically do anything other than take me to Cildara from here on out."

Morrigann's mouth twitched as he returned her gaze, his violet eyes unreadable.

"No." He spun on his heel and left her alone.

THE NEXT MORNING WAS ROUGH. STORY HADN'T RETURNED TO THE camp, choosing instead to sit sleepless in the forest. But at least it kept her away from *him*. She was just going to have to make certain she was never *ever* alone with Morrigann from now on, since it seemed he wasn't going to stop his advances.

Looks like me and Eachan are going to be best friends, she thought sourly. Though, truth be told, Eachan wasn't all that bad. When she wasn't telling Story how unsuited for Eírnin she was, or sneering at Dagen. *So basically only when she's bickering with Morrigann.*

Story had spent most of the night shivering against the cold under her cloak and considered the elf's words about the dwarves. As the dawn was pinking along the horizon, a sudden idea popped into her head—they could get to Cildara much faster if what Eachan said was true.

Stretching her knotted muscles, she walked back to the camp. Dagen lay where she'd last seen it, still snoring on its pile of rocks. Morrigann leaned against a tree, eyes closed, though she was certain he wasn't sleeping. Eachan sat on the log Story had vacated the night before, elbows on her knees, chin in her hands, staring listlessly at the smoldering fire. Judging by the bags under the elf's eyes, Story wasn't the only one who hadn't slept.

"Master Dwarf." Story toed Dagen. The dwarf grunted, spat, and rolled over, scratching its backside in the process. "Master Dwarf, I need to talk to you." She prodded it again.

"Try throwing water on it," Eachan suggested. Story raised an eyebrow, but picked up a water skein and splashed a few drops on its face. The dwarf shot to its feet, wide awake and sputtering.

"Ach!" Dagen wiped the water out of its eyes. "What! Why, Miss, why? What did I do to you? Why are you trying to drown me, Miss?" The dwarf shook its head free of the water and spat on the ground.

"Trying to drown you? It was just a bit of water, and I was only trying to wake you up." Story looked to Eachan for help, but the elf had covered her face with her hands, trying to hide an amused smile.

"Dwarves are deathly afraid of water," Eachan said with a smirk. "They can't swim. Sink like stones, they do."

Story's expression was incredulous. "So you had me

wake it up by torturing it with fear? What the heck is wrong with you, Eachan?"

The elf waved a hand dismissively. "It's just a stupid dwarf. Plenty more where it came from."

Story threw a restraining arm across Dagen's chest. The dwarf was sputtering and literally hopping mad.

"I may be stupid, hunter, but I'm smart enough to know when I'm being called stupid!"

Eachan snorted. "You're making my point for me, Master Dwarf."

Story stepped in front of it, turning her back to the elf, and gripped its biceps. "Ignore her. I don't think you're stupid. Young yes, stupid no. And I'm sorry for scaring you. I didn't know you were afraid of water." Dagen visibly calmed down. "I'm scared of things too."

The dwarf looked up at her, curious.

"Like bugs," she answered with a smile. "Creepy crawlies and the like. I know you don't have them in Ailionora; faeries do their job instead. It's big part of why I love this place."

Dagen smiled in return. "I forgive you, Miss. What did you need?"

"Well," she bit her lip, considering her words. "I know you're close to the sidhe."

The dwarf nodded its head.

"I was wondering if you could show me a short cut to Cildara. I need to get there as fast as possible." She held her breath and noticed Morrigann's eyelids popped open, though he didn't move from his spot against the tree.

Dagen considered her words, absentmindedly scratching its bum. "I don't know the way, Miss."

Story felt her heart sink.

"But the Speaker will. Yes, Miss, the Speaker will!" Dagen beamed and wrapped its meaty hand around her thin wrist. "Come, Miss, come!"

The dwarf dragged her out of the camp, nearly yanking her arm out of its socket, and up the slope of the mountain. Story called back to the other two, "You heard the dwarf! Let's go!"

CHAPTER EIGHTEEN

MANY SHADES OF BLACK

HALF AN HOUR LATER, THEY STOOD OUTSIDE THE SQUARE entrance of a mine. Wooden beams framed the opening, and a set of wooden tracks abruptly ended at the entrance. Dagen walked inside and donned a ridged leather helmet it pulled from a cart on the tracks. It reminded Story of an old pith helmet, and she watched as the dwarf rubbed a fingernail across a wick on the front end. It flamed to life, and Story blinked in surprise. There didn't seem to be any fuel feeding the flame, yet it burned steadily.

"How are you—"

Suddenly Dagen's eyes widened, and Eachan whipped around, nocking an arrow. Then Story heard it—the crashing of the underbrush, the sound of something pursuing them.

Not another mountain troll!

"Into the cave!" Dagen yelled, hefting a massive wood-handled metal pickaxe.

Story didn't hesitate, but Morrigann and Eachan lingered at the cave entrance, both staring at the treeline.

Story gave a frustrated breath. "Come on, you two. We don't have time—"

"Shh!" Eachan hissed. "Listen. It's not big enough to be a troll."

They waited a few more seconds, the tension rising with each puff of their breaths in the chilly morning air.

Bursting through the trees flew a black blur covered in mud and leaves from the forest. Scratches peppered the selkie's body from his wild flight through the underbrush. Story dashed out to meet him and threw her arms up around his neck.

"Whoa there, Ped, calm down. I'm here, we didn't leave you."

The selkie buried its nose in her hair and huffed several loud, deep breaths, misting her neck and hair with moisture.

"It's okay; it's all okay." The selkie's legs and chest quivered, and Story couldn't tell if it was from fear or from the obvious haste he had traveled through the water and up the mountain. *Probably both,* she thought, stroking his neck. *Poor guy isn't used to being this far away from water, or traveling alone.* "You look scared to death and exhausted. Don't worry, we're going save Eírnin."

She would have been worried about Adair if they hadn't known she was already safely back in Vevila. There was no way Eisrus would have sent the signal otherwise. *He would have hung onto it until the very last possible second.*

The selkie's breathing slowly returned to normal, and he nudged Story toward the forest, away from the cave.

"Oh no, not you too." She patted him on his flanks. "It's

bad enough that Eachan and Morrigann are afraid to enter the cave."

"I am not!" The two accused cried out in unison and then glared at each other.

Story crossed her arms. "Why did you both hesitate when we thought it was a mountain troll coming for us? Did you really want to face one again?"

Eachan kept her gaze fixed on the ground and dragged a line through the dirt with the toe of her boot. Morrigann wouldn't meet Story's eyes, and casting his eyes about until he saw Dagen's massive pick, he brightened. "I'm not going anywhere near that much iron!"

Dagen's bushy eyebrows shot up in surprise. "Why, good Sir, this is not iron. No, not strong enough for dwarf mining, Sir. It's an alloy of many strong metals, but not iron, no, not iron." The dwarf shot a nasty look at Eachan. "Ach! Iron is too deep and rare. Only the elf mages can call it from the earth, good Sir."

"No, trust me on this, Story can too." Morrigann tossed her a nod and a quick wink, both of which she ignored.

"Ach!" Dagen's mouth split into a grin. "Why, Miss, is this true? Can you call iron, Miss?"

"Errr, only the once—"

"Because that would be wonderful, Miss! The elves haven't called iron for us in a thousand years. Break our treaty, they did, Miss."

"Are you truly going to bring this up? Now?" Eachan's eyes flared red. "We *couldn't* call iron because of that *faerie* you seem to like so much!" She jabbed a finger at Morrigann, who pursed his lips in a pout.

"You're as bad as Story; always holding a grudge."

Dagen tromped forward and stuck its chest out. "Ach! You broke the treaty, hunter, he did not. And you did not apologize to me either! Not very nice, hunter."

"That was a thousand years ago! It wasn't me who broke the treaty, and it wasn't you who got insulted!" Eachan shook her head in disgust. "Idiot."

The dwarf stomped its foot. "No! It was me, hunter. You owe me an apology! You owe us all an apology, hunter."

Eachan turned her back, ignoring the dwarf. Meanwhile, Dagen had started hopping up and down again in anger, so Story intervened.

"Master Dwarf, I'm afraid I don't understand." She bit her lip, confused. "You say you're only a year old, but that this treaty was broken with you personally a thousand years ago. How is that possible?"

"I was there." Dagen shrugged as if that explained it completely.

Story looked to Eachan for an explanation, but she just shook her head and mouthed "idiot." Story squeezed her eyes shut and sighed. Giving up, she looked at Morrigann.

He cocked an eyebrow. "Oh, so now you want something from me?"

She glared at him; he returned it, then he smiled. "Fine." He leaned against the mouth of the cave. "Dagen was there, sort of." He raised a hand, forestalling Story's next question. "When a dwarf dies, it's returned to the earth, and all its memories are stored in the loam there. When a new dwarf is born of the earth, it comes with all the memories and life experiences of its forbearer. So, in a sense, Dagen was there. At least, the dwarf remembers being there."

Turning back around, Eachan's jaw dropped. "What? Impossible!"

Story grinned. "So I guess you do owe Dagen an apology." She nodded her head toward the cave. "Come on, you'll have plenty of time to come up with a good one while we find this Speaker of Dagen's."

The dwarf stuck its tongue out at Eachan while turning around to wiggle its bum in an odd little victory dance before heading down into the mine. Story followed without hesitation, Ped close on her heels, though he was obviously uncomfortable inside the tunnel. She looked back over her shoulder and saw that Morrigann and Eachan still hadn't moved from the sunlight outside. They appeared to be having a quiet yet vehement argument. Story let out a frustrated breath. They really didn't have time for this.

"Come on, you two! You both have to follow me whether you like it or not." And with that she resumed following Dagen and the strange head light.

"Why were you on the surface, if you don't mind me asking, Master Dwarf?" Story called from behind Dagen. She was careful to keep her eyes on the ground, lest she trip over a road tie, as she'd already done several times over the past few hours. Ped kept pace doggedly at her side, and Morrigann and Eachan brought up the rear, silent except for an occasional sniping comment.

"Ach!" Dagen spat onto the walls. "Miss, I was supposed to pick up beer from a Pine Knolls gnome brygerri. I ran into a mountain troll instead."

"What about the gnome?"

"He ran into the mountain troll first, Miss."

Story blinked. "Okay, but why were you picking up beer? I thought you hated water?"

The dwarf sputtered and whirled around, outraged. "Beer is *not* water, Miss! No, Miss, no!"

Story put her arms up. "Whoa, calm down, Master Dwarf. No offense meant. I didn't know."

It stopped hopping, apparently mollified and turned back around to resume their trek into the mines. It took yet another random turn, and Story was beginning to understand why the dwarves didn't bother to have a door or a guard at the opening of their mine. She was already hopelessly lost.

Abruptly Dagen stopped, dug into the wall with the pick-axe, and pulled out a shower of stones. It picked up a handful of small pebbles and left them on the ground a few feet forward and aft of where they were standing.

"Must leave some food out for the knockers too, Miss, or else they'll get angry."

"The knockers?"

"Our mine fey, Miss. They help us find the metals. But, Miss, they don't like whistling or swearing, so don't do it. No, Miss, no." The dwarf sat on the ground and chomped down on its own pile of rocks.

"Okay… I hadn't exactly planned on doing either. What happens if I do?"

"You get a rock shower, Miss. And not the tasty kind." It crunched down on a rock. "Miss, you wouldn't want to eat those rocks."

Eachan and Morrigann came up behind her. Story crossed

her arms, shaking her head at the dwarf. "That's a delicious looking pile of rocks. Must be limestone."

Eachan looked sidelong at her. "Aye, smells delightful. Must be a real vintage year."

"Eachan, did you just make a joke?" Story blinked at the elf, whose eyes lit up momentarily with orange sparks of amusement before fading back to silver.

"*If* you ladies are finished, we've got a little problem." Morrigann prodded the snoring dwarf with one bare toe. "Looks like young Master Dagen has turned in early for the night."

Story groaned. "What? It's too early! We've only been walking a few hours. Half a day at the most." They would *never* get to Cildara in time at this rate.

Eachan made a face. "It sleeps more than you do, Ailesit. That's quite a feat."

Story ignored the comment, pulled out some dried fish for Ped from one of his saddle bags, and hoped they'd come across an underground lake or river soon on their journey. She hadn't expected the selkie back so soon, if at all, and wasn't provisioned to feed him. Ped swallowed his fish in two bites and turning three circles in place, lay down, and soon added his own rumbles to Dagen's snores.

"Traitor," Story mumbled, as she slid down the mine wall to sit on the ground next to Ped. Though the truth was the selkie probably hadn't slept for at least a week, given how quickly he'd made it to Vevila and back. She really couldn't begrudge him his sleep.

Morrigann made as if to sit next to her, but Ped opened one eye and let out a low growl. He immediately resumed his snoring once Morrigann backed away, hands up. Story scratched Ped behind his ears and curled up next to the selkie, tucking her cloak around her. At least she wouldn't have to worry about waking up to Morrigann cuddling her with Ped back.

Selkies really are the fastest things under the sea, she thought with a smile.

A yawn split her smile, and feeling a wave of exhaustion, she wondered if they had walked farther than she'd thought. With no sun in the sky, it was hard to tell, and she hadn't brought a watch with her into this world. She pillowed her head on her arm and wished for her own bed. She decided she hated camping. Her "adventures" in Ailionora had pretty much ruined it for her.

Story yawned again, her breath slowing to match Ped's, and before she knew it, she dropped off to sleep.

Adair sprinted across the paths of Eánna's garden, splashing through the crisscrossing streams with Ped hot on her heels. Story leaned back against Eirnin and felt him encircle her with his arms as he rested his chin atop her head. Next to them, on another blanket spread out on the grass, Eilath played a gentle but merry tune on his faolán, a guitar-like instrument with eight strings. Eánna stacked a plate full of fruits and cheeses, as well as a few poultry cold cuts alongside several rolls.

Story smiled—there was finally someone who ate more than she did. Of course, the queen was eating for two now, but still... Story sighed contentedly, and Eirnin kissed the crown of her head. He was between trips at the moment and had actually been home for over a week. She didn't know when the next trip would come, but if she tried real hard, she could forget that he would have to leave again. She could pretend that time wasn't moving forward, that summer wouldn't have to give way to autumn. That a war wasn't coming.

She watched as Eánna fed Eilath a cheese topped cracker and tucked his long, white hair behind his pointed ear so she could kiss his cheek. The love that emanated from the couple was palpable.

Snuggling in closer to Eirnin, Story returned her gaze to Adair, who was still cavorting with Ped, teasing him with a large cut of fish.

"What are you thinking, dear heart?" Eirnin murmured into her ear.

Story smiled slightly. "That this is perfect, elf-boy. If my mom was here, I'd have my whole family together." She didn't need to clarify that she meant her living family; Eirnin knew how much she missed her father and the twins.

Eirnin chuckled. "I'm not so sure how that would go over. My cousin has never been the biggest fan of Almera."

Story twisted in his lap to look up at him. "Why is that? Mom always changes the subject whenever I bring it up." She gave the queen a glance to make sure she was otherwise occupied. "And Eánna, well, I don't dare mention it."

Eirnin leaned down, until they were almost nose-to-nose, dropping his voice to the barest of whispers.

"After Eilath left the city of Ailes, he was in a bad way. He kept waiting for Eánna to ask him to come back, and she kept waiting for him to come back on his own. Both wanted the other to make the first move, and both were too prideful to make the first move themselves, certain the other was in the wrong."

"But that's just stupid! They wasted a hundred years they could have had togeth—"

Eirnin kissed her quiet. "Shhh, do you want to know what happened or not?"

"I want to know what happened," she whispered.

After a furtive glance at the queen, Eirnin continued, *"During this time Eilath and Almera met and became very close friends. They bonded over music, naturally."*

Story nodded her head. It made sense. Though, how friendship led to Adair's conception was another question she wanted answered. But first, she wanted to know why Eánna didn't like her mother — and she was certain it was more than just because she'd had a kid with Eilath.

Eirnin continued, tickling her ear with his whispers. *"As I said before, Eilath was not handling his separation from my cousin too well. Almera, who cared for him, did something a little rash."*

"What?"

"She wrote Eánna a letter."

"So?"

Eirnin's eyes sparkled with orange merriment. *"To put it simply, no one, much less a queen, likes to be told where she has erred in her life choices, nor that she is a self-righteous, prideful fool. Especially not if the letter sender is a 'flippant, nosy, empty-headed dryad'."*

"No!"

Eirnin nodded, and Story covered her mouth to stifle a giggle.

"Wow, remind me never to piss off Eánna. She can sure hold a grudge."

At that moment, Adair careened into the two of them, effectively ending their conversation. She was completely soaked and wasted no time in drenching them by wringing out her braids over them. Story laughed and rolled out of Eirnin's lap to avoid the fall of water, while Eirnin scooped Adair into his arms and ran over to the garden's fishpond. Adair shrieked in mock anger as he tossed her in, *then she shot out her hand, grabbed him by his calf, and yanked him in after her.*

He surfaced, laughing and wiping water from his eyes, and proceeded to dunk Adair. As Story watched them play, a smile on her face, she noticed Eáchan and Eisrus standing in a raised archway at the garden's entrance. Both elves watched longingly as Eirnin and Adair played. Story's heart sank. She knew what Eáchan's appearance meant. Behind her, Eilath and the queen stopped talking as well. They must have just noticed the newcomers, too.

Eirnin surfaced once again, waving at Story as he treaded water. She waved back, half-heartedly. Sensing something was wrong, he looked around the garden. The smile melted from his face as he spotted his clan leader and her apprentice.

It was time to leave again.

He climbed out of the pond and nodded toward Eáchan, letting her know he would join them soon. The Hunter turned to leave but Eisrus lingered behind, still staring at the pond. When Adair finally surfaced, she sent a delicate fountain of water out of her mouth and then looked around in confusion for Eirnin. Her eyes lit upon Eisrus's under the archway, and he raised a hand, giving her a quick wave before he turned to follow his master.

Shoulders sagging in resignation, Eirnin walked back to Story, and she rose to her feet, waving a quick goodbye to Eánna and Eilath, who nodded their heads in understanding.

Meeting Eirnin halfway, Story held out her hand, trying to stifle the loss she was already feeling. "Come on. I'll help you pack."

CHAPTER NINETEEN

APOLOGIZE

OW MUCH LONGER 'TIL WE REACH THE SPEAKER, MASTER Dwarf?" Story asked, trying to keep the irritation from her voice. She'd been hearing the movement of many bodies up ahead for hours, growing louder all the time, yet she still saw nothing but the dwarf in front of her.

Dagen gave her the same answer as the last few times she'd asked. "Not far Miss, no the Speaker's not far. Patience, Miss. Soon we'll be there."

Story was beginning to wonder if she'd made a big mistake coming this way. *What if it takes longer to get to Cildara underground than going on the surface?* She resisted the urge to glance over her shoulder at Morrigann who brought up the rear, with Eachan firmly between the two of them.

The faerie hadn't said anything about her decision to travel through the caves—well, he hadn't said anything to her at all for the past two days, but then Eachan and Ped hadn't allowed him near Story. She wondered if he hadn't been stalling for time above, taking the long way. He didn't want to see his sister, true, but what if there was something more to his whole pursuit of her?

Was he just trying to seduce her to get her give up this quest so he could avoid facing Metirreonn, .or did he really want her and was just trying to kill off his competition? She shuddered at the thought. The whole situation made her head hurt, and she wished she could talk to her dad, or Eilath. Both of them made her feel safe and protected. And both gave her good advice, although she knew in this case they both would have counseled her to stay behind and finish her training with the dreamwalking mages.

But it would have been useless; there was no way she could have focused under the current circumstances, as past experience had proven.

"Ailesit, you seem distracted." Eínlin ran his blue lacquered fingernails through his beard as he scrutinized Story.

"I'm sorry. I just... I can't seem to concentrate."

They were seated across from each other, knees crossed, in the elf's pagoda-like home. A rare iron brazier burned sweet smelling incense between them. The incense was supposed to relax her and open her mind to a waking dream state. The skill still eluded her, though Eínlin and a few of the other mages had achieved it.

"In the coming war, communication over vast distances will be an asset and could tip the scales in our favor. This is important." He closed his eyes and took a deep breath. "Now, concentrate."

"But why are we going to war?"

Eínlin frowned, but didn't open his eyes. As always, he ignored her question. "Please, Ailesit, concentrate. Belly breathing will help. In through the nose, out through the mouth. Focus your energy inward..."

Story sighed at the memory. She still couldn't walk the

waking dream. *And I still don't know why we're going to war. If Winter needs a half-blood to release Chaos, and me and Adair are safe, and there are no other half-bloods, then why are we going to war? Once Uinsienn has passed there's no reason*—Story bumped into Dagen's back. "Sorry, Master Dwarf, I didn't realize you'd stopped."

"Ach, it's all right, Miss." The dwarf stepped aside and smiled. "We are here."

Story's breath caught in her throat as she looked past the dwarf to the massive cavern beyond. It was easily a mile to the other side, and honeycombed throughout the walls all around them were caves, trails, tunnels, and dozens of bridges spanning the gaping distance. On these pathways walked thousands of dwarves, all with burdens on their backs—and judging by the sparkle from the headlamps, most were carrying bags of gems.

As Story got a better look at some of the closer dwarves, a small gasp escaped her—they all looked just like Dagen! Not only dressed the same, which they were, but physically the same. Some had scars while others had longer beards, but it didn't change the fact that they all were carbon copies of each other.

"Are they clones?"

Morrigann stepped up next to her and quirked an eyebrow. "If by clone you mean earth children, then yes, I suppose. But that's an odd term. Why not just call them what they are: dwarves?"

"No, I meant clones as in… nevermind."

Eachan stood on Story's other side and took in the scene before them. "I thought I'd be happy to get out of the tight tunnels." She sighed loudly. "And look, there are thousands of little Dagens. Wonderful."

Dagen narrowed its eyes, not sure whether it had just been insulted or not. Story decided to change the subject before the dwarf could figure it out. "Master Dwarf, could we see the Speaker? Soon? Time is of the essence."

"Yes, Miss, right this way Miss." The dwarf turned to lead them down a switch-backed path toward a bridge, but not before shooting Eachan a scathing look.

They passed several dwarves along the way, and Dagen always gave way for the dwarves with longer beards, which was most of them. The rest followed suit, and Story tried to suppress a chill at seeing the same face over and over again. Just when she thought she knew this world and was used to all its differences and oddities, something like this happened.

After crossing an amazingly engineered bridge—she couldn't see how it was supported across the span—they zigzagged up the opposite side toward a massive carved archway that looked like a gaping mouth. As they neared, Story realized that the opening was actually a carved mouth with a long stone beard, eyes, and miner's helmet to go along with it. It was a face—Dagen's face.

"Ach! The face of the first Speaker, Miss. The face of all my ancestors. The face of all brown dwarves, Miss."

"Is that... is that where we're going, Master Dwarf?"

"Yes, Miss." Without another word Dagen walked into the gaping, stone mouth.

Story stared at it, suddenly afraid, though she didn't know why. She felt as if butterflies and acid were swirling around in her stomach.

"We can always go my way, dear heart," Morrigann whispered in her ear.

Startled, and feeling like she'd just been coated in slimy ooze, Story jumped away from him, squared her shoulders, and plunged through the opening after Dagen. A few steps into the short tunnel, she could hear the others following her. Just ahead, the tunnel widened into a large room, and Dagen beckoned her on. She followed the dwarf into the room and found spread out before her fifteen of the oldest looking beings she'd ever seen.

They were seated in a semi-circle facing the entry, all propped up on cushions that looked like they were made of dryad silks. All had ancient versions of Dagen's face with snowy white hair and beards that trailed all around them. Even their brown skin seemed dusted with grey. The three at the opposite end of the room appeared to be the oldest and most wizened, with the centermost dwarf looking like he was two breaths away from disintegrating into dust.

As Story took this all in, Morrigann and Eachan caught up and moved to stand on either side of her. Dagen walked to the center of the circle, sat on the floor and crossed its legs before pulling out a rock from his pocket to munch on.

"Dagen, where is Dain?" the centermost dwarf croaked in a gravelly, dust coated voice.

Dain? Story looked to Eachan and Morrigann; both shrugged.

"Ach!" Dagen spat on the ground and then stood up and placed a stone in front of the dwarf. "Eaten, Speaker."

"Ach!" The Speaker tried to spit, but all that came out was a puff of dust. "Did you eat the troll?"

"I did, Speaker. As much as I could manage, Speaker."

"Good. Then Dain is not entirely lost."

Story's eyebrows shot up to her forehead, but she held her tongue.

"Dain will live on in a new dwarf." The Speaker nodded its head and the other fourteen dwarves nodded along with it. "There is nothing more tragic than to lose a dwarf's memories and life experiences."

The Speaker shifted its head to the side, sending up a cloud of dust around it, and the two dwarves on either side of it mirrored his actions. The Speaker was looking right at Story. The remaining twelve simply turned their heads to look at Story and her companions. She felt like a bug under a microscope.

"Dagen."

"Yes, Speaker."

"Why did you bring an *elf* to Ditmar?"

Dagen frowned, spit again, and then buried its head in its hands, as if ashamed. "Ach! The hunter killed the troll, Speaker."

The Speaker's eyes widened, and it looked directly at Eachan. "Ach! Is this true… hunter?"

Eachan made a face, but nodded her head a fraction.

"You'll need to speak up, hunter. I am nine years old, hunter, and my eyes are not what they once were."

Story answered for her. "It's true, Speaker."

The Speaker's eyes fixed on her. "Ach! Who are you?"

"Miss is the Ailesit, Speaker. Miss can call iron." Dagen was munching on rocks again, his embarrassment at being rescued by an elf apparently forgotten.

All of the dwarves' eyes widened at that. "Can Miss really call iron?"

"Just the once. But that's not why I'm here—"

"Introductions first, Miss. I am Diedrick, the Speaker." It looked to its right, at a dwarf with a missing eye, and it, and each dwarf after it, rattled off its name in turn, in the same gravelly voice:

"Dierk."

"Denby."

"Dellinger."

"Darda."

"Daven."

"Danvy."

"Dyre."

"Doran."

"Derek."

"Dawid."

"Daglin."

"Ditlev."

"Digrick."

"Dagfinn."

Story's eyes widened. *I hope there isn't a quiz on this later...*

The dwarves stared at them expectantly. Morrigann prompted her with a sharp jab to the ribs, and she shot him a dirty look. "Uh, right, like I said, I'm Story, this is Eachan, a hunter, and—"

"I'm Morrigann, the Spring Prince." He stepped forward with a sweeping bow, bestowing a radiant smile on the circle. The dwarves gave an audible "oooh" in unison.

"Sir, we would greet you properly, Sir, but we can't stand anymore. Our old bones…" The Speaker gestured at all of them helplessly, and their craggy faces all showed identical expressions of embarrassment.

"Nonsense, Master Dwarves. I'm honored to meet all of you. I know many of you only have a few days left, perhaps less, before you return to the earth. I look forward to meeting you again, when your bones are young once more."

As one, the dwarves brightened. "Sir is wise, yes, Sir is." The Speaker fixed its gaze back on Story. "How can we help, Miss?"

Story took a deep breath. *It's now or never.* "I need to get to Cildara, as fast as possible. Can you help me?"

"Ach! Yes, Miss, we *can* help you."

Story's heart soared.

"The question, Miss, is should we?"

Her heart sank. "Please, you don't understand—"

The Speaker held up a hand, a gesture that definitely cost it what little motion it had left. "No, Miss. *You* don't understand. You come to us with an *elf*, an oath breaker. I am still waiting for my apology." The Speaker fixed Eachan with a steady gaze.

The elf crossed her arms, turned up her nose, and refused to meet anyone's gaze.

"You want an… apology?" Story raised an incredulous eyebrow, wondering if it could really be that easy. She glanced at the Speaker, and it nodded. "Then you'll help me?" The Speaker nodded again, sending up another cloud of dust.

"Eachan."

"Yes, Ailesit?" The elf's voice was pitched high, as if she knew what was coming.

"Please apologize to the Speaker."

"Ailesit, this is ridiculous, you can't honestly—"

"For Eírnin." Story met the elf's eyes and saw the conflicting emotions there. "Please. It's the only way."

Eachan heaved a large sigh, and her shoulders fell. "Fine." She met the Speaker's cloudy gaze. "I'm sorry."

"Ach! Who were you speaking to, hunter?" The Speaker asked.

Eachan frowned, then blanked her face. "Speaker, I am sorry."

"For what?"

"Oh, honestly—"

Story stomped on Eachan's foot.

"Speaker, I am sorry for breaking my oath to provide you with iron for forging, a thousand years ago, after *that* faerie," she pointed at Morrigann, "cursed my entire race to become mortal and die out." She crossed her arms and glared at Story as if to say "there, happy now?"

Story would be, if it worked.

"Apology accepted, hunter."

Story let out a sigh of relief. "So you'll help us?"

The Speaker gave a grating, dust-filled laugh. "Ach! No, Miss, no. Not yet. The hunter must apologize to all she broke oath with."

"All she broke oath with?"

Morrigann snickered. "I'd get comfortable, Story. This will take a few days."

Story looked at the Speaker. "But, then you'll help us?"

"Yes, Miss."

"And you can get us to Cildara quickly?"

"Miss, I know of a way that will get you there in three days, Miss."

"But Eachan must apologize to all the dwarves first?"

"Ach! Yes Miss, by name, Miss."

Story glanced at Eachan, who appeared horrified at the prospect.

The elf held up a hand to forestall Story's next words. "Aye, I know, Ailesit. It is the only way." She faced the Speaker. "I'll need a place where I can do this, and can all the dwarves come to me to make this go faster, Master Dwarf? Time really is of the essence."

"Hunter, you may stay here. Dagen will pass the call. Yes, hunter, the dwarves will come to you, hunter. Ach! We have waited a long time for this, yes we have."

At the Speaker's command, Dagen sprinted from the room, and Eachan stepped in front of the dwarf on the Speaker's right. "Dierk, I am sorry for breaking oath with you."

The dwarf nodded. "Apology accepted, hunter."

Eachan stepped in front of the next dwarf, and Story settled down against one of the walls, resigning herself to a long few days. Morrigann made as if to sit next to her, but Ped thrust his head out and growled. Raising both hands in surrender, the faerie turned instead toward the Speaker and settled down next to the ancient dwarf. He leaned forward and engaged the Speaker in an animated, yet quiet, conversation that Story couldn't hear.

Ped curled up around Story, nudging his head under her hand, and she scratched it absentmindedly. She missed Adair. She missed her mom. She missed Eírnin. Letting out a deep breath, she resolved to visit them in the dreamscape. *And since*

I can't enter a waking dream yet... she yawned and snuggled in close to Ped, pillowing her head on his shoulder and tucking her cloak tightly around herself.

It's just cold because we're so far underground... it's not winter. Yet.

CHAPTER TWENTY

RUNNING DOWN A DREAM

ALMERA SLEPT, CURLED UP IN HER CORAL BED, LAYERS OF SEA sponges beneath her as she snored fitfully. Her vibrant red hair lay in a braided mess around her, with bits of seashells, ribbons, and bells twined throughout. A mollusk silk sarong of blues and greens twisted around her legs, and her pearly white skin gleamed softly under the glowing orbs that Story knew dotted the room, though she couldn't see them—the room had only partially formed around her.

"Hi, Mom." Story sat on a stool that materialized near her mother's bed.

Almera flopped over in her bed muttering, "Where is she?"

Story felt instantly guilty and tried to take her mother's hand, but Almera twisted away from the touch. "Mom, I'm okay. I'm safe. I'll be back soon. I promise."

The dryad turned over again and then faded from the dream. Story sighed. *She must have woken up. Probably worried about me.* She swallowed thickly and tried to ignore the pit forming in her stomach. *I need to do this, to save Eírnin. She'll understand!*

Story stood and closed her eyes. When she opened them, the scene before her had shifted. Adair lay cocooned in her seashell bed, slumbering peacefully. Her breathing was slow and even, and Story smiled, relieved that at least one member of her family was not losing sleep over her.

Though she's probably still mad at me.

Story closed her eyes once more. *I wonder...*

As she opened them, her rooms at the elf queen's island coalesced around her.

But I wanted to see Eírnin. Why would I come here?

The large, high-backed wooden bench by her fireplace materialized, and there, sitting in the midst of the cushions, was Eírnin.

Eírnin!

He was awake!

Story's breath caught in her chest for a moment, then Eírnin looked up at her and smiled. The slight gaps in his teeth showed while his purple eyes crinkled around the corners. He held his arms open, and she flew into them.

"You're okay!" Story settled on his lap and peppered him with kisses, which he returned with equal fervor.

"I missed you," she said against his lips. He pulled her tighter against him, his hands sliding down her back, over her hips, and then back up again.

"Did the healers find an antidote?" She broke off to stare into his glittering purple eyes, which reflected just how she felt. She found it a bit odd to see his irises just one color, though—usually one or two others swirled around in there as she was privy to even his most hidden emotions.

Eírnin buried a hand in her braids and pulled her back into the kiss, deepening it, driving the question from Story's mind. His tongue teased her mouth open, and she melted against him, losing herself in the warmth and comfort of his presence and love.

Her dream visits with him had never been like this before—Eírnin had always been asleep since he couldn't dreamwalk. She smiled as she ran her fingers through his dark hair, pleased with the change. His lips left her mouth and traveled to her jawline and then down her neck to her collarbone as he tipped her slightly away from him.

"How are you here?" She knew she shouldn't question it, should just be happy that he *was* here, awake and alive, but she couldn't help herself. "Did Eínlin show you—"

Eírnin silenced her once again with a kiss, only this time she found herself mildly annoyed. He was deliberately avoiding her questions. She pulled away from him. "Why won't you talk to me?"

He leaned in to kiss her again, violet eyes glittering, but she held his face in her hands, preventing him. "Eírnin, stop. Please, talk to me."

Frowning, Eírnin let out an exasperated sigh—definitely not the reaction she was expecting. As she rested her hands on his cheeks, she began to feel a thin ridge form under her thumb. It was a scar. A burn scar.

Realization dawned as his hair faded from raven black to brilliant gold. His tattoos disappeared, and his face reformed before her. Only his glittering violet eyes remained the same.

Story shoved his chest and leapt off Morrigann's lap as fast as she could.

"You're unbelievable! How could you?"

He shrugged unapologetically. "How could you think I wouldn't try?"

"You said you wouldn't bespell me!" Her hands fisted at her sides, trembling with anger.

"Dear, simple Story, once again, I didn't," he chuckled, though it sounded forced. "I gave myself a glamour. You simply saw what you wanted to see. Which, sadly for me, in this case was your fiancé. I had hoped otherwise…"

"You're disgusting." She raised a hand toward him and focused, trying to cast him out of her dream. He just looked at her. She focused again and raised her other hand. He smiled.

"Having some trouble, dear heart?"

"Don't call me that!" She closed her eyes and willed him to be gone. After counting to ten, she slowly opened them. The bench was empty, and she let out a sigh of relief. For a moment she'd been worried she hadn't been able to cast Morrigann from her dream because some traitorous part of her mind wanted him there.

"You really should give me a chance." Morrigann's arms slipped around her from behind, and Story jerked away with a gasp. She dashed into her bathing room, closing and locking the door behind her. If she couldn't cast him out of her dream, she could at least put a wall between them.

"Are you worried about someone barging in on us?" Morrigann sat at the edge of her bubble-filled tub, feet dangling in the warm water. "It's your dream, Story. You control who comes and goes."

She leaned back against the door, ready to scream in frustration. "You just don't give up do you?"

"No." He canted his head to the side, regarding her with a sly smile. "Do you?"

"This isn't about me," she snapped.

"Sure it is."

"No, this is about *you*." Story jabbed a finger at him. "You only care about what you want, about what makes you happy, and who gives a damn what happens to anyone else along the way?"

Morrigann threw back his head and laughed.

"What's so funny?" Story crossed her arms over her chest.

He held up a hand and composed himself. Finally ready to speak, he stood up from the water and mirrored her pose. "Admit it, you're just like me."

Story snorted. "We've been over this—we're nothing alike. You're the bad guy."

"Really?" He prowled around the tub toward her. "In my mind, I'm the hero, and you're the villain." He stopped in front of her, eyes narrowed and a slight frown on his face.

"I *am* the good guy," Story said firmly.

"Why?"

His question brought her up short, and she stumbled over her words trying to find an appropriate answer. "Well, because... because my goals are honorable." She nodded. "Yes. Honorable. I want to save Eírnin. And before that, I saved the elves."

"And I want to save all the worlds from complete destruction." Morrigann leaned in closer, almost nose to nose with Story. "By that logic, I'm more of a good person than you."

"I don't kill people willy nilly to achieve my goals." Story jabbed a finger in his chest again.

He swatted it away. "Neither do I."

"But you *do* kill people."

"So did your father." He punctuated his words with a jab of his own. "So does Eánna; perhaps not personally, but through tools. Tools like Eírnin." His crossed his arms. "For the greater good. Or at least, what she sees as the greater good."

Story had no response to that. So she fought back the only way she could think of—she changed the subject.

"You don't make any sense! One minute you want to kill me, and the next you want to be with me? Romantically? I mean, you've already told me you're going to kill me once we get to Cildara." She gave a humorless laugh and began pacing. "That doesn't make me think this nightmare of a relationship has any real hope for longevity. Assuming I was even interested. Which I'm *not*."

If the Spring Prince was surprised by her change of attack he didn't show it. Cocking his head to the side, he regarded her carefully for a moment before finally responding. "There is an alternative to killing you."

Story whirled to face him. "If that's the case why are you just *now* bringing this up?"

Ignoring her, Morrigann resumed pacing where she'd left off. "If you were mine—my consort, that is—my father couldn't take you from me. You would be safe. You would be untouchable."

"Whoa, time-out." Story held her hands up in a "T" in front of her, blocking his path. "Not that I'm actually considering this, but you've already mentioned that your sister has a habit of offing your girlfriends. Which makes me wonder how you could possibly keep me safe from your father, if you couldn't even keep the supposed love of your long and sorry life safe from Metirreonn?"

Ignoring her barbs, he just smiled. "That's the brilliance of my plan. If *you* were Autumn—"

"Oh, *hell* no!" She shook her head to punctuate her words, laughing sourly. "Now I totally see what you're really after. You just don't like your sister, so you want me to off her since I'm pretty sure you can't do it yourself, or else you'd have done it a long time—"

"No, wait, hear me out." Morrigann gripped her shoulders, an unusually serious expression on his face. "We go to Cildara. You destroy my sister, making you Autumn, thereby enabling you to save the elfling for certain. It all works out for everyone." He looked ridiculously pleased with himself.

Story raised an incredulous eyebrow. "And in payment I'd just have to stay with you, be a sidhe. Forever?"

"Be my consort, yes."

"Even though I'm in love with Eírnin, and I'm going to bond with him?" She pursed her lips, fairly certain she knew what his answer would be.

He released her arms and stepped back. "Unfortunately, you would not be able to bond with him any longer. Bad luck, that." Morrigann gave her an apologetic smile. At her deepening frown, he cupped his chin in one hand as he ran his thumb along his burn scar, looking pensive. "But, I am not a jealous person." He gazed at her intently. "You could still be with the elfling. I would be willing to share you."

"Absolutely NOT!" The very idea of it made Story ill. "I'm not a time share condo—he gets me two weeks a year, during off-peak seasons and holidays, and you get me the rest of the time."

"Be reasonable, Story!" Morrigann threw his hands up in the air, frustrated. "I am trying to help you! I'm offering you a way to save the elfling—a guaranteed way—*and* stay alive yourself." He frowned. "I thought you'd be a bit more grateful."

"*Grateful?*" Story let out a snort. "For what? You're trying to manipulate the situation into getting what you want. Which, at the moment, is me." Story didn't shift her stance. "Though, I'm sure you'll eventually get tired of me once the chase is over. What happens then?"

Morrigann didn't say anything in return, and they stared at each other, each unwilling to bend as the minutes passed.

Finally, Story uncrossed her arms and closed the distance between them, placing a hand on his arm. She softened her expression as she met his gaze. "If you really cared about me, you'd stop threatening to kill me or make me do whatever it is you want me to do, and just trust that I'm going to do everything in my power to stay out of your father's hands."

His violet eyes were unfathomable. "After you save the elfling, of course."

Story smiled, though she felt a bit sad, without quite knowing why. "Yes, of course. I love him."

He didn't return her smile, and he didn't agree. But, Story noticed, this time he didn't say no.

She woke up the next morning feeling more worn out than she had before she'd gone to sleep. Ped was gone, and after a quick sweep of the room, she could see Morrigann was too. She felt both relief and a twinge of loss at that.

Stupid sun faeries, always making you want them around!

Eachan was on the opposite side of the cavern apologizing as quickly as possible to the line of dwarves that trailed out the door, while the fifteen dwarf elders watched silently. The oldest looking one was gone, and the dwarf that had been on its right, the one with the missing eye, was now seated in the center position.

"Miss is awake!"

Story looked over her shoulder to see Dagen sitting behind her, fingering her knife.

"Ach! Diedrick dusted while you slept, Miss. Dierk is Speaker now, Miss. Dagbart is the newest elder." The dwarf pointed her knife at the "new" old dwarf seated on a pillow near the entrance.

"I thought they couldn't move?" She eyed Dagen's hand. "And why do you have my knife?" She looked up at the dwarf's face and realized with a start that it had a large puckered scar across its nose. "You're not Dagen are you?"

"No, Miss, no. I'm Doffen, Miss." The dwarf continued to finger her knife, and she noticed it had tiny pebbles in its hand that it was rubbing over the blade. "Though me and Dagen share a birthday, Miss." Doffen crossed its eyes and looked down at the scar on its nose. "The bogey, a water fey, did this, ach!" Then it resumed rubbing the stones over the blade. "Miss, we move the Elders when they can't move themselves anymore, Miss. As for your knife, Miss, well, it's a good knife. But it's iron. It will dull easily, Miss."

"Yeah, but it sharpens easily too." Story knew she sounded overly defensive, but this was her father's knife they were talking about. *And what is it doing with my knife anyways?* She held out her hand expectantly, and Doffen, after swirling the tiny stones over the surface a few more times, mumbled a few unintelligible words and handed it back. The blade glowed faintly before fading back to its matte grey finish, as if nothing had happened.

"Lovely. Now that monstrosity will never dull." Morrigann, who'd just returned, leaned against the smooth wall of the cavern near Story—but not near enough for the iron to bother him. "Mind sheathing it? It's making it awfully warm in here for me." The faerie fanned himself dramatically with his hand.

Story opened her mouth to answer but realized she had nothing to say. Worse, she was relieved he was back. She hardly knew what to say to him after last night's dream. Had they come to an accord?

Not likely. Still can't trust him.

And yet, there was no need to be rude to him, or to torture him if the knife truly was making him uncomfortable. She sheathed the blade in a smooth, practiced motion and stood up. She felt the need to stay near Morrigann, which meant she had to get as far away from him as possible. He'd already sunk roots far too deep into her for her liking.

Brushing past Morrigann without a word, she walked down the tunnel past the lined up dwarves until she reached the mouth of the archway. Peering down the full switchbacks, she could see that the line of dwarves to see Eachan appeared endless. Her heart sank, and she slumped against the archway, fighting back tears.

I'll never get back to Eírnin in time.

Morrigann's warm hand alighted gently on her shoulder. She flinched at his touch, but then instinctively leaned into it, feeling angry with herself for doing so. A sense of calm and peace wrapped in warmth washed over her.

"Eachan hasn't slept, and she's only pausing long enough to take a quick drink when she needs to wet her throat. If she continues at this rate, we should be able to leave tomorrow." He gave her shoulder one last squeeze and left Story alone, taking the warmth with him.

CHAPTER TWENTY-ONE

SHIP TO SHORE

S TORY'S DREAMS WERE UNTROUBLED THAT NIGHT, THOUGH SHE slept fitfully and woke up the next morning shivering. Ped eventually came back, soaking wet and smelling like fish, causing all the dwarves to give him a wide berth. Morrigann stayed away from her, preferring to confer with the elders, who clearly worshipped him. This, of course, left her feeling neglected and alone, which was silly since she *wanted* to be alone. Didn't she?

Dagen was still gone and Doffen stayed doggedly by her side, answering her endless questions about dwarves, their society, the way they worked, and their customs and courtesies. She tried to focus on the conversations they had, to take this opportunity to learn about another culture, but she found it nearly impossible.

The hours crawled by as the line of dwarves with progressively shorter beards filtered through, until finally, the dwarves who arrived were fresh faced and clean-shaven.

"Miss, those are the babies. Ach! Born yesterday they were, Miss."

Story's jaw dropped. "And they're already walking and talking?"

"Born with all our blood giver's memories, we are, Miss."

"Right." She shook her head. "I just didn't think it applied to motor skills and speech too." She regarded the dwarf beside her curiously. "If you're born already knowing everything, then what's the point of living?"

"Oh Miss, no one ever knows everything," the dwarf chuckled, deep and throaty. "Ach! There is always something to be learned. We have short lives and long memories, Miss. But Miss, memories is not the same as living." It pointed at the tunnel opening. "And look who comes! Ach!"

Just then, Dagen came through the tunnel, trailed by another baby dwarf. Story didn't think she'd ever get used to the idea of babies looking like fully-grown adults. Dagen waved excitedly at her and Doffen, pointing animatedly at the dwarf next to it. Doffen waved back, so Story waved too, figuring it was the polite thing to do.

Eachan apologized to each of the dwarves in line until she got to Dagen. She paused and sipped from a golden-jeweled goblet filled with gnome beer. She wrinkled her nose at the taste and faced Dagen.

"Master Dagen, I am sorry for breaking oath with you." She paused, letting her hoarse voice rest a moment and, to everyone's surprise, continued. "And I'm sorry for being condescending and rude to you on this journey. You are not my lesser, and I would do well to remember that." She snapped her mouth shut while everyone, Morrigann included, stared at her. It was clear the words had been difficult for her to say.

"Apology accepted, hunter. Ach!" Dagen spat on the ground. "It is good to see a hunter behaving the way they ought for once, hunter. Far too long since you became oath breakers, hunter." The dwarf grinned up at her before pushing the 'baby' next to it forward. "But, hunter, you have one last apology left. This is Dain. I was its blood-giver, hunter."

Eachan's eyebrows shot up. "Dain? But I thought Dain had been eaten, Master Dwarf."

"Oh, hunter, that Dain was eaten. This is a new Dain." The new Dain waved and smiled, and Eachan's eyes widened marginally.

"So... this is not the same Dain? You decided to create a new dwarf last night, and you named it Dain, after your sibling?"

"No, hunter. This *is* Dain. It will always be Dain. Just like I will always be Dagen. This is a new Dain. New life, old memories, hunter."

"Ach!" The new Dain spat. "I'm going to make new memories now, hunter."

Eachan composed her face, but Story could tell Eachan was just as confused as she was. Perhaps some things would never be fully understood.

"Well then, Master Dain, I am sorry for breaking oath with you too." The corner of the elf's mouth tugged up slightly. "And welcome back? Or is it just welcome to the world?"

"Ach! Both, hunter. Both."

They were assembled before the dwarf elders once again, only now Dellinger was in the centermost cushion, the newest Speaker, as Dierk and Denby had "dusted" during the previous day. Story had been asleep each time, and for that she was grateful—Doffen told her dusting involved disintegrating slowly and painfully. Yet none of the dwarves seemed to fear it.

Maybe because they know it's not the end for them?

As Story looked at the dwarf before her, she was amazed by how much Dellinger had visibly aged in the last few days. She supposed she shouldn't have been; after all, physically, they were very short lived. She cleared her throat, anxious to be traveling again.

"Speaker, Eachan has apologized to all the brown dwarfs. Will you show us your shortcut to Cildara now?"

"Ach! I will not, Miss."

Story felt her eyes widen in shock, and a wave of anger washed over her. *How dare they break their promise—*

"For I cannot walk, Miss. My bones are dusting as we speak. But Miss, Doffen will take you. Doffen does not fear the grinlings nor the bogey, Miss." The Speaker smiled, causing a crack to form near its mouth. "Doffen knows the way."

"Thank you, Speaker." Story bowed her head, feeling hope swell in her chest. *We just might make it in time!*

The Speaker nodded, sending up a cloud of dust and fixed its gaze on Eachan. "Hunter, I like you. You are proud, and pride is bad, hunter. But you swallow your pride, even when it hurts, like a bad gem. I have been talking to the Spring Prince." The Speaker angled its head toward Morrigann. "And I believe you, hunter. Ach! Winter is nearing, and we must unite. Dagen and Dain and Dirk and Dagvin will go to the shores near the City of Ailes, hunter, to meet your queen and plan, hunter. They will not cross nor go near the water. Ach! We are not all so brave as Doffen."

Story and Eachan exchanged a quick glance, the elf's eyes mirroring the surprise Story felt.

"Thank you, Speaker. I..." Eachan paused, at a loss for words. "I thank you. With the dwarves at our side, we may stand a chance."

"Yes, hunter, we may, hunter. Ach!" A puff of dust exploded from its mouth. "We will also speak to the red dwarves, though they are very silly. Who knows what they will do?" Then the Speaker coughed, and another dust cloud puffed out of its mouth.

Doffen grabbed Story by her wrist and yanked her unceremoniously down the tunnel. "Come, Miss. Dellinger is dusting, and we should go to Cildara now."

Story barely had time to glance behind her to see the Speaker coughing more and more as bits and pieces were crumbling off it. Dwarves were already swarming the room rearranging the remaining dwarf elders. She didn't know why, when she knew this wasn't the complete end for Dellinger, but a wave of sadness washed over her. A part of the dwarf was still dying and would be forever lost to only memory. She felt tears spill down her cheeks.

"Ach! Don't cry, Miss. Dellinger would not want to be remembered with water, Miss."

THE DARK WATER OF THE UNDERGROUND RIVER LAPPED AGAINST the large raft. Lanterns hung from each of the four corners illuminating their way in the darkness. Doffen sat square in the middle of the wooden raft, easily ten feet away from the water on each edge. While the dwarf claimed not to be afraid of anything, Story wondered if that was just a past Doffen's memory, and that this Doffen did indeed fear water, like the rest of its kin.

Ped had jumped in and immediately shifted into his seal form, swimming briskly alongside them in the swift current. Every now and then, he dove for fish or something only he could see. Morrigann lounged at the front of the raft, legs dangling in the water, back to the rest of them, occasionally turning his head to make a comment to Doffen. But he never met Story's gaze. He'd been ignoring her since he'd used his warmth to calm her, and she tried not to dwell on the empty feeling she had.

"Eachan?"

"Yes, Ailesit?" The elf stood stiffly next to her, facing the opposite direction, keeping a self-imposed watch. Though Story thought it had more to do with not looking at Morrigann.

Story craned her head up from her cross-legged position on the smooth wooden planks. "I'm just curious... it hasn't been spring for the past thousand years has it?"

"No." Eachan glanced down at her, puzzled at the sudden question. The lamplight flickered against the elf's round face, making her Ailach appear to dance. Story felt a pang of loss, thinking of Eírnin and how in the low light the two elves looked so very similar.

Eachan resumed her watch. "I don't think our world would have survived without all four seasons in play. Or, at least, without a cold spell to kill everything so that it could be reborn again with the coming summer. Need to get rid of the old to make room for the new. I imagine it works the same way in your world too."

"Then how, with three of them locked away until I released them...?" She left the remainder of her question unasked, waiting for the elf to answer.

Eachan appeared uncomfortable, shooting a furtive glance at Morrigann. "I don't pretend to understand the ways of the Sidhe."

Story nodded her head in agreement. She still couldn't figure the Sidhe out.

"Why do you ask, Ailesit?"

"No reason. Just curious."

Eachan gave her a sidelong glance but didn't say anything. They sat in silence, the water rushing around them and Ped's occasional splash or bark when he surfaced filling the air.

I ought to go for a swim myself.

Story dangled her bare feet in the chilly river and sighed at the feel of it swirling around her ankles. She peeked up at Eachan out of the corner of her eye and found herself wishing that they had met under different circumstances—she thought that maybe they could have been friends.

Maybe.

"So, how long has Eisrus been your apprentice?"

Eachan glanced back down at her, seemingly shocked that Story was asking her a somewhat personal question. But then she surprised Story and sat down gracefully next to her, crossing her legs beneath her.

"A little over five years. He's still very young though, only twenty-three. He has many years left to train and learn."

A hint of a smile flitted across the elf's face. "Still, he is the fastest learner and by far the most talented archer I've ever trained. He will one day be the finest hunter among us."

"Oh, so you've had other apprentices then." Story could see the pride Eachan held for Eisrus; she clearly had great expectations for him.

"One." Eachan said the word slowly, suddenly closed off again, as if she didn't want to discuss it.

This only served to pique Story's curiosity. "Who?"

"Eírnin." Eachan glanced at Story and then quickly returned her gaze to the darkness behind them.

"Oh." *Nothing like pointing out the massive elephant in the room.* Story winced inwardly, then let out a quiet breath. *Well, I've stuck my foot in it, so I may as well go with it. What's the worst that could happen? We go back to not talking?*

"I didn't know. I thought that you two just..." Story looked at the elf expectantly.

"Courted?" When Story nodded her head, Eachan frowned. "No, that would have been inappropriate as he was my apprentice and I was his master. Though, by the end of the twenty years he trained under me, it was obvious how I felt, and he was not opposed, in fact, he seemed to rather like the idea. So I asked and received permission from both our parents to court when he returned from his Grand Tour."

"Grand Tour?" Story had no idea why she focused on that detail when there was so much other big news, such as *Eírnin and Eachan had gotten serious enough to court!* She tried to tamp down her jealousy, as it was unfair. She'd dated plenty of other guys before Eírnin. Plus, he'd obviously chosen to be with her, not Eachan.

"Aye, it's a traditional rite of passage for each hunter to

signify the ending of their apprenticeship." Eachan looked at her, orange and yellow flecks coloring her eyes. Apparently she'd been surprised by Story's tangent too. "It's just what it sounds like. They leave for a year on their own in the wilds, to hunt, and get the lay of the lands around us. To refine their skill. Coming back signifies they are good enough not to die. That they're finally ready to hunt alone."

"So, when he got back he decided he didn't want to date you?" Story clapped a hand over her mouth, shocked at the boldness of her question, and by the look on Eachan's face, so was the elf. "I'm sorry, that was rude and none of my business."

"No, it's all right, Ailesit," the elf chuckled, surprising Story yet again. "Aye, I suppose I'm just a bit taken aback is all." She gave Story a sidelong gaze. "I had thought Eírnin would have already told you all this."

"Um, no. All he ever told me was that you wanted to court him, but that he didn't want to court anyone."

"He clearly wants to court you."

Story decided she didn't like this conversation anymore. "I—"

"Ailesit, don't trouble yourself." Eachan held up a hand. "Please. Eírnin is grown. He can decide whom he wants to court and when." She let out a quiet sigh. "For what it's worth, he has seemed happy these last few months."

Story bit her lower lip, unsure of how to respond. She wasn't sorry Eírnin had chosen her over Eachan, but she was sorry for the pain Eachan was clearly going through because of it. She decided it would be best not to tell the elf about the engagement just yet. *No need to pour salt in the wound.*

"After his parents died, Eírnin withdrew from everyone. Even his cousin, the queen. He'd leave for long stretches of time, as if it was one long Grand Tour after another. He was becoming reckless and finally tried to take down the troll that killed his mother by himself." Eachan sighed again, closing her eyes. "He was still so young and not ready for the challenge. But he was so angry. So, so angry." She paused, remembering. "I followed him—just to make sure he'd be all right, mind you—and when it was clear that he would lose to the troll…"

"You stepped in and saved him." Story felt a bit awed. "He never told me that part of the story."

Eachan shrugged. "I don't think he likes to remember that part of his life. It was a dark time for him."

Story remembered her own dark time, after her father and the twins had died in a car accident. She definitely had an idea of what Eírnin had gone through. Something Eachan said earlier tickled her memory.

"Eírnin said Eánna wouldn't grant your request for courtship, but you said both sets of your parents had granted it?" Story raised a questioning eyebrow and hoped she wasn't pushing her luck.

The elf's mouth flattened into a thin line before she spoke again. "Aye, that. Well, after about fifteen years of waiting for him, I finally got a bit impatient. Since his parents were gone, and I was now the newest clan leader—so I couldn't very well ask myself—I asked the queen for permission to court him. I thought it would be purely a formality. You know, something to remind him that I was waiting for him. She said no." Eachan ran her long fingers through her short-cropped hair, her Irish lilt thick with emotion. "He had apparently made it quite clear to his cousin that he didn't want to be with anyone. And I believed him. It softened the blow some."

Story blinked and stared at her hands in her lap. "Then I showed up."

"Aye, ten years later." Eachan gave a humorless smile. "I guess the truth was he just didn't want to be with me."

"Eachan," Story rested a hand on her shoulder. "You can't—"

Just then, Ped shot out of the water and onto the raft, shifting to his dog form as soon as his flippers were clear, dousing both Story and Eachan with a wave of icy water from his arrival. Almost at the same time, Morrigann jerked his feet out of the river and twisted around, hand extended toward them.

"Story, look—"

But Story didn't hear the end of his sentence as she found herself suddenly surrounded by the darkness of the water. Worse yet, something had a hold of her leg and was drawing her deeper into the murky depths below.

CHAPTER TWENTY-TWO

TUG OF WAR

ALMOST AS SOON AS STORY WAS IN THE WATER, WHATEVER IT was that had grabbed her released her, and she kicked toward the surface as hard as she could. She had a moment of panic when she realized she wasn't sure which way was up and could just as easily be swimming down, and she counted herself lucky when she saw the flash of one of the raft's lanterns and swam in that direction.

Breaking the surface and gulping in a deep breath, Story swirled her arms and legs around her as she treaded water, searching for whatever had attacked her. Had she been fully human, the icy bite of the water would have made her feel dull and slow, but she counted herself lucky once again that her dryad blood kept her warm in the water.

"Story!" "Ailesit!" "Miss!" and a howl all called out to her at once. She swam to them as quickly as she could manage.

What the heck was that? And why did it let me go?

Then she remembered Eachan's words from several days

past. *"Dwarves are deathly afraid of water. They can't swim. Sink like stones they do."*

She wondered... What if whatever it was had just expected her to sink to the bottom and drown so it could eat her at its leisure?

Story swam harder, muscles protesting—it had been far too long since she'd last swum.

Her companions on the raft leaned over the edge, even Doffen, urging her to swim faster. The dwarf restrained Ped, and both Morrigann and Eachan extended their hands out to help her up.

Five feet away from the raft, something brushed her ankle, and she kicked, making contact with something solid, fleshy, and scaly.

Please don't be a sea serpent! But knowing this world filled with mythical creatures, it would be just her luck. Her bad luck.

"Faster, Ailesit! 'Tis the bogey!" Eachan leaned so far out that Morrigann had to anchor her to the raft with his own weight. Story was nearly to them and stretched out a hand toward the elf. Something slithered across her back just as her fingers brushed Eachan's, then Story was jerked back under the frigid water again.

As the dark water swirled around her, Story didn't panic; this was not like the fuath attack—one of the times Morrigann had tried to kill her—where she had to worry about passing out from lack of oxygen. She'd managed to suck in a deep breath before going under, and thanks to Eachan's timely piece of information, Story knew she was dealing with some sort of water fey.

Fumbling, she pulled her knife from its scabbard and

felt around whatever was holding her. The creature felt like a thick, scaly snake wrapped around her body while a set of arms—or flippers, she couldn't be certain—dragged her down toward the bottom of the river. Story touched her knife against the thickest part of the serpent near her thigh, and the scaly flesh immediately shrank from the touch. She grabbed the bogey with one hand to steady it, and she could feel it writhing beneath her fingers as her knife sliced through its flesh as if it were made of soft butter. Bubbles boiled up toward the surface as the iron burned its way through the serpent.

Careful to slice slowly so that she didn't inadvertently cut her own leg, she felt the knife come through the other side of the serpent and graze her thigh. The two halves of the bogey fell away, and Story kicked up toward the surface, not bothering to sheath her knife. The raft's lamplight was a tiny pinprick, and she had no idea how far down she was.

She only managed a few pulls through the dark water before all four of her limbs were seized and tightly wrapped by the same scaly creature. Or rather, creatures. *How many bogeys are there? Or,* she thought with horror as she felt another slide around her neck, *is a bogey like a hydra? You cut off its head and seven more appear?* Two more circled her torso as she writhed in their hold. *Or, in this case, seven more bogeys?*

Don't panic! She stopped struggling to conserve her air and consider her options. *What's the worst they can do? Drag me to the bottom and wait for me to drown before eating me?* The bogey didn't know she could hold her breath for nearly an hour now, thanks to her tie to *The Ailes. I can figure out a way to get out and swim back to the raft before that happens.* She knew it was just bravado, but she was barely staving off the panic that threatened to overwhelm her. Then another thought struck: *what if they eat me alive? Or drag me into a cave so deep I can't find my way out!*

She jerked against the bogeys again, desperate to escape, and then she remembered her knife. *Okay, I can't cut them, but they should still shy away from the iron. It'll burn on contact!* Hope swelled through her.

Careful not to drop it, she shifted the knife in her hand so that the blade pointed down toward the bogey on her forearm. She angled her wrist against the rush of the black water flowing around them. Her blade contacted something fleshy, and she slid the flat of it across the surface. Too dark to see anything, she felt heat and bubbles boil around her, and suddenly the resistance on her arm disappeared.

Grinning triumphantly, she moved her now free arm toward the next closest bogey, the one twisted around her leg. The serpent tried to jerk her leg away, but she pulled back just as hard, trying not to cut herself in the process. It felt like a battle in slow motion.

Just as the flat of her blade reached the bogey, her back slammed into the rocky bed of the river. The knife slipped from her fingers, and another serpent wrapped itself around her arm. She jerked and struggled, but to no avail. The bogeys stretched her limbs out as far as they could, and she lay sprawled out on the bottom of the river like a human approximation of a starfish.

Think, Story, think! But she couldn't think. All she could feel was panic as fear overtook her mind. *I'm going to die! I'm going to drown!* The fact that she would be conscious long enough to even ponder the manner of her death only served to heighten her anxiety and fear. And while she hoped for a rescue, she knew that none would be coming. Morrigann wouldn't risk it, and Eachan couldn't swim this deep. Poor Doffen had no chance of survival in the water. Story tried yanking her arms and legs again, but the serpents only held on tighter, exhausting her.

This isn't fair!

A set of needle fine teeth bit into her calf.

NO!

The bogey bit down harder and tore a chunk of her flesh away. Pain shot up her leg, and she could feel the blood flowing from it.

A bolt of terror and adrenaline infused her, waking her exhausted limbs as she arched her back and yanked against the bogeys. The one around her neck slammed her head down against the rocky floor. Her head exploded in pain as she struggled to retain consciousness. Story felt tingling needle sensations all over her body as the bogeys took bites out of her. Her hand began to spasm as a bite on her forearm shot an excruciating lance of pain up her arm.

Something hard brushed against her fingertips, and she reached out for it reflexively, as if it was a lifeline. Story's hand closed around the handle of her knife, and she dragged it toward her.

Something bit down on her cheek.

She jerked her arm inward and managed to move the bogey holding it a few inches. The knife scraped across the stones on the river floor, and the blade flared to life in a flash of light.

In that moment, the bogeys surrounding her scattered, but not before she got a glimpse of them. They were worse than she'd imagined—from the depths of her nightmares, a sickly, milky white color, rotting, slimy scales, large mouths filled with razor sharp teeth, and two skeleton arms with very human like hands. The bogeys closest to the knife had been singed by the light. Still partially blinded by the bright flash herself, Story dragged the knife across the stones again to keep the bogeys at bay.

Once her eyes finally adjusted to the light, and she was certain the flashes were keeping the serpents away, she forced her bleeding fingers to pick up a handful of stones and dragged the blade across them. Her knife momentarily flashed light, and the bogeys that had been creeping in dashed away again. Story pushed herself up with her elbows, ignoring the pain searing across her body, and with her rapidly ebbing strength, kicked off the river's floor and swam toward the surface.

It was slow going as she could only use her legs to kick. Despite the burning pain she was in, Story could still feel small flaps of skin fluttering in the current all over her body. Finally, after what felt like an eternity, she broke the surface and took a deep, ragged breath. Her lungs burned, and air had never hurt so good.

A set of warm, familiar hands looped under her arms and heaved her out of the water and onto the raft.

Story could dimly hear voices calling her name and speaking animatedly to each other, but she couldn't understand the words. Morrigann then Eachan flashed before her. They seemed to be moving in and out of light and darkness—almost as if there was a strobe light going. Her mind was a muddle, and it wasn't until someone, probably Doffen, pulled her knife and the stones gently from her fingers that she realized she was still dragging the blade across the surface, causing a flash of light every time.

Her body shivered uncontrollably. Now that she was out of the water she was freezing! She felt her outer layers of clothing jerked off by two sets of hands working quickly together. Her teeth chattered so hard she was certain she'd crack them. Just when the cold was more than she thought she could possibly bear, she felt someone lie down behind her and wrap strong arms around her. A shot of warmth and calm rolled through her, soothing her shivers away.

A sigh escaped Story's lips, and then her eyes rolled back and she saw darkness once again.

CHAPTER TWENTY-THREE

WICKED GAME

EVERYTHING WAS DARK. STORY LAY FLAT ON HER BACK IN A black void. She couldn't see anything, not even a hand held in front of her face. The only reason she knew she was lying prone, and not standing up, was because there was pressure beneath her back. A momentary jolt of panic flashed through her as she thought she was still at the bottom of the river getting eaten alive. She calmed when she took a breath of clean, crisp air.

"You're running out of time, Ailesit." Metirreonn's voice wafted through the air, disappearing as quickly as an autumn breeze.

Story sat up, and the void materialized around her. Eínlin paced back and forth across the bamboo floors of the dream-walkers' main hall. He was muttering something she couldn't hear and kept shaking his head.

"Eínlin." Story stood up slowly, expecting her body to be aching after what had just happened to her, but there was no pain.

Oh, right. Dreamscape.

The clan leader walked past without acknowledging her, continuing to pace.

"Okay, I get it, you're mad at me, but come on, isn't this a bit immature?" She reached out a hand to stop him, and it swiped right through his shoulder as if she was a ghost.

What the heck? That had never happened in the dreamscape before. *Am I dead?*

Eínlin finally stopped pacing and knelt before a beautiful sand painting on the ground. It was richly detailed, made from fine grains of sand. It must have taken days to create. Story gasped as she recognized the image depicted: Adair, sleeping peacefully in her bed, just as Story had seen her in her previous dreamwalk.

Guess I'm not the only one who feels the need to check on her.

Then Eínlin swept his hand across the sand picture, forever erasing his hours of labor.

The scene melted into Eirnin's home. He stood before her frowning.

"Of course I'm protective of you, but that's not why you can't come with me!" He crossed his arms over his chest. *"Story, I would like nothing more than to see you safe and secure for the rest of your very long life, but I would also never presume to tell you what you can or can't do."*

"You're telling me I can't come with you on this mission!" Story remembered this argument well.

Eirnin threw up his hands. "How many times do I have to tell you it's Eánna who forbids it, not me?" His expression softened, and he reached out a hand to cup her cheek. *"Dear heart, even I have to listen to the queen. This is so much bigger than just the two of us."*

She leaned into his hand, knowing that it was just a

memory, but she didn't care. *A hot tear slid down her cheek, and he gently wiped it away with the pad of his thumb before pulling her into a tight embrace.*

"I wish it wasn't, elf-boy," she whispered in his ear.

"Me too, dear heart, me too."

EVERY PART OF HER BODY HURT. NO, THAT WAS INADEQUATE; EVERY part of her body felt like it was on fire.

Story knew she was awake, but she didn't open her eyes. She wasn't sure if she had the energy, and more importantly, she wasn't ready to talk to anyone yet.

"She's fine now, you can let her go!" Eachan hissed.

"Hardly. I've only just stopped the bleeding. Look at her, she's a mess; I'm amazed she was even able to swim back up to us."

Story felt the heat that was encompassing her pull her even tighter toward the heart of the flame, and a line of sweat erupted on her brow. The thin cotton shift she had on was completely soaked, whether by water or sweat, she didn't know.

"No thanks to you, faerie."

"I didn't see you jumping in after her either, hunter."

"Because you stopped me!"

Story's ears perked up at that. *Morrigann prevented Eachan from helping me?* Another memory flashed before her—one of Doffen, who would do anything the sidhe told it to do, restraining Ped. She felt a pit of disgust form in her stomach.

I knew not to trust him! She was no damsel in distress, but still, a little help would have been nice.

When he responded, Morrigann's voice was cool and collected, as he calmly stroked Story's hair. "Yes, I stopped you because you would have been torn to ribbons by the water fey, and never come back up. You are many things, hunter, but a dryad is not one of them." He paused. "You would have been throwing your life away needlessly and would have only fed the bogey, making it stronger with your fear."

"What?" Eachan didn't sound as if she believed him.

"The bogey is fed by fear and despair, not just flesh. Yours would have made it impossible for Story to escape."

Doffen's gravely voice broke in. "Ach! If hunters had not stopped doing as hunters should, you would not have forgotten these things."

"Fine."

Story could feel Eachan pacing near them as the raft's wooden boards vibrated under her.

"Then what was keeping *you* from jumping in, faerie?" Eachan's voice was accusatory again.

"Aside from needing to restrain you?" Morrigann paused, presumably to allow Eachan an opportunity to answer, which she must have done silently with a gesture, as he then continued speaking. "I couldn't let the bogey feed on my emotions either." He stopped stroking Story's hair and pulled her tighter to him again. "Besides, I had faith in my little half-blood. I knew she'd escape."

"Yours? Since when has Story been yours?" Eachan's voice dropped a few degrees and became positively icy. "She belongs to no one. Least of all you, sidhe."

Story knew she should open her eyes, she should tell

them to stop, she should make Morrigann let her go... but she was afraid. Afraid of the physical pain that would greet her when she did, and more than that, she didn't want to leave the warmth and comfort of his arms. She was too exhausted to make herself go.

"I don't understand you, hunter." Morrigann's rich voice rumbled near Story's ear. "If you'd stop protecting the girl and leave her to me, it would free up the elfling. You could have him back. I would have Story. We'd both get what we wanted."

Story held her breath, feeling her heart hammer against her chest as only silence greeted her.

What will she say? Will she give in to temptation?

But Eachan didn't answer; Doffen spoke instead. "Sir and hunter, the Miss is awake. Yes, Miss is awake."

"Yes, I know. Thank you, Master Dwarf." Morrigann tightened his hold around Story as her eyes flew open. *He knew?*

Eachan's face flashed betrayal, whether it was aimed at her or Morrigann, Story didn't know. "You tried to trick me, faerie!"

He chuckled. "Why are you so surprised?"

Story pushed against him, weakly. "Let me go," she croaked, her voiced strained and parched. Morrigann didn't loosen his arms. "Let me go, now!" She pushed his arms again, and Eachan reached over and forcibly removed them.

When the elf's hands touched the sidhe's arms, they locked eyes, and Story caught the angry glare they shared. The moment passed, and Eachan dropped her eyes to Story's; red faded to yellow as she helped Story to her wobbly feet.

Pain shot through Story as soon as she broke contact with Morrigann. Her head swam, and she would have collapsed had Eachan not been there to steady her. Ped was immediately by her side as well, and with the aid of both of them, she was able to hobble to the far side of the raft.

"Thank you, Eachan."

"I'm sorry I couldn't do more, Ailesit."

Holding up a weak hand to forestall any further apologies, Story got her first look at the damage done by the bogey. Two overlapping half moon scars from the bites were on her hand. She looked up her arm and saw another two on her forearm and biceps. Reaching up to her cheek, she felt yet another one there. In the dim lantern light, she could see another half-dozen peppered her legs, though she was certain some were masked by the old scars on her thigh from her encounter with the fuath last spring.

"Geez, the water fey really have it out for me, don't they?" She gave a rueful laugh that hurt her throat and shivered from the chill in the air as it permeated her wet shift.

Eachan took off her own cloak and wrapped it around Story. "Your things are still wet."

"How long was I out?" It couldn't have been that long if her clothes were still wet.

"Only a few minutes."

"How am I this healed?" Even as she spoke Story knew the answer to her own question, looking past Eachan to meet Morrigann's glittering violet gaze. He was once again diminished, lacking his usual glow. He turned away and acted as if she wasn't even there.

Feeling her stomach lurch, Story blinked back tears, though she was uncertain why. Ped curled up behind her, and she leaned back against him, overcome with both physical and emotional exhaustion.

"You need to sleep, Ailesit. The dwarf says we'll reach Cildara tomorrow." Eachan stood at the edge of the raft, back straight and shoulders squared. "I'll keep watch. Don't worry, Ailesit, nothing will bother you this night."

Despite the elf's words, something was bothering Story. Instead of a peaceful dreamless sleep, she found herself very much aware and in Morrigann's garden—yet it was his garden without the iron cage she'd imprisoned him in.

Seriously? Him? I'm dreaming about HIM?

She closed her eyes and shifted herself away. She didn't care where, as long as it was *elsewhere*. When she opened them, she found herself right back where she was, in the center of Morrigann's garden, sitting in his wooden throne.

Groaning, she balled her hands into fists and pressed them against her eyes.

Fine, if I'm stuck here, I'm at least going to dream about the people I want to see.

If Morrigann can do it, so can I!

She closed her eyes and imagined Eirnin there with her— not Eirnin, the clan leader, but *her* Eirnin, the one she battled with, traveled with, and defeated the Spring Prince with. The Eirnin she'd fallen in love with.

As she opened her eyes, Eirnin's shape coalesced at the edge of the clearing. He smiled at her, his eyes crinkling at the corners, and he held his arms open. Story leapt off the throne and ran toward him, knowing this time it would not be

Morrigann in disguise. It couldn't be since this Eirnin was just a figment of her imagination, a fantasy.

"It's never as good as the real thing." Morrigann's silky voice called from behind her.

Story's concentration faltered, and Eirnin disappeared from her dream as if he'd never existed. Clenching her jaw against the hot tears that rolled down her cheeks, she stood straight, refusing to turn around and let Morrigann see her like this.

"And it's a dangerous pastime, Story." His voice was closer.

Scrubbing a hand across her face, she swiped away her tears. "I don't care. I needed to see him."

Morrigann walked around Story and faced her. "It always starts that way. You tell yourself, 'I just want to see them one more time' or 'I just need to hold them one more time'. But soon you'll find you spend most of your time in the dreamscape, fantasizing about those lost to you." An expression that bespoke sympathy crossed his face. "You need to stay grounded in the real world or you'll go mad."

"Like you?" Story flung the words at him, angry and embarrassed at being both "caught" and lectured by him. The worst part was, she knew he was right.

"Yes, like me." He raised an eyebrow and cracked a half-smile. "Would you fancy an apple?" His half-smile blossomed into a full grin as he extended a silver apple toward her.

Her mouth fell open in shock, and she suddenly found herself giggling, as if it was an old inside joke, which, she supposed, in a twisted way it was. "No thanks, as usual, I'll pass."

"Suit yourself. They're not nearly as good as the real ones were, sadly." He bit into the silver skin, and the loud crunch filled the air as a dribble of juice leaked from the corner of his mouth.

Shaking her head as she chuckled, Story asked, "Where the heck did you get that?"

"Oh, simple Story, you do like to keep me entertained, don't you?" Morrigann walked past her to his throne and settled himself down in it, slinging a leg casually over the arm. "This is the dreamscape after all, and we're dreaming about my garden from before you defiled it with iron."

"*We're* dreaming?"

"I'm dreaming, you're dreaming, hence 'we're dreaming'." He waved a hand at her. "Oh calm down, it's no different than what you do with the elf mages. It's not romantic or anything—since you seem to abhor that—it's just a chance to talk without the elf sticking her nose in our business."

"We have business?" Story asked as a sinking feeling overcame her. Was he going to back out on her? He couldn't! She couldn't get the antidote without him. A pang of guilt ran through her over her planned betrayal, but she shoved it away. Eírnin was more important!

"Indeed." He extended a hand, and a chair grew up beneath her, catching her knees and scooping her up. "Please have a seat."

"Since it seems I have so much choice in the matter."

"There is always a choice, Story." He sat in his throne, resting his ankle over one knee. "You once asked me why I imprisoned my mother and sister."

Story's eyes widened, and she held her breath. Was he going to tell her? "Yes... though at the time it seemed like a touchy subject." She shrugged. "I figured it was because Metirreonn either killed or had someone else kill the elf dreamwalker you loved. As for your mother… well, I have no idea there."

Resting his elbows on his armrests, he steepled his fingers together and regarded her for a moment with narrowed eyes before speaking.

"Autumn did not kill Ealis. I did."

CHAPTER TWENTY-FOUR

SECRETS

ROCKING BACK IN HER SEAT, STORY WAS AT A LOSS FOR what to think. "But I thought you loved her?"

"I still do." Morrigann gazed at her over his tented fingers, glittering eyes betraying none of the agony he must still feel if what he said was true.

"But then why?"

"I didn't say I killed her on purpose." He flexed his hands out before him and stared at his fingertips. "I'd get comfortable; this is a long story, Story."

He's making jokes? Now? Story could hardly believe it, but she tucked her feet beneath her and sat back in her chair. "I'm all ears."

"Yes, I'm certain you are." The faerie smiled tightly while he interlaced his fingers again. "About fifteen hundred years ago, I met Ealis, and we did the predictably forbidden thing and fell deeply in love. My mother was unhappy, to say the least. She had created Autumn as my consort, and in her eyes I needed no one else."

"So you saw each other in secret."

Nodding, Morrigann continued. "For centuries we met in the dreamscape. She was a dreamwalker, and I had always been able to keep the other sidhe out of my dreams." He closed his eyes. "Or so I thought.

"Little did I know, my sister had long been spying on us. Eventually, her jealousy overcame her when it was clear I would not soon lose interest in Ealis and return to her, as I had always done in the past." He looked at Story inviting her to ask the question he knew she had.

"Why didn't you just offer Ealis the same deal you offered me?"

"You mean have Ealis kill Autumn and take her place?"

Staring at her feet, Story nodded her head.

"I did. Like you, she refused. Apparently the idea of becoming one of the Sidhe was not amenable to her either. Though a sidhe was good enough for her to love…" His voice trailed off, and Story could hear the tinge of bitterness in it. He perked back up as if nothing had happened and waved a hand in front of him. "And then she eventually left me, as you saw." Morrigann looked at Story again, but she said nothing, unsure of how to respond.

"Shortly after we imprisoned our father, I realized if Summer did not need Winter, why did I need Autumn? I could be free to choose my own consort!" He let out a biting laugh. "My sister must have sensed my desires, and before I could act, she'd made her move on Ealis. I arrived in the city of Ailes too late, and Autumn killed her."

"But I thought—"

He held up a hand. "Please, this is difficult enough. Let me finish." Story nodded, feeling slightly embarrassed, and Morrigann continued, a faraway look in his eyes. "I wanted revenge, but alone I could never get it. My sister and I are equals, you see. I needed power, and the only power available was *The Ailes*." He paused, taking a breath. "And there it was, that big, beautiful tree behind my sister, framing her as she held Ealis's corpse. Then Autumn smiled at me with that utterly mad smile of hers.

"I didn't think—I acted. Ealis had long before trusted me with the secrets of harnessing *The Ailes's* power, and so I used it. No, I tore it away from the elves and cast my sister down into Aisdean—far better than the hell she deserved."

Pausing to compose himself, he scrubbed a gold dusted hand across his face. "It wasn't until I ran to the fallen elf that I saw her ailach was not a dreamwalker's."

Story felt her breath catch. "You mean it wasn't…"

Morrigann shook his head. "It was Ealos, her twin."

They sat in silence for a few moments as Story pictured the emotions he must have felt; relief over the fact that Ealis was not dead, but then horror as all the elves began to fall to the ground and Change, becoming mortal and losing their magic.

"Why didn't you stop it, give back the power? Their life force?"

Morrigann shot to his feet, suddenly angry. "Don't you think I would have if I could?" He raked both hands through his hair, scattering sparks of magic everywhere. "I'm certain there was a way, but I didn't know how, and none of the elf mages were really in a position to tell me." He began pacing, and Story tried to curl deeper into her chair, away from him and the rage that was wafting off of him in visible waves of glittering gold magic.

"I found Ealis crawling toward the tree. She used the last of her own magic, her life force, to try to restore *The Ailes*." He glanced at Story over his shoulder. "All she got was a loophole in my curse for her efforts. The loophole you exploited."

Biting her lip, Story was unsure how to respond. Morrigann hadn't technically killed Ealis, though she could see why he felt he had.

"Why... why do you hate the elves so much then? What did they ever do to you? Why did you work so hard to keep me from restoring *The Ailes* if that's what Ealis wanted?"

He regarded her with unreadable eyes before finally answering. "If you restored *The Ailes*, Aisdean would be opened, and my father would be released."

"Along with your mother and sister."

He nodded. "Yes, that was part of it. As for why I'm not fond of the elves, that is a story for another time." Morrigann resumed his pacing. "Unable to rid myself of the elves' power, and angry with my mother for putting me in this hopeless situation to begin with, I cast her down to Aisdean as well." He raised an eyebrow. "And you know how the rest of the story goes."

He sat back down in his throne and rested his cheek against his fist. "So, now I have a question for you." He regarded her with an icy gaze. "Ealis died thinking I'd betrayed her trust, which, I suppose I did." He leaned forward slightly. "Are you going to betray me, Story?"

"Ailesit!"

A hand shook Story, and she jerked awake, blinking her eyes against the lantern light.

"Ailesit, are you alright?" Eachan crouched before her, her eyes flooded with worry.

"Yeah, I'm fine, thanks." Story positioned her aching, stiff arms gingerly to push herself up into a seated position as Eachan reached out to help her.

"You were twitching and moaning as if you were in pain, Ailesit."

Glancing over at Morrigann, who was still seated on the opposite end of the raft with his back to her, Story shook her head. "It was just a bad dream."

Eachan followed her gaze toward the faerie and narrowed her eyes. "If you say so." She glanced back at Story. "You should know, Doffen says we are nearly there." Apparently satisfied that Story was okay, the elf stood back up and resumed her watch.

Feeling a surge of excitement, Story smiled until the realization of what would come next came crashing down on her.

Am I going to betray Morrigann? She looked at the faerie, her eyes tracing his faintly glowing outline. *Am I really the type of person who could do that?* A month ago, she was certain she could. Now, she wasn't so sure. *So much has changed.*

She leaned back against the still snoring Ped, taking comfort in the selkie's warmth.

I don't love Morrigann, and he doesn't love me. That much I do know. She let out a frustrated breath. *But he professes to 'like' me, whatever that means, and I certainly don't hate him. Besides, I'm not so sure he's the villain anymore. Or that Metirreonn is either, for that matter.*

Staring at Morrigann's back, she pondered his and Metirreonn's situation. Essentially they'd been forced into an arranged marriage—or whatever the Sidhe equivalent was—by their parents. Their thoughts, desires, and wishes had been completely disregarded.

I can't imagine being told who I had to spend my life with, to have my right to choose taken from me.

Then she remembered Morrigann's words, *"There is always a choice, Story."* It seemed he'd chosen not to follow the path forced on him by his parents. *Yeah, and look how that turned out for everyone.*

He had to be scarred on the inside after everything that had happened to him. Metirreonn, too. She'd been rejected by her "perfect" match, and it seemed that at some point, she did love him. Whether she still did remained to be seen, though Story suspected vengeance was the more powerful emotion coursing through Autumn at the moment.

The lamplight glinted off the scars on Story's legs and arms, scars she would always have now, and she wondered if that's what she looked like inside too. *A mess of ugly, badly healed, emotional scars.*

She closed her eyes and leaned her head back against Ped. *Stop it with the self-pity train, Story. It won't solve anything!*

Eachan shifted slightly, and Story found herself contemplating her elf companion as well. *Her situation is so much like Metirreonn's. Is her kindness all an act? Will she try to get me out of the way once we have Eírnin's antidote?*

Feeling eyes on her, Story looked back to the front of the raft, just catching Morrigann's glittering gaze before he looked away again.

Can I really do it?

DOFFEN POLED THEM OVER TO THE EDGE OF THE RIVER, AND AS THEY neared, Story could see a short dock jutting out from the edge of the raised riverbank.

"Nearly there, Miss. Nearly there."

Shivering under her cloak, Story placed a hand on Ped's quivering shoulder. "I know, I'm anxious to be out of here too, boy."

"Aye, that makes three of us," Eachan said from beside her.

That made Doffen laugh. "Ach! Oh hunter, your kind never have liked our mines."

Eachan merely raised an eyebrow and kept silent.

"Now Miss, when you leave to follow the tunnel up to the surface, beware of the grinlings, Miss."

"Grinlings?" Story looked at Doffen warily. *What else do they have lurking down here?*

"Ach! Yes, Miss, grinlings. They are little thieves, little pests, little villains, Miss. So don't tarry in the tunnels on your own." The dwarf wouldn't be accompanying them further as they planned to return to the city of Ailes via the ocean on Ped's back. A trip that took weeks or months overland would be completed in a matter of days.

Story was afraid to ask her next question, but given what she'd seen thus far... "What about goblins?"

"Goblins, Miss?" Doffen appeared truly confused.

"Well, you have them, don't you?" Story stared past the edges of the light, wondering what lurked there.

"Miss, of course, Miss. Wouldn't be much of a mine without goblins, now would it, Miss?"

"Great. Just great."

"Yes Miss, it *is* great, Miss."

"Huh?" Story was confused. "Aren't goblins bad?"

Morrigann's smooth voice, just on the other side of Ped, broke in. "I suspect this is where your human tales have gotten things wrong again. Goblins are cousins to spriggans, and they are helpful to the dwarves."

"Helpful how?"

"Ach, Miss!" Doffen spat and grinned. "The goblins keep others out of our mines. Yes they do, Miss, yes they do. You wouldn't like them, Miss. No, no you wouldn't."

Story chuckled. "In that case, I don't think our tales are too far off."

They reached the dock, and Eachan leapt off the raft before it stopped moving. Morrigann and Ped followed her, while Story lingered on the raft a moment to speak with Doffen.

"Miss, just follow the tunnel until it ends, Miss, then walk toward the setting sun until you get to Cildara."

"How will I know when I've gotten there?"

Doffen let out a loud guffaw and slapped his knee. "Ach! Miss, you are funny, Miss. You will know."

Story raised an eyebrow at that, but let it go. "Thank you, Master Dwarf, for guiding us. I know it was scary. At least, it was for me." Suddenly overcome with the urge, she reached out and pulled the dwarf into a tight hug.

Doffen stiffened momentarily before patting her back lightly. "Yes, Miss, yes. You're welcome, Miss. You are always welcome in our mines. The goblins won't bother you, Miss."

Story released the dwarf and felt her eyes begin to burn a bit, but knowing how dwarves felt about water did her best to hold her tears at bay. She waved goodbye and hopped off the raft onto the dock. "Be safe, Doffen."

"Always, Miss. Always."

THEY'D BEEN WALKING IN THE DARKNESS, WITH ONLY MORRIGANN'S faint glow to light their way, for a couple hours when finally the dark started to grey before them.

They were nearing the exit.

As they walked closer, Story could make out the squarish shape of the opening and felt a chilly breeze flutter across her skin. A tree limb with most of its leaves fallen was silhouetted against the opening, appearing almost skeletal. Story's feet stopped moving of her own accord.

I can't do this. This isn't me. I'm not this sort of person.

It didn't hit her like a ton of bricks, or anything profound. It was just that she was finally ready to admit it to herself. She'd avoided this decision point for as long as she could. She wasn't surprised by her realization—she was mostly surprised that it had taken her this long to come to it.

"Ailesit?" Eachan was a few paces ahead, Ped by her side.

"Give me a minute. I need to talk to Morrigann." She met the faerie's gaze, and he raised an eyebrow as she turned back into the tunnel and walked down a few dozen feet.

Morrigann followed her, and after they stopped, he crossed his arms. "Is this the bit where you profess your undying adoration for me, Story?"

Normally, she would have snorted and given a cutting remark back in their awkward banter, but now, she just stared at a spot over his shoulder, unsure of how to begin.

Just say it. Rip it off, like a band-aid! "I made a bargain with Metirreonn to trade you for Eírnin's antidote."

His expression betrayed nothing as he leaned against the tunnel wall. "I see."

She forced herself to continue. "And then I made another bargain with her to imprison you until the Uinseann was past to protect Adair... and if I'm being fully truthful, myself too. Also, I think your sister plans for you to be imprisoned a bit longer than that." She felt the heat of his gaze on her and closed her eyes. "Okay, a lot longer." Story held out her hand. "Look, just give me her harp; it's what she really wants. I should still be able to get the antidote with that." She didn't really believe it, but she'd figure something out. *At least, I hope I will.*

Morrigann regarded her quietly for a few moments, and in the low light she could see his mouth spread into a mischievous smile. "Oh, simple Story, you make me laugh," he chuckled. "I already knew all of that."

Jaw dropping, Story felt relieved, confused, and a little betrayed. "You knew? How?"

"I have my spies, and Autumn has hers. We all do." He cocked his head to the side, regarding her, violet eyes glittering in the faint light. "And honestly, how much more transparent could you be? You don't really think I fell for any of it, do you?"

Feeling her cheeks flush, Story crossed her arms. "Then why did you come?"

"To begin with, I did want to get out of that cage, and you really were the only one who could release me."

"Oh, right." She bit her lip, considering. "So does this mean you have a plan? Have had one all along?" Story met his eyes, feeling hopeful again.

He smiled brilliantly, and his natural glow increased as he placed a friendly hand on her shoulder. "I always have a plan."

Story's grin matched his, and she almost completely relaxed until he spoke again.

"But then, so does my sister." He gripped both of her shoulders, a warm glow emanating where his thumbs brushed her bare collarbone. "You must promise me that you will do as I say from here on out."

"No!" Her response was immediate, and she pulled away from him.

Morrigann held her tighter, almost hurting her. "Listen! Do as I say, and I promise you that you'll get the elfling's antidote and be able to leave Cildara safely."

Story shook her head, refusing to meet his gaze. *Can't trust him! He'll only betray me in the end. He betrayed Ealis...*

Leaning in, Morrigann tilted her chin up, forcing her to look at him. "You owe me."

Story's lip trembled as the words tumbled out. "I won't kill her. I won't become a sidhe. I won't be your consort." Tears leaked out of the corners of her eyes, and she had no idea why.

He smiled, almost gently. "I won't ask you to. Trust me."

"I can't." She felt her will begin to crack at the corners.

As if able to sense she was weakening, Morrigann cupped her cheek with one hand and leaned in so close she could smell his honey sweet breath. "Do it anyway."

A wave of warmth and calm swept over her, and Story's eyes half closed as she soaked it in. Everything in her experience taught her that she couldn't trust him, shouldn't trust him. *But he did promise…*

"Okay."

CHAPTER TWENTY-FIVE

TURNING TABLES

STORY AND MORRIGANN RETURNED TO EACHAN AND PED WHO
were both impatiently waiting for them a few feet inside
the square entrance. Story walked behind Morrigann almost in a daze—she couldn't believe what she'd just agreed to!

Though, I'm not a faerie, so I don't have to keep my promises…

"What was that all about?" Eachan narrowed her eyes as
they neared, but Story could still see the yellow, red, and purple swirls that were there whenever Morrigann was around.

The faerie reached over and patted her cheek as he
walked by. "Don't you worry hunter, that's between my little
Story and me."

The elf's neck and face flushed, while her eyes burned red
and purple. Story placed a calming hand on her shoulder. "We
were just fine tuning the terms of our agreement. Turns out I'm
not as cold-hearted as I thought. Not even for Eírnin's sake."
She looked down, almost embarrassed by her admission.

"I was wondering when you'd finally come around to

yourself." Eachan placed a mirroring hand on Story's shoulder as her eyes cooled. "You are many things I don't like, but a back-stabber is not one of them."

"Wait, so you knew too?"

"Aye, but that's not necessarily a bad thing. People always know where they stand with you," the elf chuckled. "So, I suppose the new plan is to take the antidote by force?" She pulled out her iron-tipped arrow and examined the length of it. "Excellent."

"Hold on, hold on. You," Morrigann pointed at Eachan, "put that thing right back, and stop waving it about. You'll hurt somebody."

Frowning, she returned the arrow to its quiver. "I wasn't asking *you*, faerie. I was asking Story."

Story's eyebrows shot up in surprise. *That's the first time she's called me by my name...*

"Well, you should be asking me." Morrigann squared off in front of Eachan, hands on his hips.

"Not likely!" Eachan mirrored his pose and looked him right in the eyes; she was nearly as tall as him. "Who put you in charge?"

"I did." Story's voice broke their standoff, and Eachan's head whipped around to stare at her with solidly yellow eyes. Morrigann smirked. Story had half a mind to slap him just to make him stop. Then she sighed, *why bother? It never works anyway.*

"Are. You. Mad?" the elf seethed.

"No." Story copied their pose, hands on her hips. "I don't trust him, but he's got a plan, and I have a few guarantees, and if worse comes to worst, you can shoot Metirreonn. So keep that arrow handy."

"Can I shoot him too?" Eachan angled her head toward the faerie.

Story shrugged. "If it looks like he's playing us, sure."

"What!" Morrigann's smirk melted from his face.

"Might I ask what the plan is?" Eachan fought to keep a smile off her face as she eyed the sidhe.

"You might, but don't expect me to answer." Morrigann pouted. "Now, if you ladies will follow me, if I know my sister—and I do—there will be an ambush just outside the mouth of this cave. We'll all go along quietly with our captors, who will graciously escort us the rest of the way to Cildara."

He suited action to words and strode into the sunshine, glowing all the brighter for it. "Ahh, blessed Sun. I do love the dwarves, but that was far too long without you, old friend." Morrigann's head tilted upward, and he smiled as he spoke.

Story moved to follow him, but Eachan stopped her. "I don't like this," she hissed.

"Do you have a better idea?" Story gave Eachan a chance to answer, but the elf merely frowned. "No? Well, me neither. Our options are pretty limited at this point." Story pulled her arm out of Eachan's grasp. "You can stay if you want, but I'm going."

"Oh, hold on. I didn't come all this way to quit now." Eachan hurried to catch up, with Ped trailing them.

Knowing she was about to walk into a trap, Story hesitated by the mouth of the cave. Her stomach was a roil of anticipation, and she took several deep breaths to calm herself. *It's not a trap if we know about it, right?*

She walked the few remaining feet through the dead leaves that crunched underneath her feet to Morrigann. He smiled at her invitingly and was just opening his mouth to say something when, suddenly, they were surrounded.

"Centaurs!" The word popped out of Story's mouth before she could stop herself. She'd expected tree sprites or some other fey.

"At least there is one tale you humans have not gotten completely wrong." A centaur with a black and white paint horse body had spoken. His voice was deep and rumbling, as befitted his barrel equine chest and the equally broad human chest connected to it. The centaur's paint pattern and horsehair continued up his human torso and down his arms, only thinning out slightly at his hands and face. A beautiful mane of black and white hair cascaded from his head as he tossed it to peer at his captives.

"Ah, look, if it isn't my sister's favorite centaur." Morrigann bowed slightly at the waist, though Story was certain it was meant sarcastically. "Cadwaladr, how are you? You're looking mighty spry for your old age."

No way! It can't be the same Cadwaladr who gave the prophecy, can it? Story felt her eyes widen, and she ignored Eachan's questioning gaze. *But then, he did immediately recognize me as a human... has he seen humans before? Back when there were more passages between our worlds?*

"I am fine as always, Spring Prince. Thank you for asking." His expression remained impassive as he spoke, though his hands gripped the wooden pole of a long wicked looking spear. "Your sister is most anxious to see you."

"Really? I thought she was more anxious to see what I brought with me."

Eachan had an arrow out and aimed at Morrigann before he even finished talking. "I knew you'd betray us, you faerie bastard!"

"Hey!" Morrigann feigned a wounded expression. "I

know who both my parents are, thank you very much." He frowned. "Also, if anyone should feel betrayed it's me. How *did* my sister know to set an ambush here, Story?"

Playing along, Story crossed her arms, lifted her chin, and looked away.

"Put away your weapon, hunter," another centaur called from behind. Her voice was deep, but feminine, as the bare, black-furred breasts on her chest also indicated. "You should know better than to try to use an arrow on one of the Sidhe—or have you been so long away from your own traditions that you have forgotten?"

Eachan lowered her bow and hung her head in chagrin, silently returning her normal, obsidian-tipped arrow to her quiver.

Why would she—Eachan winked at Story surreptitiously and realization dawned. *Of course!* By pulling out a normal arrow, Eachan had tricked the centaurs into underestimating her and thinking she had nothing that could harm Autumn.

Hopefully a fatal mistake—but not for us!

Her own knife was not mentioned by anyone. As far as the Centaurs were concerned, she was in cahoots with their mistress. *And maybe they just don't know about it...*

Feeling more energized than she had been in a while, almost as if she got a second wind, Story clapped her hands together. "So, Morrigann may or may not be betraying us," *please let him just have meant Metirreonn's harp,* "we may or may not have planned against him," *not at the moment,* "and you're a really, *really* old centaur who also happens to know about humans and has a penchant for giving prophecies." Story glanced at the wide assortment of centaurs around them: an Arabian, a quarter-horse, one that looked like a pony, a couple breeds she didn't recognize, and even one Clydesdale. She added, "Oh, and you have a posse. Does that about sum it up?"

Cadwaladr regarded her with placid, chestnut brown eyes. "Yes, human, I believe that covers it."

I wonder if he knows I'm half-dryad, or if he's just a cocky mister know-it-all who hasn't bothered to look beyond my superficial appearance? "Well then, I've always wanted to say this: Take me to your leader."

The centaur raised one bushy eyebrow and turned toward the setting sun. With a wave of his spear indicating they should follow him, Story and her companions fell into step behind him, the remaining five centaurs arrayed around them. They seemed to take it for granted that Story and her group would accompany them without a fight. Either the centaurs were incredibly fierce warriors, against whom they would have no hope, or they were very cocky.

Probably both, Story thought with a wry smile. They were nearly to Cildara, they had a plan, and she wasn't going to have to betray anyone to save Eírnin. On the whole, things were looking up!

About an hour later, as they crunched through the carpet of orange, brown, and red leaves toward the lowering sun, Story got her first glimpse of a wood sprite—its yellow eyes burning as it peeked out from behind a massive oak. Eachan nodded her head when Story glanced her way, confirming her suspicion. They were close.

A few more minutes passed, and several more wood

sprites were spotted. They walked past a handful of aspen and maple trees and found themselves just inside a perfect circle of oaks. That was when Story realized the only centaur still with them was Cadwaladr; the others had not entered the grove.

Her eyes darted around, and a hum of magic swept over her. *I know this place.* Her fingers tightened on Ped's back as he let out a high-pitched whine.

We're here. Cildara.

Eachan's fingers twitched, but she showed no other outward sign of anxiety. Meanwhile, Morrigann grew progressively more aloof and inwardly drawn as they'd neared Cildara—almost as if he was trying to bolster his faded powers.

Or trying to distance himself from me.

Despite all the promises that had been made and everything that had been said, she still didn't trust him and knew he still hadn't told her everything.

A few minutes passed with them awkwardly standing around, the tension building when, finally, Morrigann spoke. "Sister, you've kept us waiting long enough. Now you're just being rude." He walked toward her stone throne at the center of the grove and was just about to sit when a blast of chilly air swept through the circle, scattering leaves in its wake. A flurry of magic sparks and leaves coalesced over the throne, and then Metirreonn was there, reclining demurely, as if she'd been waiting for them all along.

Morrigann took an automatic step away from her, and she raised a perfectly manicured eyebrow that was in stark contrast to her crazed expression. "What, no kiss hello, dearest brother? Is that any way to greet me, especially after so *very* long apart?" She leaned toward him and smiled. "Didn't you miss me? Even a little bit?"

Taking another step back, he crossed his arms over his chest. "Believe me when I say I thought of you often and with very strong emotion."

Her face blossomed into a beautiful smile, and her hair, all reds, golds, and browns, like the leaves on the ground, curled up around her. "Oh, how I've imagined this moment." She straightened her trunk, coming out of her seat. "It's the one thing that kept me sane all those years."

Story would have snickered at that—no one would describe Metirreonn as sane—if not for the multiple thick roots that burst from the ground and wrapped themselves around her legs.

"What the heck?" She tried to pull away, but it was too late; she was held fast to the ground. Looking around, she could see that Morrigann, Ped, and Eachan were in the same position.

"Metirreonn! What is this? You said I'd be free to go if I brought him to you!" Story forced herself not to expend her energy on pulling against the roots that had wrapped up around her calf.

Breaking her gaze from her brother, Metirreonn glanced at Story, as if only just realizing she was there. A leafless twig coalesced on her skin, then rose from it. A small bud formed on the end and then quickly grew before unfurling into a full-sized, green, oak leaf.

The antidote!

If Story could have lunged at it, she would have. Out of the corner of her eye, she could see Eachan straining at the roots that held her, clearly wanting to reach the leaf as well.

"Patience, Ailesit. I have waited a thousand years to reunite with Spring." The roots around Morrigann's legs dragged him right up next to Autumn, and she pulled his head against her chest, raking her fingers through his hair. "Your petty mortal worries can wait a few moments more."

As she watched Morrigann do nothing to fight his sister off, Story felt an unpleasant clenching in her stomach she quickly recognized as not quite jealousy, but rather, possessiveness—as if no one else should be allowed to touch the Spring Prince like that. A quick glance at Eachan, and her brown-filled eyes confirmed she was feeling the same way.

Stupid sun faeries!

Story frowned, knowing her feelings were not solely because he was a powerful faerie—he had, contrary to her desire, grown on her over the past couple months. She cared about him and did not like seeing him manhandled by Autumn.

He can go ahead and kick his plan into action any time now.

But he didn't. Metirreonn leaned her head against the top of Morrigann's. "Dear, dear brother. What should I do with you? Kiss you? Hurt you? Hold you? Cast you down into Aisdean for a thousand years?"

Morrigann said nothing, just sat limply in her arms, eyes dead of any spark, resignation on his face.

Why doesn't he do something? Story looked between the sidhe and realized just how diminished Morrigann truly was. Alone, he still seemed powerful, but up against a sidhe in the prime of her season, magic rolling off of her in visible red, gold, and brown waves, he had no chance.

What kind of plan is this? What could he possibly do against her? Why didn't he say something before? Then, remembering their first conversation at the cage, she realized, he had.

"Let me get this straight, you want me to help you get to Cildara and steal one of my sister's leaves for an elfling I care less

than nothing for... My sister, who hates me and blames me for imprisoning her for these last one thousand years—and rightly so, I might add... And nearing the autumn equinox, no less, when she will be at both the height and the heart of her power, and I'll be at my lowest?"

Feeling her stomach sink, Story realized he'd warned her all the way back at the beginning. *He doesn't stand a chance!*

"I know!" Metirreonn's crazed laugh broke into Story's thoughts recalling her to the present scene. "I think I'd like to watch you suffer."

Air whirred by as Story flew across the ground as the roots jerked her toward a tree. Her back slammed into an oak's trunk knocking the wind out of her, and two branches curled around her arms, pulling them so tight behind her that her back arched up, thrusting her chest out painfully.

Eachan shouted "NO!" and Ped snarled, but both were immediately silenced by roots bursting from the ground and wrapping around their necks and mouths.

"This wasn't part of the deal!" Story rasped out. "You promised—"

"I promised you would leave my home safely and that my wood sprites would not harm you. *Safe* is such a subjective word, isn't it?" Metirreonn flung Morrigann away from herself and undulated across the ground toward Story. "I never said *I* wouldn't harm you. And from what I remember of humans, your fragile little bodies can actually take quite a beating before they break... permanently." Her gaze swept over Story's body, taking in her litany of scars and bruises. "But then I see you already know that. Shall we see how much further we can take things?"

In the background, Morrigann was lifted to his feet by

two more branches entwining his arms and shoulders. He shook his head as if dazed, and Story swallowed thickly, trying to push down her own fear while Metirreonn came ever closer.

"Metirreonn, please. Just give me the leaf, and we'll go. I've done what you asked, you can't—" A branch wrapped itself around her neck, cutting her off and making it impossible to breathe. *Does she know how long I can hold my breath for?*

"Hmm, where should I start?" The Autumn Princess stopped about a foot in front of her and cocked her head to the side, her empty, white eyes fixed on Story. "Perhaps with your pretty face so that my dear brother won't want to look at it anymore?" She extended one smooth arm toward Story's cheek, and Story watched with horror as it came slowly nearer.

What is she going to do to me? Then her gaze fixed on something even worse and infinitely more frightening: the leaf, Eírnin's antidote, was no longer on Metirreonn's shoulder. *No! Where is it? What did she—*

Pain exploded along the side of Story's face as the sidhe's finger made contact, and the branch around her throat loosened just enough to allow the scream that tore from her throat.

I 'LL GIVE YOU BACK YOUR HARP." MORRIGANN'S VOICE CUT through the haze of Story's pain, filling her with hope that perhaps *now* he'd get around to enacting his plan.

Metirreonn pulled back her arm, and Story slumped in her bonds as red drops of blood slid down her face and onto the roots below.

"Release Story and her companions, and I'll give you back your harp." Morrigann's face was an emotionless mask, but his eyes burned with hatred.

"And?" Metirreonn extended a finger back toward Story's face, and Story stretched her neck as far away as she could.

"And father's horn." He said this last one as if it cost him dearly.

"Done."

The roots holding Ped and Eachan withdrew, and they got shakily to their feet.

"Release Story." Morrigann demanded, as if he wasn't being held immobile on every limb, helpless to his sister's power.

"Give me the instruments first. I showed my good faith by releasing her companions." She glided over to him and caressed his face. "Come now, dearest brother, we aren't meant to fight. Let us kiss and make up." She smiled, almost gently. "Our dreams can still be realized. What need have we for mother and father?" She laid a light kiss on his lips and leaned her forehead against his. "There were once only two seasons— there can be again."

"Those are not my dreams, sister." Morrigann pressed his eyes closed. "They never were."

She lashed out with her hand, raking it across his face. "And what is your dream now? Ealis is dead, and you would replace her with a *human*? She's not even of our world." The gouges she scratched in his face were already healing over, and she leaned in close again. "You used to have taste."

He smiled up at her. "Anyone is better than you."

"I am going to pull her to pieces bit by bit, ensuring she lives just enough to leave my home 'safely' with her companions." She stroked his face, then grasped his chin savagely in her fingers, forcing his eyes up to hers. "And I will make you watch."

She turned toward Story and found Eachan and her drawn bow blocking her way. Surprise flickered across the sidhe's face, but it was quickly replaced by fear as the iron-tipped arrow buried itself squarely in her chest. As Metirreonn flew back across the grove from the force and magic of Eachan's arrow, the elf raced to Story's side. She pulled out Story's knife and cut away the branches that shackled her. They fell away easily at the iron's touch, and in a moment, Story was free.

"Thank you."

"No time for niceties, Story." Eachan thrust the knife back into Story's grasp. "Go get the faerie. I'll try to find the leaf." She dropped to her hands and knees and began searching among the carpet of fallen leaves. When Story hesitated, Eachan looked up and yelled, "Go!"

Story ran across the grove toward Morrigann, noticing that, oddly enough, the centaurs outside the grove did nothing. *They had to have heard the commotion...*

Cadwaladr, the only one who'd accompanied them into the grove, had stood quietly off to the side during everything, and was now bent over the still form of Metirreonn. He glanced up at Story as she ran by but made no move to stop her. He leaned back over the Autumn Princess, and Story could hear him muttering a few unintelligible words as sparks of glittering gold magic shot from his hands toward Metirreonn's wound.

When Story reached Morrigann, he grinned at her, and she couldn't help herself as she smiled back. "Some plan of yours."

"It worked, didn't it?"

"That remains to be seen; we're not outta here yet." She easily cut through one set of branches holding his arm, though he winced as if it pained him. She hesitated, with her knife just over the next set. "What's wrong?"

"You can't release me, Story." His breath was labored and strained. "My bonds are not like yours. I made a promise to her. If I go before fulfilling it, it will destroy me."

"She's going to destroy you if you stay!"

"Why don't you let that be my problem?" He held his freed hand in front of her face. The oak leaf was pinched between his fingertips. "Don't forget this, otherwise it was all in vain."

With trembling fingers, Story took the leaf. "I can't just leave you here."

"Yes, you can." Morrigann smiled at her again. "Oh, simple Story, haven't you figured it out yet? This *was* my plan. It was the only way. Autumn will never willingly let me go." He traced the contours of her battered face and gently tucked a braid behind her ear, running a fingertip along its rounded edge. "Please don't make me regret my decision." He buried his warm fingers in the braids at the base of her neck and leaned his forehead against hers. "Don't let my father get you or your sister. After the Uinseann, all will be well again." He pulled away and gazed into her eyes. "Now go."

Feeling hot tears well up in her eyes, she scrubbed them away with the back of her hand. "But—"

He laid a warm finger across her lips. "You promised to do what I said."

Story pushed his hand away and was about to respond when they heard Metirreonn stirring.

"Ailesit, we're running out of time!" Eachan called.

"I have the leaf!" Story returned her gaze to Morrigann and brandished her knife. "I don't care, I'm not leaving you here with that crazy—"

Her words were silenced as Morrigann's free arm encircled her waist, pulling her tight to him, and his lips crushed down on hers. Fire tore through her, and all conscious thought fled her mind as the faerie and his sun-filled kiss consumed her. Her knees gave out, and if he hadn't been holding her, she would have fallen to the ground, unable to take the full force of his magic.

Story was yanked away from his embrace and pulled unceremoniously onto Ped's back. Eachan locked eyes with Morrigann as he mouthed the words "thank you." The elf nodded in return.

"No!" Story struggled against Eachan's hold, but realized she was much weaker now—Morrigann had drained her with his kiss. "Let me go! We can't leave him!"

"We have to leave now, Story! There is no time!" Eachan held her still, and as Story tried to get one last look at Morrigann, Metirreonn sat up, aided by Cadwaladr. Her blank white gaze swept across the scene, taking in her fleeing captives, and though weakened by the arrow protruding from her chest, she still managed to raise a finger and point it directly at Story.

"The girl... the human... is a half-blood." The faerie collapsed back against the centaur.

All was silent for a moment, then Morrigann's head whipped around, and he yelled, "Run!"

Ped didn't need to be told twice and took off as fast as his four legs could carry them. Story's last view of the grove were of Morrigann's fear-filled face as he seemed to see something approaching that Story could not, and of Cadwaladr surging to all four hooves and barreling toward them with a leveled spear.

They cleared the edge of Cildara when Cadwaladr's voice boomed. "Kill the half-blood!"

The sound of more thundering hooves joined the chase. Eachan had an arrow nocked and flying straight into the neck of the nearest centaur before Ped cleared his first log.

"To the mine, selkie!"

"No, back to Ailes." Story's mind felt muddy and slow,

but she knew going back to the cave was the wrong way. They should head straight to shore, to water—their travel would be so much faster that way.

"The mine!" Eachan said firmly. "It's closer. We have no chance of outrunning the centaurs to the water." She turned around and launched another arrow. "But the goblins will keep the centaurs out of the mines. They'll let us pass. Well, they'll let you pass, and as we're with you..." She strung another arrow and aimed at the Clydesdale. All other conversation was cut short as she focused on her task.

Story lay slumped over Ped's neck, weak and useless, while branches whipped by as the selkie ran and the centaurs gave chase down the mountainside. Eachan continued to shoot, but her arrows weren't endless, and the centaurs kept their distance, trying to flank them and cut them off from the cave entrance.

Why do they want to kill me now? Before, they just sat there... Then she remembered, of course! *Cadwaladr gave the prophecy of the half-blood sacrifice releasing Chaos. The centaurs would rather see a half-blood dead now than in Winter's grasp later.*

Story was nearly jolted out of her perch as Ped leapt over another log and then ducked under a low branch. The selkie was breathing hard, his tongue out and lolling to the side. He was also slowing.

"Damn! I'm out of arrows." Eachan bent low over Story's back. "Fly, selkie! Fly like the wind! We're almost there."

The square opening of the mine flashed between the trees in the distance, no more than two hundred yards away. The three remaining centaurs, led by Cadwaladr, closed in now that Eachan was out of arrows. A spear as thick around as Story's wrist was suddenly quivering out of the trunk of a tree they sped past.

"There's one spear down. Two more left." The elf jerked Ped to the right with her knees as another spear embedded itself in the ground where he'd been about to step. "Make that one left."

To Story's surprise, Cadwaladr stopped short and gripped his spear. Eachan gave a rare smile as she looked over her shoulder. "He'll have to be much closer than that if he wants a real shot at us." She turned back around and looked at the mine entrance, her mouth blossoming into a full-fledged grin, eyes filled with orange and green. "Better yet, we're nearly—"

Story was hit by a spray of warm, silver blood as Eachan's voice cut off abruptly. They both stared down at the fist-sized spear protruding a few inches from the elf's chest. Ped hurled himself into the mine entrance and tripped to a halt just inside.

Story and Eachan tumbled off, while Cadwaladr remained where he stood, a hundred feet or so away, flanked by his two remaining centaurs. They didn't move any closer, but they didn't move away either. Story and her companions were trapped in the mine.

Story crawled to the elf's side, the ground slick with blood. "Eachan!"

"Story..." the elf gurgled, lying awkwardly on her side, the majority of the spear's length stretching out behind her. It seemed to have missed her heart but had definitely punctured a lung.

"...not much time left."

"No! I can help you." Story pulled herself upright and extended a hand toward the spear.

"Don't pull it out... I'll bleed to death, and I have to—" she coughed up blood. "—have to say some things first."

"But I can heal you! I healed Ped—"

"I know… But you were at your full strength, and you had *The Ailes* near you." Eachan took a labored breath. "Not this time, Story… You can barely stay up yourself."

Story opened her mouth, and Eachan held up a trembling hand to forestall her. "Stop arguing for once." She spat out a mouthful of silver blood. "Take the leaf directly to Eícetan… He'll know what to do." She paused, her breath shallow and wet as she slowly drowned in her own blood. "Please tell Eilantos I'm very sorry I couldn't finish his son's training… Eisrus is the best archer I have ever seen. But don't tell the boy that… he'll get a big head."

She closed her eyes and took a few more shallow breaths, and that's when Story noticed the elf's silver tears. She reached out and took Eachan's hand in hers. It was cold, and growing colder as her body called blood in from her extremities to her core to heal and protect when, in reality, it was killing her by flooding her lungs.

"Please don't leave my body here…" Eachan coughed up more blood.

"No." Story squeezed her hand tighter and fought back her own tears. "Of course not. I'll take you home."

Eachan smiled. "I know you will. I think… I think we could have been friends… Perhaps." She coughed again.

"Definitely." Tears spilled over and ran down Story's cheeks unchecked.

The elf closed her eyes again, gasping for a breath that wouldn't come.

Is this it? Is she gone? Story leaned over her, still holding her hand, feeling both helpless and useless. *Why her? It should have been me—I'm the one they wanted dead!*

Eachan's face crumpled in pain as she gasped for another breath. "Why…"

Story wanted to shush her, to tell her to save her energy, *but save it for what?*

"Why…" the elf began again but was interrupted by another fit of coughing.

"Why what?" Story was afraid to ask, but who was she to deny someone of their last words?

"Why… why couldn't he love me?" Anything else Eachan wanted to say was interrupted by another coughing fit filled with blood.

Though there was no question as to who *he* was, Story had no answer for the elf. What could she say? *I'm sorry he loves me and not you?* Instead, she continued to hold Eachan's hand, stroking it lightly with her fingers, until the great hunter no longer coughed, no longer struggled for breath, and more importantly, no longer cried.

CHAPTER TWENTY-SEVEN

CARRY THAT WEIGHT

COLD. IT WAS SO COLD. HOW MUCH TIME HAD PASSED? STORY didn't know. Minutes? Hours? Years? Long enough for Eachan's body to grow completely cold and stiff. Long enough for the sun to set and the moon to move across the sky. Long enough for her heart to break a thousand times over.

Eachan was dead. Morrigann was facing a fate worse than death. A herd of centaurs stood, unmoving, outside of the mine waiting to kill her. She had no light, no guide, and no idea how to get back home. She and Ped were sure to be lost in the caves if they weren't attacked by grinlings or the bogey first. Either way, they would die. As would Eírnin once Winter's first frost reached him. And Eachan and Morrigann's sacrifices would have been for nothing.

Those last thoughts, more than anything, paralyzed her with fear and despair. Story's thumb automatically continued to trace circles on Eachan's cold skin, as she mumbled "I'm sorry, I'm sorry, I'm sorry…" over and over again, as though it were a mantra. Perhaps it was—what was a mantra but something to keep focus? If anything, it kept her from losing herself to hysterics and sobbing.

It wasn't until the sun came up and its rays glistened on the white frosted ground outside that Story finally moved. Shooting to her feet, and then promptly tripping over Ped as her legs struggled to get feeling back in them, she stumbled to the mine's entrance.

"Winter's first frost..." Her eyes surveyed the land around her as her heart thudded a panicked rhythm; everything was covered in icy white. "I'm running out of time!"

She knew logically that the mountains would frost before the valleys and—even more importantly—before the elven isles as they were further north, but logic didn't matter when she was faced by the very thing that would kill Eírnin.

"Think, think, think, Story... What can you do?" She paced near the entrance of the mine, not failing to notice the centaurs followed her every move. Why they hadn't tried to spear her again she didn't know—but something about being *inside* the mine was protecting her, and so as far as she was concerned, leaving the cave with them around was not an option.

Ped stood near her and whined, thrusting his head under her hand, begging for attention. She scratched him around his ears and down his long nose. "Well, boy, looks like it's down to us." She scratched under his chin, and he leaned in closer so she could move down his neck. "I know you're fast, but are you faster than the bogey?"

He growled and gave a short bark, as if affronted.

"Oh, right. Silly me," she chuckled and patted the top of his head. "I forgot; you're the fastest thing in the water, aren't you?"

He barked again, then promptly lay down and rolled over onto his back so she could scratch his belly.

Raising an eyebrow in surprise, Story squatted down and obliged him. He'd never done that before—at least not for her. He always let Eírnin pet his belly, but not her, never her. "You finally like me now too, eh?" She scratched up his chest and down again, and his leg thumped the ground whenever she hit a nerve. "So, if I got us down to the river, would you be able to swim us out to the open water and back to Ailes? And I'm talking in record time here, boy."

Ped jumped to his feet, barking excitedly. He ran a few paces down the cave and ran back, pausing only long enough to lick her face before repeating it all over again.

Story held her hands up after his third trip. "Okay, okay, I get it! You want to try. And as I don't have a better idea..."

Licking her face again, Ped trotted down the tunnel a few steps and paused to wait for Story.

"Sorry, boy, we can't go just yet." She looked down at Eachan's body and took a deep, calming breath. The first thing she had to do was remove the spear.

After removing the stone head, she tried to gently pull the shaft out from the back, but it wouldn't budge. As much as it pained and sickened her to do it, she had to brace her feet on the body—it helped if she didn't think of the corpse as Eachan—and used the full strength of her legs, back, and arms combined to pull the spear out.

The spear's shaft made a sickening slurping sound when she managed to finally dislodge it from the body's back. It was covered in gore, blood, and tissue. Dragging it to the mine's entrance, Story hurled the pole toward the centaurs.

"I hope you all rot in hell!" Then she fell to her knees and broke down weeping. "It's just not fair. It's never fair." She knew talking to herself wouldn't make her problems go away, so after a few self-indulgent moments she scrubbed the back of her hand across her eyes and got back to her feet.

She walked back to Eachan, grateful she'd died with her eyes closed—Story didn't think she could handle it if the elf had been staring up at her with lifeless eyes.

She removed the hunter's kit and dug through it until she found a few lengths of rope. Pulling off both her own cloak and Eachan's, she wrapped and secured them around the body with the rope. She transferred the remains of Eachan's kit to her own and shared what little food was left with Ped, though it turned her stomach to eat.

"You ready, boy?"

The selkie crouched next to the elf's body, and Story lifted it gently onto his back, once again glad for the additional strength *The Ailes* had gifted her through their bond. She tied the body securely to the selkie and then pulled out her knife. Eying the mineshaft's rocky walls, she murmured, "I wonder…"

Scraping the blade along the rock, it flared up, flashing light all around until she pulled it away. Smiling, she put the knife against the shaft's wall once again. "Well, at least we have light."

The walk down to the river was silent aside from the scrape of Story's knife along the mine's wall. Nothing attacked them; she never saw a goblin, though she thought she heard some digging behind the walls at one point. Regardless, she kept going and was grateful this shaft was a straight shot to the underground river. She was certain she'd have become hopelessly lost if she'd had to navigate any turns.

The half-day walk afforded her plenty of time to think. Well, if she was being honest, to wallow in self-pity.

First my family.

Then Eírnin.

Now Eachan and Morrigann.

Everyone I care for dies.

Who's next? Adair? Mom? Eilath and Eánna?

Ped? Pinni's already gone.

How many more will die protecting me?

She couldn't help but wonder if Ailionora wouldn't be better off if she'd never come. Eírnin never would have been poisoned to use as leverage against her. Morrigann would not be facing an eternal hell at his sister's hands. Winter would never have been released, and the threat of Chaos destroying all worlds would never be realized.

I've ruined everything. I destroy every life I touch.

Sure, the elves were no longer dying out, but at what cost? Would it have been better for their race to see an end if it meant preserving all the others of every world? By Eánna's and Rhiannonn's logic it would have been.

I had no way of knowing what would happen when I restored The Ailes...

But Morrigann had. He'd warned her, after she caged him and accused him of attempted genocide.

"My crimes, you say? My crimes? Oh how very little you still

know about our world… Simple-minded still. You have no idea what you've unleashed. Of what is to come."

And despite his warning—as well as Eánna's, Rhiannonn's, Eínlin's, and others—she'd still run off, heedless of the very real danger she was causing not just herself but all the worlds. Worse, she'd involved Adair, essentially dangling herself and her sister in front of Winter.

What was I thinking?

The truth was, she hadn't been. She'd let her emotions completely rule her. She should have seen Autumn's trap for what it was.

She was never going to let me live. She couldn't risk letting her dad get me either. She might be crazy, but she's not that crazy.

Despite it all, would she still have gone after the antidote for Eírnin?

Yes. I couldn't have lived with myself if I didn't. But I would have planned it better. I wouldn't have just run off recklessly, simply reacting to the situations thrown at me.

At least, that's what she told herself. The reality was, she had no idea if things would have worked out any better if she'd spent a few days plotting and gathering information, and ultimately forming a plan.

As it is, I still might not make it back in time.

She banished the thought almost immediately, but it was too late, her eyes were misting, and she felt grief consume her once more.

THEY FINALLY ARRIVED AT THE WATER'S EDGE, AND STORY PICKED UP a loose rock for her knife before they walked out on the dock. She stared into the water, holding Ped back—he was eager to dive in. She had no way of knowing if the river led deeper into the caves or eventually let out to the open water—to the Ailes Sea, if memory served her. Worse, though Ped could breathe under the water, they'd have to surface at least once an hour, or she'd drown.

What happens if the tunnel narrows so much that there is no surface? What if there's a waterfall? What if there's no way out? What if the bogey is faster? What if…

She swallowed. Knowing she really had no choice but to go forward or sit on the dock and eventually die, she mounted Ped. Tying herself to Ped's back, so that even if she did lose consciousness, or worse, drown, at least the leaf would make it back safely, she bent over Eachan's body. She felt a fleeting wave of guilt as she realized that if this worked, her journey home would be shortened to only a few days, since she was no longer forced to travel over land.

Since a certain faerie is no longer with me.

Sighing, and trying to ignore the wave of sadness, she patted Ped's neck. "Are you ready, boy?" She took a deep breath as Ped plunged them both into icy cold blackness.

FOUR OR FIVE DAYS PASSED—STORY COULDN'T BE SURE SINCE MUCH of the first part of the journey was spent in darkness. The near total darkness, with only occasional flashes of light from her knife, combined with almost complete physical and emotional exhaustion, plus no way to sleep for longer than an hour at a time was almost enough to drive her to the brink of breaking completely. And though she didn't really feel physically cold from the water, she was completely and utterly numb.

Unsurprisingly, it was the sun that saved her. When they finally emerged from the caves and into the open ocean, Ped surfaced, and the soft sunshine warmed Story to the core, calming her enough so she could sleep for a few collected hours on Ped's back while he patiently swam across the surface. The fact that there was no frost to be seen on any of the shores also helped, though Story knew that could change at a moment's notice—weather was fickle and unpredictable. Much like the Seasons who controlled it.

Food was no longer a problem, though if she never had to eat raw fish again it would be too soon. Also, being alone with one's tormented, guilt-ridden thoughts for nearly a week was never a good thing. When the city of Ailes finally showed up on the horizon, Story found she was relieved, anxious, and filled with trepidation. The closer they got, the more her anxiety rose, and she found she wanted to turn right around and go back.

I'd rather face Winter, I think...

How would she explain Eachan's body? How would she explain to Eírnin everything that had happened?

Will he still want me?

How could she explain any of her actions to the queen— risking everyone and everything for Eírnin?

How could I not risk it?

As Ped swam the final distance to the isles, Story gasped. Both shores were swarming with life. A vast encampment was teeming with bodies of gnomes and dwarves. The gnomes were camped near the shores, while the dwarves stayed as far away from the water as possible, on the outskirts. Elves in the dress of the warrior clan were dotted among them, and judging by the weaponry and assorted armor, there was no mistaking what this mass of people was.

"An army…"

Ped reached the hunters' isle and swam past it on his way to the healers' isle. Story felt her heart tug when she spotted Eírnin's home, but it flashed by and was gone. She watched with growing anxiety as they weaved through the channels between the different clan islands. An occasional elf would spot her, but Ped was moving too fast for her to see their reaction.

Still, it came as no surprise when they rounded the corner to Eícetan's island, backlit by the setting sun, and saw not just the clan leader on the dock waiting for her, but Eilantos, Eínlin, Eilath, and of course, the queen herself, Eánna.

CHAPTER TWENTY-EIGHT

THE REMEDY

THE WIND WAS CALM AS THEY PULLED UP TO EÍCETAN'S DOCK. Story didn't dare meet anyone's eyes; she was too afraid of what she'd see in them. Instead, she held out her hand toward Eícetan.

"Here's the leaf." It was in perfect condition, unspoiled by its trek under the water, or from being crushed in her pouch for nearly week. It looked just as it did when it was on Metirreonn's shoulder, perfect.

Like magic.

Eícetan plucked it from her fingers and, without a word, spun on his heel and jogged up the wooden dock to his home and, presumably, Eírnin.

Time to face the music.

Story looked up and met each set of eyes in turn. Eilantos was worried, probably for his son. Eínlin was both relieved and curious. Eilath was sad, worried, relieved, curious, and several other emotions she couldn't sort out.

Eánna was angry.

She rarely showed Story, or anyone outside Eilath, her emotions, and her face was calm and placid as ever, yet her eyes burned red with fury.

"Ailesit. You've returned." Her voice was clipped and unsympathetic. "Was that Eachan?" The queen raised one of her arms off her very swollen belly, a visual reminder to Story of just how much time had passed, and pointed at the body.

Blinking back tears as she and the body bobbed gently in the water on Ped's back, Story forced herself to hold the queen's gaze as she answered.

"Yes."

Eilantos let out an audible sigh of relief, and his eyes faded from yellow, to green, before settling on blue. Even though Eínlin must have told him his son was with Adair in Vevila, he had still clearly been worried. Eilantos reached down and moved Story's fumbling fingers out of the way and untied the wet rope himself before hoisting the body onto the dock. Eínlin held a hand out to help Story up from the water, and she accepted it graciously. Relieved of his burden, Ped leapt from the water and changed into his massive dog form before he hit the dock and galloped toward Eícetan's hut.

An icy wind kicked up and fluttered everyone's cloaks, except for Story's as she no longer had one to wear. Soaking wet and out of the water, Story felt the cold like a human. Bumps rose on her exposed flesh, and her teeth began to chatter, still, she didn't move and met Eánna's angry gaze fully.

"She died protecting me. The centaurs were trying to kill me once they found out I was a half-blood." Story's voice began trembling but she kept speaking. "She took out three of them before Cadwaladr got her with his spear. He was aiming for me, and she was in the way." She paused before continuing. "She asked me…" Story's voice broke. "She asked me not to leave her in the mines. I promised to bring her home."

Hot tears streamed down Story's face, but she didn't reach up to wipe them away. "This is all my fault."

"Yes, it is." The queen's gaze continued to bore into Story's. Then Eánna's face softened. "But what is to say she would have survived or succeeded without you there? I foresee many things, but the future is always shifting." Her eyes faded to silver, and she turned toward Eilantos. "Please see to the preparations for her memorial. We will hold it at dawn."

"Yes, my queen." Eilantos inclined his head, gently picked up Eachan's body, and placed it in a nearby gondola before climbing in and poling away. Story's gaze was riveted on the boat; the further it got away the more empty she felt. It didn't make any sense. That wasn't Eachan. But the body was the last tie she had with the elf, who, for better or worse, she'd come to care deeply for and respect.

And it's my fault she's dead.

"We will talk more soon, Ailesit, for there is much to discuss. But for now, let's go see my cousin, shall we?" The queen raised one elegant arm toward Eícetan's home, and Story could hear the scattered jingle of metal bracelets under her creamy wool cloak.

Before Story could answer she found herself wrapped up in Eilath's arms as he gave her a tight bear hug. He leaned his head near Story's ear and whispered, "I would have done the same in your place, child. She's only angry because she has to be."

Nodding as she hugged him back, Story understood. Eánna was queen after all. She had to concern herself with her entire race, not just her cousin. Story, who had chosen to live among the elves and subject herself to the queen's rule, had deliberately disobeyed her. It didn't make Eánna's anger toward her hurt any less though, no matter how well deserved it was.

Eilath was whispering in her ear again. "Thank you. For looking out for Adair. For sending her home. Worrying about you is more than enough." He squeezed her tightly one more time and released her. While Story wiped her eyes and nose on her filthy sleeve, he pulled off his blue, calf-length cloak and wrapped it around her shivering form. It fell nearly to her bare feet.

Taking the queen's arm, Eilath escorted her up the dock. Eínlin turned toward Story and held out his arm. She grasped it cautiously, and Story and the clan leader followed in their wake.

"I am glad you are back, Ailesit." Another blast of cold air blew his long, white beard over his shoulder and knocked the hood of his cloak off his head. "Things have been... interesting since you've been gone."

"How so?" Story didn't really care. Her eyes were fixed on Eícetan's hut which lay a scant hundred meters ahead. She wanted to run the rest of the way, but Eínlin's iron grip on her hand made it clear she would do no such thing.

"Brown dwarves began showing up, as I'm sure you saw."

"Yes." Though that hadn't been wholly unexpected to Story; they had said they would help.

"They must have spoken with their cousins, so then gnomes started showing up, and before we knew it, things were as you see now." He raised a bushy eyebrow, distorting his pinwheel ailach. "More come daily. There's no method to the madness. The warrior clan has their hands full trying to sort it all out and organize them." He chuckled. "Eíbhilin has been ranting and raving about what a sorry lot they all are, and how they'll never shape up to anything, and how we're all doomed. I've never seen him happier."

"Okay..." Story didn't quite understand what the point to all this was.

The dreamwalker stopped them in front of the hut's opening and patted her hand. "My point is, Ailesit, not everything that happened was bad. You and Eachan accomplished more together over a couple months than the rest of us, led by Eírnin no less, did in three times the amount of time and with many more resources." He cocked his head to the side regarding her curiously. "The other races may not fully trust elves yet, but thanks to you and Eachan, it would seem they're finally willing to give us a chance again." He released her arm and smiled, eyes twinkling orange. "I expect to resume your training tomorrow immediately following the memorial. Don't be late."

The Dreamwalker left Story alone in the doorway, and she peered inside the dark hut. As her eyes adjusted to the darkness, her heartbeat quickened. And then there he was, just like the last time she saw him, both in person and in the dreamscape.

Eírnin slumbered, arms at his side, on a mat on the floor of Eícetan's hut, with Ped curled up at his feet. Eírnin's skin was pale, as if he hadn't seen the sun for months, which, Story realized, he hadn't. His face had a few days growth of stubble on it—someone had been shaving him, though the hair on his head was a few inches longer.

He would have hated it that long. Story smiled at the thought, and that cracked whatever had been holding her back. She ran to his side and only briefly noticed Eánna and Eilath standing unobtrusively at the far side of the hut with Eícetan and his apprentice working over an ancient, cast iron kettle.

Sitting in the dirt by Eírnin's side, ignoring the cold seeping in from the ground, Story took his hand in hers and squeezed it three times. His pulse was weak and erratic, but it was still there, and she clung to it. She followed the lines of his face over and over again with her eyes and bit her lower lip to keep herself from crying.

"I'm back, elf-boy. I'm sorry it took so long." She bent over and kissed his knuckles, ignoring how cool they felt to her touch. "I hope I wasn't too late."

A whistling sound startled her, and she jerked her head up to watch as Eícetan's apprentice poured a hot, brown liquid from the kettle into a ceramic mug the Healer held.

"Thank you, Ealian." He shifted his gaze. "My queen?"

Eánna nodded, and he walked over to Eírnin, picking up a wooden funnel along the way. Kneeling down near the Hunter's head, Eícetan set the mug down carefully and then gently opened Eírnin's mouth, placing the funnel's small end inside.

"What are you doing?" Story had a fairly good idea, but hoped she was wrong.

Eícetan picked up the mug, confusion clear in his eyes. "Healing him."

"But that's scalding hot!"

"It has to be, Ailesit." He held the bottom of the funnel in Eírnin's mouth with one hand and tipped the mug toward the wide opening.

"It'll burn him!" Story gripped Eírnin's hand even tighter,

knowing that if she didn't, she'd rip the mug out of Eícetan's hand and throw it against the woven walls of the hut.

Don't let your emotions rule you this time, Story!

"Aye, it has to." Eícetan poured the boiling liquid into the funnel and cursed under his breath as some of it splashed out and burned his own hand. When the mug was empty, he stood back up, gave the mug and funnel to his waiting apprentice, and adjusted his sarong.

"Well?" Story's gaze flickered between Eírnin and Eícetan.

"Now we wait."

"I hate waiting."

It turned out they didn't have long to wait. As it had when the poison first took him, Eírnin's body began to convulse and spasm. Ealian was already cradling his head, so Story just clung to his hand.

"What's happening?" Story's heart thudded heavily, as she felt momentarily thrown back to that awful day when he was first taken from her.

"The poison is getting burned from his body, Ailesit." Eícetan's hand came to rest on her shoulder. "It will take a while."

And it did.

Hours crawled by while Eírnin continued in his seizure. Unable to do anything else for the Hunter, Eícetan turned his attention to Story and her physical wounds. At first, she told him to leave her alone and focus on Eírnin, but he persisted, and eventually she ignored him and let him do whatever it was he wanted to do to her. So long as he didn't make her let go of Eírnin's hand, she didn't care.

He spread some kind of salve on her bite scars after she

told him in short, clipped answers what had caused them and how they came to be partially healed. Eánna and the clan leaders exchanged a meaningful look at her revelations regarding the sidhe but said nothing. Eícetan put something else on the side of her face which cooled the burn from Metirreonn, and then bandaged it with a loose gauze, wrapping it around her head to secure it. Eánna and Eilath's eyebrows had risen in unison when they heard what caused her various wounds, though they said nothing. Story was certain they'd ask her about it later during their "talk."

Finally, the seizure slowed until there was just an occasional muscle spasm or twitch, and then, eventually, there was no movement at all. Eírnin lay perfectly still, and Story found herself leaning in toward him and holding her breath.

Please, please, please!

And then the faintest bit of pressure on her hand.

One.

Two.

Three.

Eírnin's hand moved on its own. It was weak and she could hardly feel it, but it was all him. Story wasn't imagining it. She felt her mouth break into a wide grin and tears of joy pricking the corners of her eyes.

His eyes slowly, ever so slowly, cracked open, and she could see his sea-green and purple irises peeking through.

Then he smiled his lopsided, cocky smile, and her heart felt truly warm for the first time in months.

CHAPTER TWENTY-NINE

COOL BLUE REASON

THE WATER SWIRLED AROUND STORY AS SHE SWAM AROUND IN a circle, propelled easily by her flippers.

Flippers?

She contorted her body in what was surely an unnatural manner for a human or a dryad and confirmed what she'd been feeling.

Yup. Flippers.

Her gaze followed the lines of her smooth, black sealskin until she couldn't move her head around to look any further.

If I'm a selkie, then I'm dreaming.

She propelled herself through another loop in the water, twisted into a roll, and flattened her side flippers out to flat spin through the water. No wonder selkies preferred their seal form—this kind of swimming was like flying!

Best dream ever!

She swam around for a few more minutes, reveling in the freedom of it, when she noticed a dark form drifting listlessly through the water. No, actually, it was bobbing up against something on the surface, and as Story looked up she realized that "something" was everywhere.

Ice?

With a flick from her tail, she shot over to the bobbing object and almost immediately regretted her decision. The shapeless blob coalesced into a torso, two arms and legs, a shock of short, black hair waving gently in the water, and pointed ears.

Eachan!

Stomach clenching, Story stopped herself, and the sudden motion in the water shifted the corpse so that it turned to face her. Its eyes were gone, as were jagged hunks of skin as Eachan's body slowly decomposed. A crab crawled from the eye socket, and Story opened her muzzle in a silent scream. She propelled herself back and away as fast as she could, searching for the nearest hole in the ice to escape.

I have to get out! Waking herself didn't work, so she swam faster, using her entire body to shoot through the water.

There!

Surfacing, she took a deep breath and only just barely managed to get her head back under the water before a massive, white paw, over a foot in width, came crashing down where her head had been a moment before. She drifted under the ice shelf and saw through the cloudy ice the distorted shape of a giant, white bear lying in wait for her.

Polar Bear… and I'm a seal…This is a horrible dream!

She flipped around in another circle and tried to calm herself enough to wake up. Breathing deeply, she closed her eyes and focused on being back in her room, curled up safely around Eírnin.

Water continued to swirl around her, and she frowned. *Why can't I wake up?*

Looking up, she saw the bear was still there, unmoving. *Well, I'm not going out that way.*

Glancing around, she saw a portion of ice that was significantly darker up ahead. Perhaps it was under a rock, or a cave? Something that would afford her some protection? She swam toward it, and as it got nearer she was able to confirm that, yes, the ice shelf was thicker here, but when she got closer, she saw one area where light shone through.

A fisherman's hole? Am I under an igloo?

Nearing the hole cautiously, she slowly edged her whiskery nose into the air and inhaled deeply. The smell of the bear was thick in the air, but as nothing had grabbed her and dragged her out of the hole to eat her, she raised her head out of the water just enough to peek around the room.

It was a cave, or rather a den. Most likely the bear's den. She was about to duck back under the ice when something caught her eye. On an ice shelf on the other side of the cave lay a glittering gold violin.

Unthinking, she hoisted her lumbering body out of the water. Before she could worry about how she was going to get around on flippers she realized she was back in her human/dryad form, naked and shivering against the cold. She cast a quick look around and, not seeing the bear, tiptoed across the snow and ice to the instrument she knew so well.

The violin wasn't alone. Next to it on the shelf was a small Celtic harp. Story traced her finger along the spine, admiring the intricately carved curling leaves on it.

This must be Metirreonn's harp. But why would Morrigann keep the instruments here?

Next to the harp was a large brass bugle with an icy blue tassel hanging from it.

So then this has to be Winter's —

She jumped as a low clatter sounded from behind her, and she withdrew her hand from the horn. Glancing slowly over her shoulder, afraid she'd find the bear there, her gaze fixed on something far more horrifying. On the other side of the cave, beyond the thick, icy stalactites and stalagmites scattered throughout the space, were two large blocks of ice at rest next to each other. They were clear, so Story could see perfectly what they contained inside.

She ran toward them, slipping and sliding on her bare feet and colliding with one of the stalagmites before finally coming to a stop in front of the ice blocks. Her breath was ragged and shallow, her pulse erratic, and fear threatened to seize her. Placing one of her hands against the ice, she imagined she could just feel the heat wafting off of Morrigann's glittering gold hand on the other side.

But, of course, she couldn't. The Spring Prince was perfectly preserved inside, hand outstretched, as if he was reaching for her. An expression of surprise, pain, and fear was painted across his face, the scar on his cheek stretched and contorted as his mouth was frozen open in whatever shout he'd been giving.

His eyes moved.

Story yelped and jumped back in surprise, slamming into a pillar of ice. Its chill burned her bare skin, but she didn't move, horrified as the realization hit her.

He's still awake and aware in there!

Morrigann's eyes focused straight ahead on her, almost pleading, or was it warning?

Glancing over at the ice block next to him, Story confirmed that, yes, it was Metirreonn, complete with an iron arrow still buried in her chest. Her blank, white eyes also seemed to be focused on Story, but she couldn't be sure. Regardless, it was creepy.

She returned her gaze to Morrigann, and he seemed more anxious than before.

"What are you trying to tell me?" She shuddered and finally peeled herself away from the frozen pillar, rubbing her hands up and down her arms. She missed her sealskin and the warmth it provided her. She eyed the block of ice, searching for any crack or fracture she could exploit. "How do I get you out?" She knew it was probably a pointless question—she couldn't affect real things in the dreamscape and have them work in the real world. At least, that's what she'd been told.

Morrigann's eyes darted to his left.

Story turned her head to the right and leaned over, craning her neck out past Metirreonn's block. "You want me to look in there? In that other room?"

His eyes widened momentarily, and then resumed flashing back to his left, over and over again.

Maybe whatever I need to let him out—if it can be done—is in there?

Taking a few hesitant steps toward the entrance, she felt her hair stand on end—there was a *lot* of magic in that room. She stood in the roughly hewn archway and peered inside. Darkness shrouded the room, but on the other end, she could see a body. By the way the chest moved up and down in the shadows she could tell it was alive, but it appeared to be sleeping.

Sucking her breath in as a thought struck her, she leaned in to get a better look.

Could this be Winter?

She froze as a puff of warm, moist air rolled across her back. Dropping to the ground, Story rolled away from the massive polar bear just before its jaws snapped where her head had been.

Have to get back to the water hole! My only chance is to out swim it!

Pushing to her feet, she slid behind a pillar of ice just as the bear turned around. She stared, frozen by fear, taking in its massive size. It was over twice her height and, if she had to guess, easily two thousand pounds. Digging its short, powerful claws into the ice, the bear launched itself after her. It slammed into the ice pillar, and she tried to run back toward the hole, but her feet couldn't get any traction. Chunks of ice rained down around her, and a deafening roar sounded from behind her. Risking a look back, she slipped and fell onto her belly just as the bear leapt on top of the spot where she would have been.

Damn! It's blocking the hole!

Scrambling on her hands and knees, she scuttled across the ice and pulled herself up with the aid of a stalagmite. Her entire body was aflame from ice burns, and her teeth were chattering, but she didn't have time to worry about any of that. The main cave entrance was only a few feet away and coated in a thick layer of snow that would give her more traction than the ice had. She launched herself toward it, knowing the bear wouldn't be very far behind.

Who the heck uses a giant polar bear to guard their lair? As her feet hit the snow, and she ran outside into the swirling storm, she frowned grimly. *Winter, that's who.*

She felt the ground shudder behind her, and turning to her right, she ran up the mound over the cave. She couldn't remember if you outran bears by going up or down hills, but she figured she'd find out soon enough. She was too focused on staying alive to dwell on the fact she was certain Winter had imprisoned his children, and that she'd found his home—who else could (or would) freeze Morrigann and Metirreonn in blocks of ice? She filed the information away to analyze later.

The snow was falling thicker now, and she nearly ran headlong into a solid stone rectangle. Bracing her hands in front of her, she stopped her forward momentum and tried to grip on the stone for support, but it was too slick with ice to get any real support. She turned around quickly, sending up a scattering of snow at her feet, looking for the bear, but saw nothing.

That doesn't mean anything—it's white, and the snow is so thick in the air...

A massive paw, larger than a dinner plate, materialized, and Story turned just enough to move with it, absorbing most of the blow with the side of her body. She flew through the air, raising her arms up to protect her face and cushion the impact. Landing in a snowdrift, she would have normally considered herself lucky, if not for the fact that most of her body was now buried in the snow.

Trapped, she struggled to pull herself out and looked around wildly for anything she could use as a weapon or to dig herself out. Her breath caught in her throat as she took in what she saw.

Two concentric rings of rectangular stones stood on end, like dominos. Some of them had a stone lintel over the top, but others had tumbled to the ground. Though she'd never been there, she knew it from pictures.

"Stonehenge..."

"No, little half-blood, this is Uagruth." A low, rumbling, and masculine voice drifted among the swirling snowflakes. "For a time, it was called Anord." The voice was closer now, and Story strained her eyes to see where it was coming from. "Though those days have long been forgotten."

"Who are you?"

The voice chuckled. "I had heard you were simple, but come now, haven't you figured it out yet?"

"Winter?" Story asked, though as her heart sank, she knew.

"Yes. Though you may call me Geamhradann."

The voice was nearly on top of her now, and she struggled to get free of the rapidly piling snow. The bear's massive head coalesced in front of her, peering out from the snowstorm that had perfectly camouflaged it.

"Hello, Story. I've heard so much about you from my children," the bear said. "I am so looking forward to meeting you." Geamhradann raised one massive paw, gave what was clearly a bear's version of a smile, and then swung the paw down onto her head.

CHAPTER THIRTY

PRECIOUS

A CRASH OF THUNDER JERKED STORY AWAKE. FREEZING COLD and shivering, she immediately stuck her hand out and verified that Eírnin was still there, next to her, breathing and alive. Feeling all over her own body with her free hand, she could tell there were no new wounds, though, when she touched her ribs and winced, she wondered if she hadn't somehow bruised them in the dreamscape. There was still so much she didn't know about how it all worked.

Guess I'll start to rectify that tomorrow. Eínlin was sure to put her hard to work, making up for lost time. *Still,* she thought as she brushed away a lock of hair from Eírnin's forehead, *it was worth it.* Then she frowned, thinking of both Morrigann and Eachan, and found herself wondering if she was a horrible person for thinking like that. *They both willingly gave their lives for him...* But that didn't make it hurt any less.

Eachan did it because she loved Eírnin. Morrigan did it because... Story dispelled that train of thought. She didn't want to think about or guess as to the faerie's reasons for doing anything, much less helping her.

The dream was hazy and fading from her memory, but she recalled Morrigann's tortured expression frozen in the ice.

He's frozen in the dreamscape... Does that mean he's frozen in real life too?

Flashes of being pursued by a giant, white bear filled her mind, and she rubbed her forehead, trying ease the pressure.

Winter is a polar bear? And his name is... Geamhradann?

Lightening flashed outside the open doors that lead to her balcony. The thunder crashed shortly thereafter. The sky was dark and angry, and as Story got up to shut the doors the rain hit. Rather than close them, she stood there, in only her shift, and let the icy rain assault her exposed skin. It felt like thousands of tiny pinpricks all over her body, and it felt good. It felt alive. *She* felt alive.

Opening her arms wide, she walked out onto the balcony, her thoughts skimming over the events of the evening. Back on the queen's island, Eánna had brought Eírnin up to speed on what had happened since he'd been gone, though just the highlights. He'd get a full briefing in the morning. He didn't seem a bit surprised that Story had gone off on the quest to get his antidote, though his slight frown and yellow swirls in his eyes had shown his disapproval over her choice.

That's only because he didn't like me risking my life for him. Eánna hadn't mentioned the fact that she'd expressly forbidden it, and that Story had acted against her orders.

He'd held Story close almost from the moment he woke up. Eírnin seemed to understand her need to be in constant physical contact with him right now, her desperate need to reconnect after what was months of emotion-filled separation for her. Though to Eírnin, their separation had only been for a moment, a blink or two of his eyes. He had no memory of his coma.

The hardest part of the evening came when Story had to tell him that Eachan was dead. She hadn't told him many details, mostly just what she'd already told the others, in that Cadwaladr had done it, and that she'd died protecting Story. Eírnin's eyes had swirled red and blue, and he looked like he wanted to punch a wall. Instead, he hung his head and wept for his fallen mentor. It was the first time Story had ever seen him cry, and she hoped she'd never have to again.

As Story held Eírnin close and tried to comfort him, Eánna had quietly slipped out. Whether he was overwhelmed by all the information—and the queen still had more to tell him, as he was a clan leader now—or simply exhausted from the beating his body had taken during his hours-long seizure burning out the poison, he was soon fast asleep in Story's arms.

She'd held him for a while, simply happy over the fact that he was alive and back in her arms. But, eventually, her own stench and the desire to bathe and change into clean clothes won out. Lifting him gently, she'd placed him in her bed, tucking him in snugly. After she was clean and changed, she snuggled in behind him, wrapping herself around him tightly, never wanting to let him go. She'd fallen asleep, feeling safe and secure.

Until that dream, she thought sourly. The icy rain ran down her back, face, and arms in rivulets, and she realized she was shivering violently. A blanket was tossed around her, and she was scooped off her feet into Eírnin's arms.

Eírnin kicked the doors shut behind them and walked quickly over to the fireplace on the other side of the room. "Are you trying to make yourself ill?" Setting Story's shivering form down on the white, woven rug in front of the marble fireplace, he built the fire back up until it was roaring. Then he sat on the rug next to her, pulled her wet body onto his lap, wrapped the blanket around both of them, and held her tight, warming her.

"Well?" he asked again.

Story didn't answer. Instead she buried her head against his neck and cried. It took him a moment to realize her shaking was no longer from shivering but from weeping, and that those were tears he was feeling on his neck, not rain water. When he did, he pulled her tighter, and ran his hands up and down her back trying to soothe her.

"Shh, please, dear heart, don't cry. There's no reason to cry."

His words only set her to sobbing more.

"Please tell me what's wrong." He pushed her away gently and tipped her chin up. She looked into his blue and yellow swirled eyes, and he asked, "How can I help?"

The tears continued to stream down her face as she answered. "I love you so very much. I can't even put it into words."

He smiled. "Is that all?"

Closing her eyes, she took a deep and tremulous breath. "I've done things, things I'm not proud of." She met his eyes again, now burning orange. "I need to tell you what happened while you were sleeping."

He smiled gently. "You know you can tell me anything, right?"

Story bit her lip, worried. *What if he rejects me? What if he won't love me any more? What if he hates me? What if...*

His eyes faded from orange to green as he continued to smile at her, and she felt an odd sense of calm wash over her. She realized he no longer cared what she had to say—that he was just happy and content to be with her, and that alone gave her the strength she needed.

Snuggling back in against him, Story told Eírnin everything. Every conversation, every kiss, every feeling, every moment of her journey, not sugar coating or leaving out anything.

When she finally finished, the rain had stopped, and everything was silent. She was afraid to look up, afraid of what she'd see. But she couldn't help herself, so, pulling away, she peeked at Eírnin's eyes. A bit of brown jealousy flashed by, and perhaps a hint of yellow and purple, but on the whole, they were still the same, a peaceful sea green. There was no red to be seen at all. He leaned in and kissed her gently before pulling back and quirking up the corners of his mouth in a slight smile.

"You're not mad at me?"

"What do I have to be angry about?" His smile blossomed fully. "In the end you still came back to me. That's what matters."

Story felt a ring slip onto the third finger of her left hand. Surprised, she held her hand up to her face and looked at the ring. It was silver in color and did not actually form a true ring with ends that met but, rather, was a strip of metal with two smooth, green stones set on either end. The silver had been bent and formed such that it twisted around until the two green stones passed each other, so that when on her finger they appeared to be stacked one on top of the other. When she angled her hand to the side the round stones looked like a set of serene, sea-green eyes.

"What is this for?" She glanced at Eírnin and then returned her gaze to her hand.

He laughed. "Oh, this is a bad start. If you don't recognize an engagement ring—"

"Engagement ring?" She raised her eyebrows in confusion. "But... I haven't seen any other elves with engagement or wedding rings."

"Aye, that's because it's not a part of our culture."

Story was even more confused now. "Then why do it?"

Eírnin laughed even louder and pulled her into another hug. "Because, dear heart, it's a part of yours!"

"I never told you that..."

"I spoke with your mother about it a while back."

"When?"

"When I first asked her for permission to court you."

He smirked, and Story blushed, but also found she was pleased and stared back at her hand. It wasn't exactly a traditional engagement ring, but she didn't care. If anything, this one meant so much more because he'd gone through the effort to find out about her culture's traditions, and so much planning to get the ring made.

She smiled up at him and, wrapping her hands around his neck, kissed him soundly. "I love it, it's perfect. It reminds me of your eyes."

"Aye, it reminds me of yours too." He pulled her hand up to his lips and, eyeing the ring, kissed her fingertips. "The red dwarves did a good job, I think." His lips moved up to the back of her hand before he turned it over and pressed another kiss onto her wrist.

Story closed her eyes and soaked in the feeling of his lips moving slowly up her arm until they reached her shoulder. She needed this, to feel connected with him again. Eírnin lingered at her shoulder a moment, and as she ran her fingers through his air, she almost pulled his mouth up to meet hers. Story forced herself to be patient and was soon rewarded.

Eírnin's kisses slid up her neck and across her jaw, leaving a trail of fire in their wake. She was almost quivering with anticipation when he paused at the corner of her mouth and smiled.

Story was done being patient. Her mouth captured his hungrily, and their kisses intensified. His hands tightened on her back, and she struggled to get closer to him, even though she was already pressed up as tight against him as she could physically be. She pushed him back forcibly onto the rug, and he chuckled.

"Maybe I should go into more comas..."

Smacking his shoulder, Story glared at him. "Don't even joke about that!" But there was no real anger in her words. She was too happy at the moment.

"I'm sorry, dear heart." He winked. "But not sorry about this." He pulled her down, and for a time, her world was filled with nothing but Eírnin. Kissing him, holding him, and caressing him. After a few moments, Story pulled away, both of them breathing heavily, and one look showed Eírnin's eyes were solidly purple.

"How soon until we get married?" She was only half kidding.

Eírnin laughed and pulled her tight into his embrace. "Not soon enough, that's for certain."

Laughing with him, Story was just leaning in for another kiss when her door burst open.

"Ailesit, the queen—" Eavan stopped short and

immediately averted her eyes and turned around. Story and Eírnin sat up and exchanged a worried glance.

"You can turn around, Eavan. It's fine. We're decent."

Eírnin stifled a snort, and Story shot him a quelling look. Eavan turned around, but still kept her eyes averted.

"I'm sorry, Ailesit. I didn't realize… It's just that the queen requested your presence immediately; actually, she requested both of you. I was about to go to the Hunter's rooms next to wake him…" She trailed off again, clearly mortified, and Story would have laughed it off, except for the urgency in the handmaiden's voice.

"What's wrong?"

"I don't know, Ailesit. The queen just said to hurry. She said to meet her in the healing room."

Story and Eírnin both shot to their feet, and after wrapping the blanket around herself—it was drafty in the palace—they both hurried after Eavan. Story had never been to the healer's room on the queen's island, but she assumed it was where a member of Eícetan's clan stayed in the event the queen ever needed healing. Panic gripped her as she wondered what had happened.

Is the baby coming early? Is Eilath okay? Did something happen to Eínlin? He was one of the older elves remaining…

They took a sharp turn, and Eírnin slipped and nearly fell on his stocking feet. Running past a few more corridors, Eavan's sandaled feet clapped against the marble tiles. She took one more turn and then stopped in front of a plain, wooden door that had five parallel lines carved into it.

The healing clan's ailach.

Eavan indicated that this was the correct door with one hand and then left. Story and Eírnin exchanged another worried glance, his eyes completely yellow now, and he reached out to pull the door open. She followed him into the dimly lit room, and when her eyes finally adjusted to the low light, she gasped.

Lying on a woven mat in the middle of the room while a healer worked on him was Eisrus. Or rather, what remained of him.

He looked as though he'd been mauled by a massive wild animal of some sort. If not for the slight rise and fall of his chest, she would have thought he was dead. Eisrus's entire body was covered in mud and dried, crusted, silver blood. His face was a mass of bruises. One eye was swollen shut and the other was gone.

Rushing to his side, Story dropped her blanket and reached out to hold his hand. Horror washed over her as she realized then that his entire right arm was missing too.

"What happened?" Story looked up at the queen, who was on Eisrus's other side.

"We were hoping you could tell us that, Ailesit." Eánna's voice was not angry, but it was demanding.

"I swear I don't know! Morrigann gave him a bit of his warmth, and Eisrus was only supposed to let go of it once he and Adair got to Vevila safely." Story's heart hammered in her chest and her hands shook. "There's no way anyone could force him to release it." She looked between Eánna and Eírnin, almost pleading with them to believe her. Eírnin squeezed her shoulder and gave her a tight smile.

Closing her eyes, the queen sighed. "No, they could not force him to release it. So they took his arm. Once it was dead..." She trailed off, and no one needed her to finish her sentence.

Story felt panic rise in her chest. "But who would—"

Eisrus moaned and worked his mouth as though he was trying to say something. Story leaned in closer and could just make out his whisper.

"He has her. He has her. He has her…"

"Who has her, Eisrus?" But Story was certain she already knew.

"He has her…"

"Who!" Story gripped both of his shoulders and leaned closer. "Who has Adair?"

"Winter." The word escaped his mouth as a sigh.

Story released his shoulders and fell back against Eírnin. He caught her and held her as she shook.

"No, no, no! Not Adair! It should have been me! This is all my fault, all my fault!"

Eírnin smoothed down her braids and rubbed his other hand up and down her back, trying once again to soothe her as she fell to pieces.

"Who found him, cousin?" he asked the queen.

"I did." A male voice answered for Eánna.

Story sniffed and wiped a few tears from her eyes before looking toward the sound of the voice—it was vaguely famil-iar. A brown-skinned and electric blue-haired dryad stepped out from a dark corner, and Story realized she recognized him.

"Corcoran!" He was one of her half-brothers. She'd only met him once before, months ago during her first visit to Vevila, and had immediately liked him and his sunny nature. But none of that was in evidence now—he was as worried as she was. *And why wouldn't he be? Adair is his little sister too.* "How did you find him? Was he in the water?"

"No. In the woods south of Faerie Land. I was bringing

someone to see you who said he'd had enough of swimming." Corcoran's frown deepened and pointed into the shadows behind him where his cloaked companion stood.

"Someone to see me?" Story was beyond confused at this point and sick with worry and guilt over Adair's abduction. A part of her mind connected that it must have been Adair she saw sleeping in Winter's lair.

How did I not figure that out before now?

The person standing behind Corcoran stepped out from the shadows and lowered his hood. Giving her a half-smile, he raked his fingers through his short, red hair. "Hey, Story. Long time no see."

Story's knees gave out, and she would have collapsed to the floor if Eirnin hadn't been holding her so tightly.

"Josh?"

To Be Concluded

PRONUNCIATION GUIDE

Adair	(Aa-dye-ear)
Ad'har	(Aa-dar)
Ailach	(Eye-la)
Ailionora	(Eye-le-o-nor-rah)
Ailes	(Eye-lees)
Ailesit	(Eye-lay-sit)
Aisdean	(Eyes-dee-un)
Almera	(All-mee-rah)
Borgmester	(Borg-mess-ter)
Cadwaladr	(Kad-wall-a-der)
Da'nan	(Da-naan)
Eánna	(Ay-un-aa)
Eáchan	(Ay-uh-shun)
Eachan	(Ay-shun)
Ealian	(Ay-lee-un)
Ealis	(Ay-lees)
Eámonn	(Ay-uh-moon)
Eásphor	(Ay-us-for)
Easin	(Ay-seen)
Eavon	(Ay-vun)
Eazoa	(Ay-zoe-ah)
Eínlin	(Ay-een-leen)

Eíswin	(Ay-ee-swin)
Eídolin	(Ay-ee-doe-leen)
Eíbhilin	(Ay-ee-bee-leen)
Eícene	(Ay-ee-seen)
Eilath	(Ay-lath)
Eisrus	(Ayz-russ)
Eirnin	(Air-nin)
Eírnin	(Ay-eer-nin)
Faolán	(Fow-lan)
Fuath	(Foo-aath)
Geamhradann	(Geem-hraa-dun)
Metirreonn	(May-teer-ee-un)
Morrigann	(More-gaan)
Rhiannonn	(Ree-an-non)
Sidhe	(Shee)
Tilpasse	(Till-pass-ee)
Uaine	(Oo-aye-n) (rhymes with wine)
Uasail	(Oo-ah-say-il)
Uinseann	(Oo-un-see-un)
Uistean	(Oo-eyes-tee-un)
Vevila	(Ve-vee-la)

ACKNOWLEDGEMENTS

Though I'm certain I will forget someone, I need to thank those of you who had a hand, be it large or small, in helping make this book happen: Aaron Allston, Amber Biles, Erin C., Ivana Faustino, Brandon Garner, Gabriella Garner, Ronald Garner, Geek Media Expo, Katherine Hanifen, Dustin Hegwood, Mandy Hortenski, Jeremy, Kathy Johnson, Conley Lyons, Maggie Masetti, Tonya Mayberry, Kylee Miller, Kelli Neier, Stephanie Oplinger, Y.M. Rivadeneira, Micheal A. Stackpole, Megan "Alpha" Snyder, Caitlin Shindler, Rich Sigfrit, Loren and Tina Spendlove, The Steelwells, Betsy Waddell, Lil Watson, Laura Williamson, Bryan Young, Anna and Timothy Zahn.

Also, I wouldn't be anywhere without YOU my loyal readers. Thank you for your continuing support for this series – I hope it lives up to your expectations.

And, of course, I need to thank my Heavenly Father, without whom none of this would be possible.

BOOKS IN THE WAR OF THE SEASONS SERIES

ABOUT THE AUTHOR

Janine K. Spendlove is a KC-130 pilot in the United States Marine Corps. In the Science Fiction and Fantasy World she is primarily known for her best-selling series, *War of the Seasons*. She has several short stories published in various speculative fiction anthologies, to include *Time Traveled Tales*, *Athena's Daughters*, and *War Stories*. Janine is also a member of Women in Aerospace (WIA), BroadUniverse, and is a co-founder of GeekGirlsRun, a community for geek girls (and guys) who just want to run, share, have fun, and encourage each other. A graduate of Brigham Young University, Janine loves pugs, enjoys knitting, making costumes, playing Beatles tunes on her guitar, and spending time with her family. She resides with her husband and daughter in Eastern North Carolina. She is currently at work on her next novel.

CONNECT WITH ME ONLINE

Twitter: @JanineSpendlove
Facebook: www.facebook.com/JanineSpendlove
Blog: www.waroftheseasons.com

Also from Silence in the Library!

OPERATION: MONTAUK

"Readers will be on the
edge of their seats from start to finish"
—James Foy, Deseret News

"Is this book a must read? Yes.
Emphatically so."
—Andrea Levine, [insertgeekhere]

BY BRYAN YOUNG

THE AUTHOR OF "MAN AGAINST THE FUTURE"